THE DISCIPLINE OF NURSE RIDING

Although about thirty years of age, Miss Delahaye was dressed as a schoolgirl. She wore a crisp white blouse which showed clearly her swelling black bra beneath; a striped tie; and a grey pleated skirt, very short so that her stocking tops of black lace, and the straps to her garter belt, were fully visible, as was a triangle of black shiny silk at her crotch. The only jarring note was her shoes, sumptuous and high-heeled.

'Well, miss,' drawled Miss Gageby, 'you are a little slut, aren't you? Black undies, indeed – you know that's forbidden – and just look at the state of your room. You shall have to pay for that before we even begin your treatment. I think you know what to expect, and for your sluttishness, you shall have the humiliation of a trainee nurse attending you. Fetch the whippiest cane from your cupboard, miss!'

THE
DISCIPLINE OF
NURSE RIDING

Yolanda Celbridge

This book is a work of fiction.
In real life, make sure you practise safe sex.

First published in 1998 by
Nexus
Thames Wharf Studios
Rainville Road
London W6 9HT

Typeset by TW Typesetting, Plymouth, Devon

Printed and bound by
Cox & Wyman Ltd, Reading, Berks

ISBN 0 352 33291 3

Contents

1	Strict Terms	1
2	The Naked Cane	15
3	Mermaid's Kiss	37
4	Deepest Need	59
5	Whipping Twins	77
6	Cupped and Stretched	93
7	Rubber Wrapped	109
8	Honey Birch	129
9	Hell Fur Leather	151
10	Bare Fists	173
11	Nursebound	195
12	Down at Heel	215
13	11.59	235
Envoi	Old Scores	255

1

Strict Terms

'Hello again, Miss Riding. I gather your last job did not quite work out.'

Prudence Riding looked timidly at Mrs Kneller, of Kneller's Office and Executive Agency. Outside, the traffic of the Fulham Road hummed merrily; inside the office, it was hushed and reverent, as in a headmistress's study.

'It's disappointing . . . We had such high hopes. We do have a genuine concern for our girls, Miss Riding.'

'I know, and I'm grateful, Mrs Kneller. It's just that . . . well, it wasn't my fault, really. I think my work was quite good. There was a misunderstanding . . .'

Prue trailed off miserably.

'It seems the last job ended as a misunderstanding, and the job before that, Miss Riding.'

Mrs Kneller sighed, but smiled tolerantly.

'I know that a girl your age has more pressing priorities than typing and computing and office life, but we must all accept that we live in the real world.'

She gestured vaguely to the teeming city below her window.

'That is the real world, Miss Riding. Not the world of clubs and . . . social life, but the world of work. London! Opportunity, for the dynamic woman who wants to build a career. The real world,' she repeated, licking her lips. 'You'll forgive me for lecturing you, but really, we do try to take a personal interest in our clients – we are not just some soulless temp agency – and, well, I am at a bit of a loss to know what you *really* want.'

Prue crossed her long, smooth legs, which were generously showing, encased in sheer fishnet stockings, under her short black velvet skirt. Mrs Kneller blinked as she caught a glimpse of garter straps and frilly stocking tops, and the triangle of lacy pink panties that clung skimpily to her lady's place. Mrs Kneller's eyes narrowed, and Prue smoothed her skirt down, decorously, to within a few inches of her smooth rounded knees.

'The thing is, Mrs Kneller,' she sighed, 'I try my best, I really do. But I have to honestly say that I haven't found the right niche. When I was very little I fancied being a pilot, soaring up in the air above all the people; but that's silly, and impossible anyway, because I get the most awful vertigo. What I have really always wanted – what I'm afraid I'll never manage, because I know it's hopeless – is to be a nurse! Nursing, taking care of harmed people, healing them with love and kindness – that has always been my dream. And just because I haven't got the qualifications, the exams and things – well, they are always saying you need enthusiasm in a job, but it seems enthusiasm isn't enough. You need pieces of paper. As if bits of paper could replace a kind and willing heart! I mean, I can type, and do computers and things, but then, so can everybody else. Perhaps I'm just not dynamic enough. But I feel I'm in a rut. I could try another job, and another, but I sort of have the feeling I know how it will turn out. I do my best, but, O . . .'

Prue stopped abruptly, and sighed.

'Prudence – I may call you Prudence? – nothing is hopeless. We mustn't think of what might have been, nor what should be, but what is. You are a lady with a vibrant personality, you have the basic skills –

2

the road of secretary, personal assistant, and so on, can frequently propel a woman into the executive ranks, you know. But you must start diligently, it doesn't happen overnight. Your appearance, for a start, is to your advantage – I'm not being impertinent in saying you have rather striking good looks, and a fine figure, and a keen intelligence, and, the real world being what it is, those things go a long way in making up for lack of bits of paper, as you put it.'

Prue sighed again.

'That's just it, Mrs Kneller. I always have the impression that I'm not being taken seriously, that I'm some kind of . . . sex object. And then I get looks, and hints, and people get jealous or fancy me, or fancy somebody else who fancies me, and . . . well, that is where the misunderstandings come in.'

Mrs Kneller punched keys and stared at her computer screen, frowning and clicking her tongue.

'We could try . . . this one, or this one, I suppose. Big companies, good prospects, decent City addresses. But it would really be more of the same, Prudence. You must perhaps try to feel more committed. Sometimes, social life must take a back seat to the real world.'

'I'll try anything, Mrs Kneller, you know that.'

'That's just the point, Prudence. To say you'll try anything sounds as if you don't care from the start. It sounds as if you are not discriminating, not sure of yourself, not *focused*. Try to stop focusing on nursing, and instead on the business ladder. Wait a minute . . .'

The keys of her computer clicked in agitation.

'Well . . . this is curious. It just came in. It seems they are looking for someone very like you. In fact I could say they were looking *just* for you, Prudence.'

Mrs Kneller looked over her glasses and scrutinised Prue's low-cut cashmere sweater, in a modest fluffy grey, but which did little to hide the fullness of her breasts, nor the scalloped pink bra that underwired them and thrust the smooth bare flesh to proud prominence, with the long blonde tresses cascading with casual insolence over the breast-skin.

'Yes,' she said, and beamed. 'I think we can safely recommend you to the principals quite unreservedly. Our reputation is sound, Prudence! A job for you, and – as a trainee nurse!'

Prue's hands flew to her open mouth. Mrs Kneller clicked the computer keys some more, and pursed her lips, frowning.

'It's a bit mysterious,' she said. 'There isn't really very much information.'

'I don't care!' cried Prue. 'I'll go for it! Even if it's abroad – Europe, overseas, wherever.'

'Well, it's not exactly overseas,' said Mrs Kneller. 'It is in the north of England. Northumberland, to be precise. A health hydro on the coast, near Berwick. Very nice, if a little windswept. Lots of sand-dunes and seagulls and that sort of thing.'

She peered again over the top of her glasses at Prue's costume; the dangerous high heels, the cashmere draped as though casually over the thrust of the breasts, the tight skirt that seemed to cling to her firm strong thighs, as though afraid it might be detached by a passing breeze . . .

'You'd have to take some warm clothing, I expect. Sensible shoes and long skirts, and, you know, things they wear in the country. You dress very nicely for London, but I dare say Northumberland might seem a bit quaint to you.'

'I don't mind! As long as I can wear a nurse's uniform! Of course I'll get some kit for the north of England! I'll phone up straight away – one of the catalogue firms I use – it's so easy, just roll out your credit card and –'

Prue stopped uncertainly, and Mrs Kneller caught her hesitation.

'A little bit overspent, perhaps?' she said with a glint

4

in her eye. Prue shifted uncomfortably, her stockings making a slithery noise as her thighs rubbed.

'Perhaps just a bit. But my last salary came in last week, and my gold card is OK, I *think*, and my overdraft . . .'

She sighed deeply.

'But if I get the job, once I get paid, I mean it'll be OK, you know?

'Will it, Prudence? Nursing doesn't pay very much, and the job at Cloughton Wyke Hydro pays next to nothing. I said it was curious . . . You see, there aren't very many details – I'll give you a hard copy of what I have on the screen – and it simply mentions "strict standards of hygiene and discipline, moral, physical, and financial, for nurses and guests alike". It's the financial part that is puzzling; it sounds rather puritanical, doesn't it? As though they don't want to be a sort of Foreign Legion for frivolous women, but want serious staff who are solvent and not beset by money worries which might distract them from their duties. I can see the point, I'm afraid. Still,' she said, cheerfully, 'the description of their ideal candidate fits you to a tee, Prudence – and I don't think I am betraying any confidences in telling you that their requirements stress the physical endowments of the candidate . . .'

Prue found herself again on the Fulham Road, armed with the details of Cloughton Wyke, which was little more than a photograph of an imposing residence near the clifftops, with an expanse of the North Sea stretching behind it; a cursory résumé of a nurse's duties, which seemed to include just about anything; a reference to pay, which was derisory, and 'benefits', which seemed considerable. A short text emphasised dedication, commitment, and love of duty, and the need for a 'clean balance sheet as to moral character and social and financial commitments'.

There was a phone number she was to call, to the nurse who was the London agent for Cloughton Wyke Hydro – a Miss Macardle. She got out her purse and inspected her credit cards, flicking through them as though hoping to find an ace in the pack, then the latest bank statement, already dog-eared from its long, uninspected confinement.

'Cheer up, love, it may never happen!' cried the newspaper vendor on the corner of Sydney Street.

She grinned ruefully, and proceeded to South Ken tube station, where she found a phone box and dialled Miss Macardle's number. While she listened to it ring, she looked at the postcards which decorated the box like trapped snowflakes. All advertised services, by females for males, and all offered variations on the theme of 'severe discipline' or 'stern corporal punishment'. The conceit made her smile, more so when she saw one advertising 'strict Nurse will attend to naughty boys' hygienic and disciplinary needs,' and it showed a well-formed lady in a rather fetching nurse's uniform, all crisp and starched, and brandishing a long, fearsome cane with a crook handle. Her gaze stayed a long time on that card, until the number answered, and a soft Scottish voice said hello.

'Miss Macardle?' blurted Prue above the traffic noise.

'You must be Miss Prudence Riding,' said Miss Macardle.

'Why, yes –'

'I've just popped an application form in the post to you. You'll get it tomorrow – send it back as soon as you can, it's just a formality, you understand, and then I shall be in touch by letter.'

'Of course – thank you, Miss Macardle, but how –'

'Must dash, Prudence. See you soon.'

Prudence caught the District Line back to her shared flat in Baron's Court, and spent a fitful evening in anticipation of next day's post. In the morning, she heard the letters drop to the floor, and was first to collect them, scooping them up in front of her flatmate with an air of triumph. Her letter was a handwritten note in green ink, from Miss Macardle, saying how pleased she was at Miss Riding's interest in the post as Nursing Trainee at Cloughton Wyke Hydro, and would she please fill in the application form carefully. The form seemed standard enough, although it did not require many details of career to date or academic achievements; rather, it dwelt on personal attributes, and there was a long section to describe why the applicant wanted to be a nurse. Also, the applicant was requested to affix a recent photograph, a full-length one if possible, and a very detailed set of physical measurements and weight, which were to be accurately taken of the body unclothed.

Prue excited some ribald laughter as she shut herself in the bathroom, which didn't lock, stripped herself and, armed with a tape measure, took all her measurements – bust, bottom, inside leg, thigh, calf, and others that were quite exraordinarily detailed and verging on the intimate – and of course her flatmates found an excuse to barge in to pee, and affected gleeful surprise when they saw her at her apparently narcissistic exercise, whose delicate procedure she refused to interrupt; she was obliged to endure the quips of a succession of noisily peeing girls, as she struggled to hold the tape measure correctly.

She sat down to fill in the section on her motivation, and wrote truthfully about her longing to be a carer, and a healer of bodies, and added as an afterthought, a healer of minds, too. She hesitated over personal details, then glumly wrote, parents unknown, gave the name and address of her surviving foster parent, and the name of her only known relative, her sister Wendy, though without her address. Her face fell as she filled in that part, and more so when with trembling fingers she put down details of her bank, credit, and debts. The form warned in the politest possible way that no dissembling on these points would be tolerated, and all information discreetly but scrupulously checked.

'O, I probably won't get it after all,' she said cheerfully to her flatmates. 'Murphy's law . . .'

But the next day's post brought a further communication from Miss Macardle, inviting Prue to tea at the Ritz that very same day. She was to call and confirm; she did so at once, shaking her head at the snowfall of disciplinary postcards which had reached as far as the public telephones of Baron's Court, and agreed to meet Miss Macardle's assistant for a 'preliminary' at four o'clock. Assuming things went well, she would in due course attend Miss Macardle herself for her examination. Far too early, she walked into the Ritz as though she were intimately familiar with it; had to ask directions; at last found herself sitting opposite Miss Macardle's assistant, a slim, handsome female only a couple of years older than herself, fashionably dressed in a discreetly expensive business suit of dark blue wool, with mauve silk stockings, the jacket very narrow indeed at the waist, as though she wore a corset – though her trim, supple figure gave no hint she needed to. Her hair was cut quite short and straight, framing strong, high cheekbones.

With a slight northern lilt, she introduced herself as Miss Pickering, and said that this 'preliminary' was by way of a cosy chat, to explain certain things to Prue of which she might be unaware, and 'sound her out' generally. Tea was served, and Miss Pickering said that she was pleased Prue ate well, for the chill Northumberland air made for a hearty appetite, and a nurse needed all her strength. They made small talk, and Prue became quite voluble, encouraged by Miss Pickering's friendly and sincere manner. Miss Pickering kept asking questions about her attitude to 'discipline', and Prue insisted that she thought discipline was terribly important in every aspect of life.

Toying with a sandwich, and her eyes downcast, Miss Pickering murmured she was glad, and was sure that Prue understood that discipline frequently involved correction, sometimes quite stern correction, and nowhere more so than at a hydro, where the spartan virtues of hygiene and good order were at a premium, for 'subjects' and staff alike.

'Correction,' said Prue, her mouth full of cucumber and watercress sandwich. 'I suppose you mean bread and water diet.'

Miss Pickering smiled.

'No, Prudence,' she said. 'We prefer to call it treatment, by the way, and proper treatment is not deprivation, but . . . enhancement. I know from talking to you that you are a very kind person, and that you are just such a nurse as we are seeking. Subjects come to us with messy lives and personal problems, in sore need of cleansing and correction. We are very traditional in our approach to healing, and do not subscribe to some of the more bizarre modern ideas, or, in plain northern English, pure folderol. Our methods are plain and simple, and extremely efficient. They are old-fashioned – in short, Prudence, subjects in need of correction frequently receive it in a very direct and physical form. One of our basic principles at Hydro is that you have to be cruel to be kind.'

'I don't quite –' Prue began, and Miss Pickering hushed her, helping herself to a honeyed scone.

'Mmm!' she said, taking a large bite, and waiting to swallow before speaking again, but all the time looking deep into Prue's eyes.

'You know that, in this country, schools for young men, and young women too, used to thrive on a regime of strict corporal punishment.'

'You mean . . . *beating*? The cane? Why yes, I was aware, but that was in the old days.'

'In Northumberland, Prudence, we are rather fond of the old days,' said Miss Pickering. 'And the old *ways . . .*'

Prue listened in silence, her eyes wide, as Miss Pickering explained, smiling, that fair but strict corporal punishment was a treatment much appreciated by the subjects at Hydro; that male and female subjects paid handsomely to enjoy individually tailored correction, using a wide variety of tried and tested methods, and usually including use of the cane or strap, or just the bare hand.

'The effects are cleansing, and ennobling, even,' she said, with a very serious glint in her eye. 'A person inured to corporal correction is toughened enough to face life healthy and serene. When the body is taught to endure, so can the mind also. That is why our subjects return to Hydro over and over. You don't believe me? But there is a light in your eye, my girl, that says you do, that says you want to believe me, and furthermore that a nurse's true and noble duties now interest you more than you realised.'

Abruptly, she rose from her chair, a mischievous smile playing on her lips.

'All this tea,' she said. 'I must go to the bathroom, and I expect you want to go too, Prudence.'

It was a summons; Prue obeyed, and followed Miss Pickering to the scented bathroom, where both ladies took a cubicle and peed. When Prue had wiped herself and replaced her clothing, Miss Pickering pushed open her own cubicle and summoned her. She had her skirts up, and her mauve silk knickers down, revealing a ripe pair of perfect taut buttocks, and a fount that was gleaming clean of mink hair. Above her bottom, her waist was pinioned in the tightest of corsets, a mauve or lilac colour, gleaming satin and squeezing Miss Pickering's waist to a delicious pencil thinness. Prue gasped; below the corset's frilly hem, the woman's bottom was a lattice-work of dark red blushes.

Miss Pickering took her hand, and guided it to touch her cool, smooth bum-flesh.

'You see?' she said. 'Regular treatment is regular cleansing. This was my last correction, with the cane, and this, a bit fainter, was with the Northumberland birch – you can still see the points where the birch tips caught me. The blossoms of corporal punishment do not last for ever, of course, but I can assure you that while they do, they are a source of pride and satisfaction, and when they fade, each and every subject is avid for the croup to blossom afresh. Myself included, Prudence . . .'

Prue stroked the mottled skin of Miss Pickering's bum over and over, whistling softly.

'It's as though I can see a painting in your marks, Miss Pickering,' she said. 'Like flowers, or flames, or smiling lips. But it must have hurt you so.'

'O, there is a painting, Prudence!' cried Miss Pickering suddenly, and looked at her with eyes bright and joyful as diamonds. 'The painting of the lash on bare bottom is the noblest that can adorn any woman, or that one woman can award another! The whip or the birch tongues on helpless bare skin, Prudence, those are the sweetest kisses a woman can receive, or give . . .'

Miss Pickering pulled up her mauve knickers, smoothed her corset, and replaced her skirt, and smiled brightly. Her face glowed. They made their way back to the tea-table, and Miss Pickering took Prudence's hand.

'Tell me what you thought, honestly,' she whispered.

'I . . . I thought your bum was . . . well, it was lovely, in such a strange, shivery way. Like a true work of art.'

'Aptly put – a true nurse is an artist, and I hope you shall become such an artist. I sensed your spirit, Prue – you *are* excited at dealing cool and correct treatment with your strong hand, to the bottom of a willing and submissive subject, I must add, either male or female. You are one of us in your heart. Will you, Prue? Will you give nursing – true nursing – a try?'

'I . . . this is all so fast.'

'Sometimes, truth comes fast.'

Prue gulped a deep breath, and sighed. Miss Pickering's eyes glowed with understanding.

'Yes, Prue?'

'*Yes!*'

Miss Pickering smiled and squeezed Prue's hand, and Prue smiled too, her eyes moist with joyful commitment.

'Wonderful,' said Miss Pickering. 'Good. Now, Prudence, there is the examination by Miss Macardle, our Nursing Mistress here in London. It is a formality, a small thing, but – well, you've seen the real *me*, and I know you will understand. Our new nurses must be examined for a firm will, a firm hand, and a firm endurance. They must be able to stand and *under*stand the treatment they award their subjects. It's the lightest of things, a formality, but it means that you yourself must take –'

'Yes! O, miss, I agree!' Prue blurted, her face quite flushed. 'I don't mind – I *do* understand. I'll submit to Miss Macardle's examination, gladly. I mean I don't mind showing I can take a . . . a nurse's whopping – that must sound all silly – like *you*. I *so* want to be a nurse.'

Miss Pickering's smile became radiant.

'Then need I say more?' she asked, and Prue pursed her lips, shaking her head solemnly, and her eyes wide.

Miss Pickering leant forward to kiss her on the cheek. Her eyes sparkled, and she said there was one other matter.

'It is money, I'm afraid,' she sighed. 'In your application, you told the truth, Prudence, and it seems you are rather in a hole as regards . . . well, debt.'

Prue's face fell.

'You see, Hydro requires its staff to be cleansed both physically and morally, and debt is a rather distracting form of immorality, according to our High Mistress. Nursing is a business, and treatment a transaction, where the highest moral probity is required, like banking. It follows that our nurses must be cleansed of any debt, so that they may approach their duties in purity.'

'But how –' Prue began.

'Hydro is not without the resources, and the will, to help clean the slate of errant nurses. However, in this as in all things, there is a price to be paid for error.'

She paused, while understanding gradually dawned on Prue's puzzled face, then smiled grimly and nodded.

'Yes. You have already agreed to Miss Macardle's examination of your endurance; it will prove sterner than you had envisaged. The examination will become a test, Prudence, and, as the price of cleansing your debts, a treatment.'

'I am to be beaten for my debts,' Prue said slowly. 'Beaten . . . properly.'

'You are.'

'And they will be cleansed as my body is cleansed.'

'They will. With no obligation on your part, save to serve Hydro and do your duty. You are free to terminate your service without prejudice, but we trust you not to be unkind to us, and to yourself.'

'Then I accept. I shall be – *will* be – a true nurse.'

'Welcome to Hydro, Prudence Riding,' said Miss Pickering joyfully. 'And I hope Miss Macardle doesn't lay it on too hard, this first time. You were right, in the bathroom. It *did* hurt me so . . .'

'You must be cruel to be kind,' murmured Prue.

They left the hotel, to effusive farewells from the staff, and rather familiar glances at Miss Pickering from both male and female guests; no bill was presented. On her way to Green Park station, Prue passed another telephone box that seemed sinking under the weight of strident postcards: Mistress, Headmistress, Nurse, Teacher – all strict, severe, dominant, merciless. She paused and read every one.

13

'You in the business, then, darling?' said a man presiding over a stall of souvenirs and fruit.

Prue smiled and took an apple and bit into it, her eyes daring him to protest.

'Yes,' she said. 'Yes, I believe I am.'

2

The Naked Cane

'Do come in, Prudence,' said Miss Macardle warmly, at
the door of her discreet fourth-floor flat. 'My, you *are* a
big girl! And I suppose that is why you have been sent
for a big girl's correction. Miss Pickering couldn't speak
too highly of you. I sensed she would have liked to
administer your treatment herself . . .'

Her Scottish lilt was as soft as her grey cashmere
sweater and skirt, and she was youthful – perhaps ten
years Prue's senior. Miss Macardle's dark hair was
fashionably styled, and her eyes twinkled above
discreetly rouged lips and a modest pearl choker as she
took Prue's coat. Prue looked at herself in the glass; she
had a pleated navy linen skirt, a V-necked navy sweater
and white blouse, black stockings and sensible blue
slingbacks. She observed that Miss Macardle wore dark
crimson shoes with heels of startling height and
sharpness, on white satin stockings. She did look like a
very elegant headmistress, with little half-frame gold
spectacles and, as a raffish touch, a pink frilly lace
petticoat that swirled an inch below her hemline.

'Big girls are often thoughtless, and get into pickles,
eh?' said Miss Macardle coyly. 'There is no shame,
Prudence – even I am thoughtless myself sometimes.'

Prue blushed and did not answer.

'Well, we've time for a cup of tea before we get down
to business. No need to explain the whys and wherefores

of your examination, Prudence – you are to receive a full treatment, and what must be done must be done. You're in agreement, of course.'

'Yes, miss,' said Prue, and blushed again.

They sat down on the sofa and Miss Macardle prattled merrily as she poured tea and served scones.

'Home-made!' said Prue.

'Of course,' said Miss Macardle. 'The old-fashioned ways are always best. My subjects always appreciate the little traditional touches, especially where a well-disciplined body is concerned. I take it you understand me.'

'You mean to spank my bottom, miss,' Prue whispered.

'Quite so!' trilled Miss Macardle, peering affectionately over her spectacles, as though Prue had successfully solved a crossword puzzle. 'Don't be alarmed. It will be uncomfortable – in fact I shall hurt your bottom quite hard – but you will feel the better for it, and thank me. It'll be a spanking to warm you up, but I'm afraid it will be rather more – our Scottish methods are quite scientific.'

She gestured towards a little card-table whose ornaments were covered with a linen cloth.

'I shall show and explain the implements soon,' she said brightly, 'but in the meantime do tell me what you have been up to lately, and especially what got you into this pickle.'

She placed a friendly hand on Prue's knee, and didn't seem to mind that her grey skirt rode up to show her frilly white stocking tops and her bare thigh beneath.

Prue began to speak hesitantly, of all the uncertainties of her life, of buying things to ease her confusions – clothes, mostly – of the nagging pain that she had a sister, Wendy, that she did not and could not know how to contact. The laws on anonymity of adoption were strict, and she dreamt that, somewhere, Wendy was

16

trying to find Prue, but with as many obstacles and as little chance of success; all she knew was that she had been fostered with some well-to-do people, away from London.

'I know in my heart that I would recognise her at once if I met her, that she is my spitting image!' cried Prue.

Miss Macardle asked about boyfriends.

'Well, I have had quite a lot, I suppose,' she admitted, and explained about her difficulties at jobs, about being a sort of sex object, and how the trouble was she half enjoyed it, aware that she teased and feeling guilty about it.

'It is normal for a girl to enjoy that,' said Miss Macardle. 'I must ask you, when you sleep with your boyfriends – and I assume you do – do you come? I mean, reach a satisfactory climax?'

'Why, yes! Of course!'

'And what makes you climax? Are their caresses always expert? Or do you . . . help yourself a little?'

Prue blushed fiery red.

'Why, yes . . . I admit I do. Touch myself . . . you know, to bring myself off while they are doing it. If they notice, it usually excites them more, funnily enough. It is just that it would seem unkind for me not to, when they go to such an effort to pleasure me – I mean, they give me pleasure, and it is right and kind that I should respond with my own. There is so little kindness in the world, it always makes me happy when I can be kind to a boy . . . and then they give me such joy in return, by getting all hard and . . . you know.'

'None of them ever suggested spanking games, as part of your lovemaking?'

Prue giggled.

'Gosh! I feel soppy. No, miss . . . well, there was one, and he liked to take me from behind, doggy-fashion, and would slap my bum as he was doing it.'

'Did that include putting his penis into your bumhole, Prudence?'

'No! Certainly not! It would be awfully sore, wouldn't it? But he did spank, I suppose you'd call it that, and it made me all red. But I didn't really notice it, didn't really feel it as pain, just part of the general feeling, the loveliness. And I didn't need to touch myself to come with him. But when Miss Pickering talked of the cane, and the birch . . . I must admit it seems a bit frightening, and hard to explain that people would willingly accept it.'

'Millions of people like to eat the hottest Indian food, or chilli peppers, with their eyes watering and their mouths and stomachs on fire. How would you explain the logic of that? Yet they come to crave such sensation. The principle of corporal chastisement is exactly the same, the difference merely which body part is stimulated.'

'It's just that I have this awful memory . . . I was in Hyde Park once, near where they ride their horses, and I was strolling along, and this couple came along on horseback. Real toffs, handsome people, very haughty, and all done up in the right kit. Anyway this little puppy had strayed from his mum, and was wandering around whining and crying, and I was going to pick him up to cuddle him. He took fright and ran away, right under the feet of this couple on their horses! The horses reared up, and the male was thrown off. He landed on his feet, but he was livid, and lashed me with his riding crop! Across my breasts . . . it hurt awfully, and he was going to trample and kick the poor little puppy, but I grabbed the puppy and said he could beat me if he wanted, but he wasn't to harm the defenceless animal. The woman was waving her own whip, and trying to lash me, but I was out of reach, and she was egging him on, "Go on, Rufus, give the girl a thrashing," and he lifted his crop again, but then he saw there were some parks police nearby, and he cursed and swore, and said, "Come on, Jocasta, let's go, and leave the bitch with her whelp" . . . and they went away. The puppy was OK, I found his owner, but I'll never forget those names, Rufus and Jocasta, and the horrible cruelty on their faces as they brandished their whips.'

'Such people are themselves imperfect, and in need of vigorous correction,' said Miss Macardle gravely, 'for they must be made aware that the beauty of chastisement is kindness, not hatred. All hatred is self-hatred, Prudence, and this Rufus, in lashing you, was showing his own profound need to be cleansed by the lash of another.'

They returned to the subject of Prue's over-enthusiastic spending, and the way out of her difficulties proposed by her new employer . . .

'I feel so rotten,' she admitted.

'And that is why I am here as your Nursing Mistress, Prudence,' said Miss Macardle softly, 'to help you get over that disagreeable feeling. No lady is perfect – we are young and beautiful like you, we think the world our oyster, and sometimes we do silly things, or get into *debt*.'

Her voice was chilling at this dreadful word.

'But,' she continued cheerfully, 'debts, moral or even financial, may be purged, often simply. That is why we use correctional aids –' she gestured again towards the ominous linen cloth '– to help us control ourselves by *submission*.'

Prue stammered that she was sure Miss Macardle was very wise, and would give a proper correction. Miss Macardle smiled and drew back the linen cloth, and Prue gasped.

'Have some more tea,' said Miss Macardle. 'Now, this is a Scottish tawse, Prudence. Feel it – feel the strength of the leather.'

Shivering, Prue touched the black leather strap, with its three tongues an inch thick and four inches deep.

'It hurts a lot but takes time to mark, so it is designed for rather lengthy punishment. This, however, is an English cane, as used discreetly in the better schools, and chastisement with the cane is very sharp and very painful. Have you ever been caned, Prudence?'

'N ... no,' said Prue. 'Nor tawsed, either. Only spanked.'

'Hmm,' said Miss Macardle. 'Finally, we have a paddle. It is American – sometimes used in fun, you know, because it makes a great noise. You can see it has air-holes in its body – that is to minimise resistance and ensure maximum impact on the bottom ... or other part of the female body.'

She fingered a little wooden oval, like a ping-pong bat.

'I got it from an American, actually, at Goodenhall air base, which is tremendously hush-hush. I got to know some of our dear American cousins. They were very sweet.'

'Must I be beaten with one of those awful things, miss?' said Prue.

'Not with one, Prue, but with all,' said Miss Macardle.

She got up and closed the curtains.

'There is no birch,' said Prue tremulously.

Miss Macardle smiled.

'I am not cruel, Prudence,' she said. 'The Northumberland birch might be too stimulating for an untried bottom like yours, and would defeat my object. Now,' she continued briskly, 'what I think is best is to take you over my knee first, for a hand-spanking. I think forty would be enough to warm you. Then the tawse – for that you'd better stand up and touch your toes, like the schoolgirl you so charmingly resemble just now. And we'll round matters off with a juicy caning, and for that you'll be allowed to bend over the sofa to support yourself. I ought to warn you, Prudence, that I am quite

20

serious about disciplining young ladies, and cane severely. I am not cruel, but nonetheless a stern Mistress.'

Prue swallowed in extreme agitation.

'I'm ready for my beating, miss,' she said shyly. 'I'm new to this, I have been spanked, but never by a proper Mistress, and –' she gulped '– I think I have needed this all along, to feel my bum properly beaten I mean, and have my . . . my silly airs thrashed out of me.'

'Excellent!' said Miss Macardle. 'And then you'll have a good appetite for your supper – I have a nice hotpot.'

'Why, suppertime will not be for hours, miss,' said Prue, apprehensively.

Miss Macardle smiled and nodded agreement. Then she pulled her skirt and pink frilly petticoat up, and gestured that Prue should position herself across her thighs. Prue rose and did so, breathing deeply and smelling the scent of her chastiser, pungent as though in eagerness to award the beating. She buried her face in the cushions and felt Miss Macardle lift her skirt up to reveal her knickers. She peeked round, and caught a glimpse under Miss Macardle's petticoat; she saw a rich swelling of smooth milky skin, and realised to her surprise that Miss Macardle herself was wearing no knickers – furthermore, that she seemed to have no hair at all at her lady's place. Miss Macardle saw her glance, and merely smiled.

'That's right, Prudence. I don't wear knickers, and I go bare . . . down there. It is a matter of hygiene, air on the skin, and improvement in the circulation. A nursing mistress must set a healthy example! But now to business. Try not to squeal too much, Prue, for you'll need your lungs to squeal at the tawse and the cane. But squirm and clench your bottom all you want. I expect you won't be able to stop yourself.'

Miss Macardle was right. As the first slaps fell very firmly on the stretched fabric of her knickers, she felt

21

her bum twitch, and flinch, and then wriggle in pain as her buttocks clenched under the stinging blows. Miss Macardle spanked her quite rapidly, with no pauses, and Prue felt tears welling in her eyes, and her gorge rising.

'Ooo!' she heard, a strangled moan from her own throat.

Thereafter she swallowed hard, and tried not to make noise. She tried, too, to count the blows, but her bottom smarted so much that she lost track after the twentieth. But as her belly squirmed against the cool satin of Miss Macardle's stockings, and she felt her Mistress's muscles tense as she delivered each spank, Prue began to moan again, but with a purring 'mmm', as though she were actually enjoying it. And she felt a distinct stiffening of her damsel and nipples.

'That's forty!' said Miss Macardle. 'You took it quite well, girl. I expect you'd like a little rest before we proceed to the paddle, and, Prudence, don't think me cruel, but I shall take you on the bare for the rest of your punishment.'

Prue sat up and wiped the tears from her glowing cheeks, grimacing as her bottom touched the sofa.

'My bum bare! O . . .'

'Look at your knickers, girl – they are in a state. They'll have to come off, for hygienic reasons if nothing else. And besides, a chastisement is more purifying when taken on the bare.'

Prue looked down, and touched the crevice of her panties. Her panties were sopping wet with the juices of her excitement! She blushed, and sprang up.

'O, Miss! I'm so ashamed! I've wet myself!'

'No, Prudence, you haven't done that,' said Miss Macardle, 'but you'll want to visit the bathroom anyway.'

Miss Macardle accompanied her, and took charge of the wet garment, which she left to soak in a basin, making no move to leave while Prue made water. She sighed with relief, and Miss Macardle said that they had both drunk a lot of tea, so when Prue had finished, her hostess squatted too, and peed quite unconcernedly as Prue wrung out her knickers. Miss Macardle said they were all girls together, weren't they? Prue turned and lifted her skirt to inspect her bare bottom. She looked at it a long time, with soft eyes. Back in the sitting-room, she draped the garment on the fireguard to dry, and then it was time for her paddling. Prue resumed her position on Miss Macardle's lap, and handed her the heavy wooden paddle. She flinched as the instrument slapped her naked flesh.

'My,' said Miss Macardle, 'you have reddened quite nicely. But there is a long way to go, my girl. You have a very sweet croup, you know.'

The paddle looked like a comical thing, but was heavy, and each blow made Prue flinch. She ground her teeth together to stop squealing, but could not stop the occasional 'mmm', escaping her throat. But she was not purring now. Still, she beamed when Miss Macardle murmured, at the thirty-third stroke from the paddle, that she *was* a brave girl. At the fiftieth, she sat up and rubbed her glowing nates.

'Brave?' she said nonchalantly, but sobbing. 'O, I don't think so, miss. Punishment is just like any other transaction, isn't it? You pay the price.'

'Yes,' said Miss Macardle. 'Guilt is nothing. A debt must be settled and that is all. Never forget, Prue, that a sound naked thrashing is the best cleansing for a girl, and the same is true for males ... always at a lady's hand.'

'A male ... beaten by a girl ...' murmured Prue.

She saw that her inner thighs were quite glistening with her liquid, and that she had dampened Miss Macardle's stockings and skirt. Then she peeked again, and saw that not all of Miss Macardle's oily pool was from Prue's quim alone. Miss Macardle's shaven fount gleamed wetly in the firelight. The Mistress rose, and picked up the tawse, stroking it as she would a lover. Her breath was slightly hoarse, and her face flushed. Prue could see little rivulets of wet on her stockings beneath the hem of her petticoat.

'You like my stockings?' murmured Miss Macardle. 'I have quite a collection – stockings and corsets, and bras and – O, oodles of hygienic things! How well a good corsetier understands a woman's needs! A woman's body must be pampered and rubbed and stretched, and firmly controlled, just as a woman's bottom must have regular moral correction. Now for the tawse, Prudence. You are nicely warmed up, and your bum is well coloured. So I think you should take your skirt off completely, otherwise it will flop over your bottom and spoil my stroke – yes, that's it – now knot your blouse up around your sweater, and bend over in position, that is, legs well spread and touching your toes.'

Trembling, Prue obeyed, and felt the air cool on her exposed wet fount. She tensed and braced herself for the tawse's lash, and jumped at the first stroke.

'O, miss!' she cried. 'It's dreadful!'

'Yes,' panted Miss Macardle. 'It is quite horrid. And just think, you must take another forty-nine strokes. Your poor bum will be quite black and blue – it is not just a figure of speech, I assure you – and a pretty purple too.'

She continued to flog Prue's naked buttocks, and now Prue squealed piteously and her whole body wriggled as the whiplashes scored her. Miss Macardle's aim was deft, and made sure that no inch of Prue's bare was unmarked, from the tender furrow between her clenched buttocks – she would wait for the moment when Prue relaxed her fesses a little, then suddenly strike! – to the soft skin of her thigh-backs.

'How is that, Prue?' said Miss Macardle, not pausing in her flogging.

'O,' gasped Prue, 'it is not so bad, Mistress, I mean, the pain is awful, especially right at the top of my bum, and on my thighs. You know how to hurt! But the pain almost feels a part of me now ... it is *my* pain. I wouldn't mind if you opened the curtains, and let the whole world see that I can take it like a lady!'

'Mmmm ...' said Miss Macardle.

At the fiftieth stroke, her tawsing was at an end, and Miss Macardle laid aside the leather thong. She picked up the cane. Her breath was very rapid and panting now, and she said to Prue that there should be no pause. Prue rubbed her smarting bum and grimaced, twisting her tear-stained face, but obediently positioned herself over the sofa back, clutching the ends with her fingers and with her legs splayed wide on tiptoe, on Miss Macardle's direction.

'It hurts more on tiptoe,' she panted. 'You can't squirm as much to dissipate the pain. Now it'll be a dozen with the cane. And one for luck. Feel it, Prudence. Feel the wood that is going to kiss your naked skin, as she has kissed so many others. Now – anything you have felt will be nothing to the cane. Are you sure you can stand it?'

'I must,' said Prue. 'I shall, miss! Cane me, miss, cane me bare, as hard as you can, and make me really squirm, then I shall be content that I have settled my debt. I feel guilty – you must suffer that my treatment hurts me so.'

'O ...' sighed Miss Macardle, and Prue felt her hand gently stroke her bottom.

'Unless you get pleasure from flogging, miss,' said Prue.

'I am a professional nursing Mistress, and my pleasure is giving treatment. If I got pleasure from hurting,' Miss Macardle said, 'why, that would be immoral, and I myself should have a debt to settle.'

Suddenly the cane whistled, *vip!*, and the first stroke

caught Prue full across the centre of her fesses. The pain lanced her like a white-hot javelin; her legs jerked straight behind her as her back arched, and she clutched the sofa, burying her face in the cushions to stifle her scream.

'Mm! Mm! Mm!' came her muffled gasps of anguish.

The second stroke landed, taking her in the same place, and then the third. Her legs shuddered and jerked straight, and her belly and fount squirmed in agony, as though to burrow into the sofa away from the dreadful cane cuts. For the fourth, Miss Macardle shifted her aim, and took her on the backs of her thighs – again, three strokes to the same place. The next three were right at the tender tops of her buttocks; it was all Prue could do to stay on tiptoe. Then – two hard cuts right to her furrow, the tip of the cane brushing right against her bumhole! And the final two returned to the centre of her buttocks, her glowing core of pain.

When it was over, Prue heard the cane clatter to the floor; she remained groaning in position, until she felt Miss Macardle's arms around her, helping her to her feet and embracing her with a passionate hug.

'O, Prudence, I am so proud of you!' cried Miss Macardle. 'Your poor bare ... I've never seen any croup so purple and hot from my cane – as though the cane sensed a lover in you, and *wanted* to kiss you!'

Prue smelt the tempting hotpot from the kitchen and looked at the clock – two hours had indeed passed. She smiled at Miss Macardle through her tears and said she had well paid her debt, hadn't she?

Miss Macardle said that now she had to go to the ladies' room, and Prue said she must too. She strode through this stranger's house entirely naked from her belly-button down, as though she owned it, and could do what she liked, in the insolence of her punished nudity. In the bathroom, she stepped aside for Miss Macardle who squatted first, lifting her skirts and

26

revealing that delicious shaven fount, glistening with her secretions which she made no attempt to hide. Prue hopped from one foot to the other; Miss Macardle noticed, and smiled.

'Desperate, eh? We all know the feeling. If you can't wait, Prudence – here, come. We are girls together now, united by the lovely friendship of the cane.'

Prue was clasped by the waist and brought to a squatting position on top of Miss Macardle, and, by stretching her own thighs wide, she could comfortably squat and do her business through the aperture of Miss Macardle's thighs. Her aim was not accurate: both women were so intent on their pent-up evacuation that neither minded the splashes, and when Miss Macardle gave a final sigh of relief, neither made the first move to disengage from their curious position.

'You have certainly paid your debt, Prudence,' said Miss Macardle softly, 'but . . . I haven't.'

Prue felt the Mistress's hands stroke her lower belly, just by the curls of her fount, and tingled at the gentle touch. She asked with trembling voice what Miss Macardle could possibly mean. Miss Macardle's fingertips brushed her swollen clit, and she did not resist as the Mistress touched the lips of her fount, and let her fingers rest there, slowly massaging the oily place.

'I watched your bare bum squirming so prettily under my cane, Prudence, and . . . I took pleasure. Shameful pleasure.'

She took Prue's hand and put it to her own wet gash.

'You see?' she said. 'I am all wet . . . with naughty stuff. Just like you, you lovely wicked girl. And I must pay.'

Prue rose, trembling and sighing. Without a word, she took Miss Macardle by the hand and led her to the drawing room. She put her new Mistress over the sofa back and lifted her skirt and petticoat. Prue picked up the cane, still warm from her own bottom. Miss

Macardle splayed her stockinged legs, and whispered, 'Yes . . .'

She took a dozen strokes before her squirming became a violent shudder; at the thirteenth she moaned, and her hand slipped between her thighs, where she began to rub herself, as though oblivious of any presence save the cane's.

'Harder, harder . . .' she gasped at each lash.

Prue's fount flowed wet and hot as she watched Miss Macardle diddle herself, her naked bottom writhing hard under the cane, and then her own fingers went to her pleading damsel, rubbing it as she flogged: until at the thirty-third canestroke, Miss Macardle cried out in a spasm of writhing pleasure, and Prue's legs wobbled as the hot joy of her climax poured through her like molten gold. Both women panted hoarsely for some moments before Prue laid down the cane and kissed her Mistress's reddened bottom.

'Did you diddle, Prudence?' said Miss Macardle. 'I hope so.'

'Mmm . . .' said Prue.

'Thank you for my chastisement, miss,' said Miss Macardle as she rose. 'I have needed that for a long, long time. It is not the same when you do it to yourself. Sometimes, it must be another lady, one who *understands* . . .'

She asked shyly if Prudence thought she had a nice bottom, for a mature woman, and Prue said it was superb. Miss Macardle beamed, then knelt, to kiss Prue's naked quim.

Their supper awaited, and both women, now decorously dressed once more, attacked the savoury hotpot. Their punishments, and their passionate diddling, were not mentioned. Afterwards, Miss Macardle said that Prudence could look at her clothes and 'hygienic' underthings. Prue went to the bedroom and was delighted at the array of corsets and waist

cinchers, bras and garters and myriad-coloured stockings, and panties of every daring cut, all of which Miss
Macardle explained had a hygienic purpose. There were
more sombre, corrective implements too: whips, of
course, but chains and pincers and shackles, hoods and
masks, gauntlets and an array of brightly painted dildos
of fearsome dimensions. Prue stripped and tried on
garment after garment, under Miss Macardle's approv-
ing scrutiny.

The only interlude came when she put on a
particularly vivid corset, in garish mauve, with matching
panties and stockings. Miss Macardle helped her strap
herself far more tightly than she should have, just for a
giggle – her scented body was close to Prue's and her
arms around her ... Miss Macardle quietly lifted her
skirts, pulled Prue's panties down, and the two women
faced each other. Miss Macardle took a fearsome
double dildo, without words, nor fuss, nor surprise, and
inserted each prong into her own quim and Prue's right
to the hilt; then she strapped the instrument in place
with a tight leather thong which pressed their bare
bellies deliciously hard together. Their lips and breasts
silently pressed, they slid their hands down each other's
bellies, fingered their soaking wet quim lips and damsels
until both cried in new spasm.

Miss Macardle sighed as she replaced her skirts, and
kissed Prue on the lips with surprising possessiveness.
She smiled warmly as Prue carefully cradled her gift of
mauve panties, stockings and corset; a four-thonged
whip, pixy hood, and the double dildo which had
possessed her gash! But Miss Macardle looked at her
watch, then held her by the shoulders, her arms
outstretched, and licked her lips pensively.

'I sense that you are very special, miss,' she said. 'I
think you have the body and spirit of a nurse, perhaps
a Mistress.'

'For that,' said Prue, trembling, 'I feel that my

29

bottom must taste the birch . . . the Northumberland birch.'

'You are brave,' said Miss Macardle, 'and virtuous.'

'Will you, miss? I mean, here? Now? Flog my bare with your Northumberland birch? I will take it proudly.'

Miss Macardle stroked Prue's bottom, and said that her flesh must mature for the birch, like a fine wine.

'And while I have a range of birches, the only true Northumberland birch is kept by the High Mistress herself.'

At that moment the doorbell rang.

'First,' said Miss Macardle, 'we must see if you have the spirit of a Mistress, as well as the body. You will change clothes.'

While Miss Macardle answered the doorbell, Prue put on the clothing as instructed, trembling with pleasure and excitement. Her costume was like a fantasy vixen's: thigh-boots of gleaming black leather, with incredibly high heels and pointed toecaps, and spurs! Then a very tight corset which thrust her breasts up very high but scarcely covered them at all, so that half of each nipple peeped coyly over. Leather gauntlets that came up over her elbows; skimpy panties made of fine chain mesh, which left the orbs of her buttocks almost entirely nude; a studded leather choker, and earrings which were six-inch nails. To complete the ensemble, she was obliged to don a leather hood, with apertures for her eyes, ears, and mouth only. She heard the front door open.

'You are late!' cried Miss Macardle. 'You pathetic creep! I can't be bothered with a miserable worm like you. What? Roses? You snivelling pig, trying to gain favour with cheap bribery? Why aren't you on all fours, you dog? I should whip your bum raw, but you are not worth the effort.'

'O, please, Mistress,' Prue heard a male voice whine.

'Come in. I have a colleague who has heard all about

30

your pathetic ways, and she knows what will cure you. I shall watch your treatment, and you'll pay double for the privilege, otherwise you can go and never return.'

'O . . . yes, Mistress . . . thank you . . .' whimpered the male.

There were shifting and rustling noises, and then Miss Macardle entered the bedroom and clapped her hands in approval of Prue's adornment. She handed her a cat-o'-nine-tails, and a four-foot schoolmistress's cane with a crook handle. Then she winked, and said this was one of her more intractable subjects, and Prudence must show her mettle by treating him exactly as he deserved. Prue's heart beat as she re-entered the salon to find the male, naked and bound with leather cords to a flogging frame which had been concealed under a tablecloth. His head hung in abject shame and submission. His bare buttocks were stretched high, and his thighs and feet splayed, so that his ball-sac was clearly visible dangling there. Miss Macardle reached into her quim, then into her anus, and withdrew two sopping, mashed wads of chewing gum, then stuffed the glistening mass into the male's mouth. Promptly afterwards, he was gagged, with a leather thong and a large steel ball in his mouth. He was utterly, thrillingly helpless, and Prue understood what was required of her.

'Chewing gum is hygienic, and helps a male subject to reflect on his errors,' said Miss Macardle solemnly, 'particularly when well-moistened. My lady's place likes spearmint, while my nether hole prefers raspberry.'

The male lifted his head and looked at Prue, mutely pleading. He could not have missed the vengeful gleam in her eyes, and he began to whimper with abject, terrified happiness. Prue lifted the cane and struck the helpless bare arse. He moaned, and Prue then laid two more rapid strokes on his bare, drawing pink almost at once. He gasped with two short yelps and, lowering her voice, Prue hissed that he was to make not –

31

one – sound – (each syllable accompanied by a whistling canestroke), otherwise the whole treatment would begin over again.

'You have already taken six strokes,' she snapped, 'but the beating is counted as from now.'

She saw a tightening of his balls – the penis was beginning to stiffen. She laced him again with the cane, right in the deep pink of his earlier strokes.

'One!' she said, bending close to his ear. 'And it shall only stop when I say so, and when you have been truly reminded of the cringing vermin you are, sir! No matter how much you wriggle or squeal or protest, it'll do no good: I don't know you, and I don't want to know such an abject thing. To me, you are just a bare male bottom to be flogged to submission by your rightful Mistress, and your bottom will take her full merciless treatment – you worm! You slug!'

At her words, his penis strained in full erection! Prue continued the flogging, with hard and remorseless strokes, developing a rhythm and not bothering to count her fervent strokes. Miss Macardle left the room for a while and returned, to observe the quivering male fesses reduced to dark crimson, then a terrible mottle of purple and black, and squirming madly as the male's legs shot straight at each stroke, to be restrained by his thongs.

'Excellent, miss,' came Miss Macardle's voice. 'Try the cat on his wretched shoulders, he doesn't like that at all.'

Prue obeyed, and began to flog the male's bare shoulders, raising crisp pink, then crimson as the cruel thongs stroked his helpless skin . . . like a sailor strapped at the mainmast, bum and back wriggling juicily. Then she took the largest dildo, parted his buttocks, and rammed it hard into his bumhole, right to the hilt. The male writhed frantically, with hoarse, anguished gasps. She strapped the leather cord round his waist, and ordered him to hold the dildo inside him. Miss Macardle smiled approvingly.

Prue was sweating with her exertions, and flogged the man even through eyes blurred with sweat. She began to apply both the cane and the cat at the same time, to his buttocks and back. Sometimes she stopped, and asked in a hiss whether he could stand any more. His head would shake violently to indicate that he could take no more, at which Prue cried, 'Impudent boy! You dare to dictate to your Mistress!' and the flogging would recommence. At length, Miss Macardle looked at her watch and said it was time to stop, as a Mistress should not tire herself on such a worthless arse. Twenty-six strokes with cat and forty-five with cane were quite enough for the wretch, as a male's bum was weaker than a female's. Miss Macardle unfastened his restraints, apart from his anal filling; he knelt before Prue and licked her boots, an attention she rewarded by pushing her sharp toecap right into his mouth, and then raked her spurs right across his bare purple flesh. He moaned in an ecstacy of humiliation. He turned to lick Miss Macardle's shoes, and she threw his jacket over his head.

'The usual tribute, but double, remember,' she snapped, 'and if you touch my skin with that miserable flesh of yours, you shall never receive my treatment again.'

She lifted her skirt and parted her thighs, revealing her naked fount. He fumbled for his wallet, extracted six fifty-pound notes, and rolled them into a cigar, which he placed between his lips, then pushed them into Miss Macardle's gaping quim. At no time did his trembling lips touch the taunting pink vulva that glistened with Miss Macardle's excitement. His final instructions were to keep the dildo in his anus all the way home, and for two hours after he got there, removing it under no circumstances before that time was up. He dressed, red-faced and his cheeks wet with tears, and began to burble his thanks, when Miss Macardle rose and kicked his bottom with the utmost contempt until, still burbling, he was out the door. Miss Macardle smiled at Prue and extracted the wad of notes from her quim.

'I like that touch,' she said. 'So near and yet so far. How he would love to kiss my lady's place! But it would never do to let a subject take liberties, or enjoy himself. A nurse's treatment must be impersonal, hence friendly, which is the nicest satisfaction. I am sure you are aware that men pay for sex, Prue, or what they imagine to be sex. It rarely satisfies, since the mere orgasm is scarcely one per cent of the joy of intimacy ... the intimacy which they crave, but which they rarely receive, since a woman so easily simulates it. But a beating cannot be simulated! Three dozen with the cane is three dozen with the cane – an event, independent of the feelings of the practitioner, and so both parties to the transaction are satisfied. The male wants to be thrashed – he is thrashed! He wants to be insulted and despised – he is insulted and despised! The beating of the bare bottom achieves a delicious intimacy, precisely because intimacy doesn't come into it! Instead, punisher and punished share a complicity, which is infinitely more hygienic.'

She peeled off four of the banknotes and gave them to Prue, telling her it was her just share.

'You start at Hydro on Monday, as Nurse Riding. The High Mistress Hygienic is a dear friend of mine, although you won't see her much – the Hydro is very strict and hierarchical – but her eye will be on you. You'll be well looked after, and well trained, in every way ... Take the things I gave you. O – and one of my cards.'

Prue looked at the proffered card, and it was not the same as the one she had before from Miss Pickering. This one showed a photographed woman dressed in the costume, or at least the underthings, of a nurse: waspie

34

corset, high boots and thrusting conical bra, with stockings and suspenders. She was holding a cane and a syringe over the bottom of a trussed naked male.

STRICT HIGHLAND NURSE TRAINS NAUGHTY BOYS IN ALL FORMS OF HYGIENIC DISCIPLINE, it read, and the nurse was none other than a stern and glowering Miss Macardle.

'O,' she said, 'I didn't mean to give you that one. Never mind, take it.'

She grinned impishly.

'A respectable Mistress has to have a bit of light relief sometimes, and phone boxes can come in awfully handy . . .'

3

Mermaid's Kiss

Cloughton Wyke Health Hydro was approached by a winding road up to the clifftop, from where the dusk lights of Cloughton sparkled seductively in the distance. Beyond that were miles of reeds and waving sand-dunes, and the grey twilit ocean. The property was surrounded by a tall hedge, backed by rows of poplars, and there was a small gatehouse at which the taxi halted, to announce their business. The attendant – a lady dressed in a black fur coat against the evening chill, and with legs in black dress nylons – picked up a telephone and spoke briefly. Wearing black shiny boots, she emerged from her cubicle with a bucket and spray-gun, and sprayed the wheels of the taxi before raising the heavy barrier pole and allowing them to proceed. As they approached the great white crenellations of the mansion, through wide lawns, gardens and orchards, Prue looked back and saw that behind the poplars was a wire fence about twelve feet high, ringing the whole property. Even in the darkness, everything looked immaculate, and the wire fence gleamed. As she stood by the front door in the comforting nest of her cases full of clothing, Prue watched the taxi chug into the night, and nervously rang the doorbell.

'You are late, miss!' were the first words Prue heard at her new home. 'The Mistress of Hygiene takes a dim view of unpunctuality.'

She looked up and saw a young woman of about her own age holding a clipboard and dressed in a cross between a maid's and nurse's uniform. She said the 'new nursemaid' should follow her. She introduced herself as Nurse Heckmondthwaite and, without offering to help Prudence with her cases, she about-turned, flicked her pretty rump and strode briskly off on clacking high heels. Her uniform was white: a very short skirt and a tight blouse, under which her torso seemed unfettered by underthings. At her waist was coiled a curious tube of black rubber, with a knobbly bulb at the end.

Her blouse and skirt were made of thin, shiny rubber, although her stockings were cream-coloured, of finely meshed nylon, with a chocolate-brown back seam. Prue could see bare white thigh above her plain stocking-tops and suspenders, but could not see if she was wearing rubber knickers too, or any at all. The nurse had slim and finely muscled legs beneath her shiny cream stockings. They walked along a polished tile corridor, in pastel pink, and smelling medicinal, with vases of pretty flowers livening the pink walls, on which mural paintings depicted naked, or nearly naked females at various hygienic exercises. Prue asked the nursemaid if only females were treated here.

'Why, no, maid!' exclaimed her companion tartly. 'You'll see plenty of males – and not just pictures.'

Prudence was shown into a long corridor, this one painted white, like a real hospital. All along it were doors with little windows, like cells, and into one of these she was shown. It was a pleasant, if spartan room, with a bed, washbasin, table and an easy chair. The floor was dark-green linoleum with a little fluffy pink rug, and there was a steel-frame hospital bed, with crisp fresh linen and dark-grey blankets. There was a little vase of peonies on the table, which Prue thought nice, and the curtains were a cheap but bright flowery cotton; the window looked out over the grounds, and in the distance the night sea glinted.

'You can unpack later,' said Nurse Heckmondthwaite. 'I expect you'll want to get straight to bed, as reveille is at six in the morning. First, I'll take you to Matron's office, and have you enrolled.'

They proceeded down the corridor, at whose end the nurse pointed out the 'privy'; Prue glanced in, and saw a row of open shower stalls, equally open Turkish squatter commodes, a plunge pool, and cabinets which the nurse said were steam and sauna baths, and were in service twenty-four hours a day. A hot, acrid smell emanated from the privy, and Prue asked what a sauna was. The nurse explained that, like a steam bath, it was a hot cabinet, to cleanse the skin and revitalise the inner organs, only it had dry instead of steam heat. During a bath, the skin was stimulated by beating with birch twigs, beneficial to the circulation and 'moral wellbeing'.

'The sauna and steam bath are an essential part of hygienic therapy,' she said, 'alternated, of course, with an ice plunge. And the birch treatment is most important, for male and female subjects alike. It is Finnish: Finland is not very far away.'

Prue shivered, and said she believed the birch was a very painful punishment, and that there was a certain baleful magic about the word *birch*, and she had read of schoolboys being birched naked as punishment. She blushed when she said it. Nurse Heckmondthwaite smiled with thin lips, and replied that the birch in bathing was therapy, not punishment, but that therapy and punishment were truly the same thing.

'There *is* a magic to the kiss of the birch, above all other instruments of healing,' she said, 'and it is wonderful, not baleful magic. The cane kisses with one tongue, the birch with many.'

She recommended Prue take a short sauna before bed, as it would relax her after her journey.

They entered Matron's office, where Nurse Heckmondthwaite curtsied; Prue did likewise, and was introduced to Miss Bream. The Matron was a woman of about thirty, with a crisp white uniform of starched cotton, a pink pinafore over it, and, like the nurse, a very short skirt which rode up above embroidered cream stockings which appeared silk. Unlike the nurse, Miss Bream did wear a very obvious corselage under her blouse, for her bosom struck Prue as quite ... inordinate. The woman's breasts were massive, and cunningly supported and thrust outwards by what must be a very stout corset, which also pinned her waist to pencil thinness. Even under blouse and pinny, her nipples stuck out so huge and pointed that they seemed to wear a separate little corset of their own. Her hair was cut severely short at the back and sides, a lick of hair curled back from the forehead, in a boyish style. She too wore alarmingly high shoes with pointed toes and heels. Miss Bream looked over her pince-nez spectacles and nodded at her, then looked at the paper Nurse Heckmondthwaite handed her, and frowned.

'Late, eh, Nurse Riding?' she said, in the blunt accent of the north. 'Can't have that. Unhygienic behaviour has to be nipped in the bud, my girl. Tenner fine, I'm afraid.'

Prue looked puzzled.

'Nurse Riding . . . that's you, girl.'

'O . . .' Prue beamed, then frowned and said in embarrassment she was not sure she could afford so much.

'Out of your wages, then,' said Matron, 'only it's four pounds extra for the paperwork. Of course you may take a treatment instead – four strokes of the cane. I dare say you'd prefer that.'

Prudence gasped, but neither the nurse nor Matron seemed to think this anything extraordinary.

'A . . . a caning?' she exclaimed. 'On my first day?'

'Certainly. But four is hardly a caning. Don't tell me you are unaware of our hygienic rules, and don't tell me you've never been caned before. This isn't the namby-pamby Home Counties.'

'Of course I have, Matron,' Prue exclaimed proudly.

'Well, then. Four is only a tickle. Think it over; if you opt for treatment, you can take them in the morning after breakfast.'

'I . . . I think I will take the treatment, Matron,' said Prue, her heart beating. 'Since I am a nurse, now.'

'Very well. Four, then. On the bare, of course.'

'O! Of *course*, Matron,' murmured Prudence.

The rest of her interview did not take long; she signed some papers, was given a rulebook to study, and her basic uniform, a pile of clothing which smelled lovely and crisp and fresh. Matron said her training would take a week, but that she would be learning 'on the job'. Prue blurted that she was so looking forward to being a kind nurse, and wearing her lovely crisp uniform, and healing patients . . .

'Nurse Riding,' Matron said crisply, 'we do not have "patients" at Cloughton Wyke, we have subjects. And our subjects need no kindness from their nurses: they need, and get, hard and proper discipline.'

At her room, Nurse Heckmondthwaite bade Prue goodnight, and said that after breakfast, she would be shaved and given her deep cleansing, before being sent straight to her apprenticeship. In the morning, she had only to follow the other nursemaids to the breakfast hall.

'Shaved?' said Prue.

'Your whole body,' said the nurse, 'lady's place and all. Unless you are already shaved down there. Nursemaids may keep their fluffy heads, the Mistress thinks girlish vanity is not unhealthy, within limits. Goodnight, nursemaid.'

Prudence stripped, looked at herself in the mirror before wrapping herself in her towel. She ran her fingers through her curly mink, and looked at the fleshy pink

41

lips peeping coyly beneath. What a pity it had to be shaved! And yet . . . there had been something curiously exciting about Miss Macardle's bare mons. To be bare seemed suddenly desirable, with the lips of her gash no longer coy . . .

The privy seemed deserted at this midnight hour, but when she opened the door of the sauna to a blistering wave of hot air, she saw another body in it, lying face up and naked on the upper bench. Prue grinned and felt a bit silly – she had her towel, but, of course, one bathed naked, didn't one? Gingerly, she unfolded her towel and sat on it, on the lower bench by the other girl's toes. At once, the heat caressed her like a glove. The other girl sat up.

''Lo, nursemaid,' she said. 'Be a duck and fling some water on the stove, will you?'

There was a bucket and ladle, beside a selection of sponges and birch flails, which Prue thought looked more like branches than mere twigs. She obeyed, was rewarded with a ferocious hiss and gasped as a wave of hot humid air seemed to flatten her. The other girl laughed.

'First time?' she said gaily. 'New, eh? I'm Jess. My real name's Jezebel Rise, but everyone calls me Jess.'

Prue introduced herself. Jess was a brunette, her hair neatly pinned back in a bun, and her body glistening with droplets of sweat. Her breasts shone like dew, and they were deliciously formed, thrusting out full, and hanging quite proudly to her ribcage, as though stretched and inflated. Prue was reminded of Miss Bream, and wondered if some mysterious hygienic process was at work. Between Jess's legs, the fount gleamed like a polished vase, smooth as her whole bare body. Her shoulders and buttocks were impressively broad, as her waist was narrow. Pinned in her pierced nipples were two large silver rings.

'Still got your rug, eh?' said Jess boldly. 'Well, you'll feel better once it's off. Any hair under the pits?'

'Just a little,' said Prue nervously. 'I shaved the other day, and waxed my legs too, but –'

'I shave every day,' said Jess, 'usually in the sauna, 'cos you don't need lather. Doesn't take long once you get used to it. Surprising how hairy a girl really is, when you look into all the nooks and crannies. The Mistress Hygienic says we may be descended from apes, but shouldn't look like them. My bumhole gets so hairy! It's so much nicer now – smooth and slippery and more efficient if you see what I mean. I'll razor you here, if you like, once the sweat softens you up. Save the trouble tomorrow morning, dry shaved in full view of the nurses. Usually they do it after your bumsquirt, or "colonic irrigation", in hygienic parlance, which we all must have.'

Prue sighed with the pleasure of the heat seeping into her, and began to rub her hands over her sweating body. She felt quite wet very suddenly, and Jess said it was the steam: one did not want the heat to be too, too dry. Eager to make conversation, Prue said ruefully that it was her first night, and already she had incurred punishment, and was to get four strokes of the cane, on her bare.

'Four,' said Jess. 'Why, that's not punishment, it's a tickle. Surely you've been caned before?'

'O, dozens of times,' lied Prue.

'Well then! Bum up and bear it! I had two sets of eighteen, in rapid fire, a couple of days ago, with only five minutes' pause between sets. My, it smarted! And still does! Here, look.'

She twisted round and showed Prue her buttocks, which were mottled deep crimson.

'How awful!' said Prue, forgetting her thrashing of the male, which did not seem awful. 'Is it always on bare?'

'Always. What other caning is there?'

'Nurse's discipline does seem strict. What had you done?'

43

'Had to bathe a lady subject, and I didn't have the water cold enough. One set for that, and then to excuse myself I explained there weren't enough ice cubes in the fridge, and that got me an extra set, for whingeing. Can't say I didn't deserve it. Actually, I got my own back 'cos, on our next session, I gave her forty with the tawse, as part of her hygiene – *and* made her wear a discipline after – that's a hair shirt. Here, do you like my nipple rings? I got them last week, when I passed my test for second level. If I make third level, I'll be able to have my quim pierced too, and have a ring there, and maybe even a *guiche*, you know, a nice little ring between your gash and your furrow. The more tin, the more respect! And a tattoo . . . mmm!'

Prue said she felt quite faint, and Jess said it was time to take a plunge. She took Prue's hand and led her from the cabin to the pool, where she pulled her into the icy water. Prue shrieked at the shock, then broke out in giggles and sighs as she realised how lovely the cold was. They splashed in the water and she felt her nipples go all hard and tingly; Jess's nipples were hard too, and big, like little brown teacakes. Suddenly she touched Prue's fount.

'You don't mind if I have a feel?' she said. 'Just to see how thick you are, for your shaving. My, you do have a big mink! When you're bare, you know it will always grow again, and even thicker – should you want to look like an ape.'

Prue said she did not want to look like an ape; it seemed taken for granted that the vivacious brunette was indeed going to shave her now, and Prue felt attracted towards the young nursemaid, and was in no mood to resist. They returned to the cabin, and Jess invited her to join her on the top bench, where it was hottest. Before she sat, she picked up sponges and birch rods, and said that it was good fun to 'loofah' each other, then tickle with the 'twiggies'. Prue felt the sponge scrub her belly and breasts, then her back, then thighs and when Jess came to her quim, she scrubbed quite tenderly and for quite a long time, until Prue felt all tingly down there.

'That is nice,' she said dreamily, and began to do the same to Jess, finding that her sponge lingered most on the stiff nipples and fleshy quim-lips, which hung quite wide and showed the neat glistening pink within, in pleasant harmony to the pink of their lathered bodies. Jess quite brazenly put her fingers to her gash and opened the lips further, inviting Prue to 'scrub deep'. Prue did so, and felt the hard little button of Jess's damsel tremble as her strokes brushed her. Jess breathed deeply.

'I think we are ready for twiggies,' she murmured. 'I'll show you how it's done.'

Prue turned round, and felt the birch rods sweep lightly across her back, making her shiver with a stimulus that was halfway between pain and tickling. Then she turned to her front, and received the same treatment on her shoulders and belly, and then full on her breasts – to her surprise, she liked that best, and felt her nipples harden even in the wilting heat. Seeing her arousal, Jess began to beat her harder, and Prue did not object, not even when Jess parted her thighs and began to flagellate the soft inner skin, and allow the birch tips to brush the lips of her quim, which were now noticeably swollen and standing free from their tousle of mink-hair. Jess whispered that the cane was a sweet kiss, but the birch the embrace of love itself. Then she said it was time for her shaving, and Prue waited, sorry that her 'birching' was over, while Jess fetched her razor.

She made Prue lie down on her back and spread her thighs wide. Prue shut her eyes and drifted into blissful dreams as she felt the cool swish of the razor against the tender skin of her lady's place, and then she opened her eyes and saw Jess intent on her task, feeling the nipple rings stroke gently over her belly as the razor purred at her fount, and thought only of Jess. She reached down and began to stroke Jess's hair, and then was ordered to lift her thighs right up to her breasts.

Now Jess applied the razor to her furrow, and her bumhole itself, and Prue gasped as the razor tingled right on the tender skin of her arse-bud. She did not object, nor flinch, but felt her juices begin to trickle on her thighs and mingle with her copious sweat. Jess signified her work was over by planting a single kiss, with closed lips, right on Prue's gash, and, in passing, her chin brushed Prue's tingling damsel, making her cry 'oo!' and sigh. When it was her turn to birch her new friend, her hand trembled.

Jess opened her thighs, and held up her breasts, inviting Prue to 'tan teats' first of all. Prue did so, gingerly at first, but then harder and harder at Jess's insistence, until the breasts were deep pink and the nipple rings jangled loudly at each birch-stroke. Jess asked if Prue liked her teats, and were they big enough from the vacuum treatment, and soon she would be able to 'wear the lyre' like Miss Bream. She said Prue had lovely firm teats, and treatment would make them a dream. Prue concealed her puzzlement.

'O! O!!' Jess moaned. 'It's so nice. Who needs men, when we girlies can have such lovely fun together? Jerks, the lot of them, only fit for having their bums whipped and squirming with the spuling tube in their holes. How I love the wet slap of a cane on a male's bare croup! Don't you love to spank boys, Prue? You must have done, a bit. And that is why we are all here, really, isn't it? Because we love nurse's discipline, the harder the better.'

Prue lied cautiously that she had never spanked a boy before, but said that the idea did excite her. She asked what a spuling tube was, and learnt that it was the same as an irrigation – the Mistress loved German hygiene, with all these fearfully scientific names, and *spultherapie* was one of her favourites.

'You will make a very thoughtful nurse, Prue sweet,' Jess purred. 'The teats are so sensitive, in every way. To kisses and strokes ... and when it's done right, a teat-whipping under the lyre is pure beauty. How I long to feel it myself! Now let's have a taste on my thighs and my gash, and don't forget my bum. You know, when you pass the test for level three, you are permitted to take vinegar baths, like the subjects. Balsamic vinegar is wonderful for cleansing and toughening the skin. I've had one – sneaked in after Mrs Shapiro had hers, and had a whole half-hour before I was caught. Got thirty with the cane for that! – balsamic vinegar is costly, and supposed to be reused for the next subject, you see. But it was worth it, my bum hardly felt a thing. And I had my revenge, the next time *la* Shapiro got a vinegar bath, I had a really big pee in it first! O, yes, *that*'s good –' as Prue swished Jess's thighs and swelling quim-lips.

'Now for the juiciest bit,' said Jess, her eyes heavy with pleasure. 'My bum, please, and make her smart well.'

She turned round and spread her buttocks wide so that her clean-shaven furrow and anus bud were fully exposed.

'All over,' she whispered, 'and hard, nursemaid.'

Prue had lost all pretence at 'hygienic' treatment, and began to flog Jess's naked fesses with all her might. The birch rods, soaked in their sweat, were quite heavy, and dealt a resounding wet slap at each impact on Jess's trembling bare, which began to crimson very rapidly, the new caress overlaying her older colouring. At each stroke, Jess shivered and gasped, 'Yes ... yes ... harder,' until Prue's sweat was as much from her flogging exertion as from the sauna. She was scarely surprised to see Jess's fingers flick down between her open thighs and across her quim, where she quite blatantly began to caress her hard little damsel.

'You don't mind me diddling,' she panted, 'it's just that you whip so beautifully, Nurse. We're not supposed to – hygiene isn't supposed to be pleasure – but everybody does. It is all hypocrisy . . . O yes, up there, catch my bumhole, *how* it stings! Who is to prove we take pleasure? O, lord yes, that's good, I'm going to spasm . . . O yes, yes, beat me, Nurse, beat my bum, sweet Prue!'

Prue continued her flogging which was now more than dutiful, as she felt her own quim and belly fluttering in the excitement of the other's pleasure, and her own fingers found her clit as she watched Jess tremble in her spasm. Panting, Jess sat up and turned to place another kiss on Prue's gash, this time open-mouthed and with her tongue flicking on Prue's distended nubbin.

'Such a big clitty,' she exclaimed. 'Do let's diddle.'

She began to lick Prue's damsel with rapid and expert flickers of her tongue, sending shudders of pleasure up Prue's spine. Prue's fingers now began to rub and tweak her own tingling stiff nipples, and she felt herself close to orgasm. She heard Jess pause to whisper:

'Northumberland, such a strange place, with all the legends of the sea. Sometimes, at night, you can hear the foghorns calling to ancient drowned ships, like *this* – it's called a mermaid's kiss . . .'

To Prue's surprise and pleasure, she began to moan, or chant, softly at first then louder and louder, her open mouth fully cupping the lips of Prue's quim as the tongue continued its devilish flickering on her stiff clit. The vibrations seemed to shake every atom of Prue's body, as Jess bellowed with a mournful yet voluptuous sound that was just like a sonorous foghorn! Prue shivered in approaching ecstacy, and as Jess moaned her hymn of worship, she spilt over into a gasping luscious frenzy of orgasm.

48

No words were necessary; the two women paused to kiss full on the mouth, their wet tongues embracing, and then Jess pushed Prue's head between her own parted thighs. Prue did not resist, but fastened her mouth on Jess's quim lips and with her tongue found the stiff damsel. Flicking against it, and causing Jess to shake with her pleasure, Prue began to moan softly against the swollen quim lips, filling her lungs and roaring as she felt Jess flutter and moan in her new climax. Prue's fingers were busy on her own clit, still throbbing and stiff, and as her moans grew to a bellow, and Jess clutched Prue's hair and pressed her head to her quaking belly, both women climaxed a sweet second time.

Suddenly the door clattered open, and the two shocked tribadists saw, wreathed in steam, the glowering figure of Nurse Heckmondthwaite.

'This noise!' she cried. 'Enough to waken the drowned. Caught in flagrante, you wicked maids! You, Riding – I knew you were a bold one, arriving late. Well, it seems you have more to look forward to in the morning than a mere scratching of four. Four dozen will be more like it.'

'It was my fault!' cried Jess. 'I'll take the flogging.'

'Shut up, Nurse Jezebel,' snapped Nurse Heckmondthwaite. 'You shall take *a* flogging, but Miss Riding here shall take *the* flogging, along with her nursemaid's irrigation.'

She uncoiled her rubber tube and stroked the bulb insolently under Prue's trembling chin.

'And if I'm nice to Matron, I think she will permit me to administer both at the same time.'

'Redheads!' whispered Jess. 'They are all the same. Vitriol is so unhygienic!'

'I didn't know Miss Heckmondthwaite was a redhead,' said Prue. 'Her hair is brown, like yours.'

49

'Didn't you see the roots?' sneered Jess. 'She's embarrassed – why, I don't know, she is just as much of a goop whatever colour her hair is.'

The two nursemaids squatted beside each other in the privy, amidst the bustle of early morning ablutions. The women all wore their nakedness easily, and few bothered even to wear bathrobes for the short walk from bedroom to privy. Some who carried themselves proudly were adorned like Jess: with body piercings, metal armbands on waist, arm, thigh or ankle, variously gorgeous earrings or necklaces, or tattoos on their buttocks, bellies and even breasts.

There was a momentary hush as a new nursemaid entered the privy, and all eyes turned to her. She was nude like the others, but her nudity was so adorned that her body seemed almost clothed. She sauntered amongst her comrades as though inspecting them, and flicking a wet towel playfully at an occasional rump or bosom, which was greeted either by a pleased simper or a sullen scowl. She was dramatically tall, a good six feet in her heels, and her upswept hair was jet black. She was very slim, and her body rippled with lithe muscle, except for her fesses and teats, which actually jutted from her body in a way that looked like a surreal artwork, had it not been for the sensuous quivering of their firm, distended flesh. Alone amongst the nursemaids, she was not barefoot, but wore black shoes with sharp heels and toes, which seemed to be waterproof, of rubber Prue thought.

On her forearms and upper thighs she wore golden bands like an apothecary's snake, and the same on her left ankle, extending up her calf like a boot. Her extruded belly-button was pierced, and wore a black jewelled brooch, with a little gold tongue and eyes, and this was the head of a tattooed snake which grew across her fount and belly from her wide, thick quim lips. In the centre of her swelling buttocks, she wore an array of sparkling studs, each one seeming separately pierced, and around them a tattoo which was whorls of stars and moons, growing from the cleft of her furrow and embracing her fesses like a swirl of gold dust. She wore a ring through her quim lips but, as well as that, they were held apart by two clamps attached to tiny gold chains which fastened to the bands on her upper thigh.

Her open quim showed bright glistening pink within, and the effect was not so much shocking as proudly intimidating, as though daring a challenge of some sort. Jess whispered that being 'tent-pegged' was a rare privilege: by baring her quim so boldly, she was proclaiming her sovereignty. Chains criss-crossed her belly, leading from her quim ring to her nipples, which seemed very wide, like young apples, and were encased in black metal covers like pointed thimbles. Two further chains looped round her neck from her nipples and supported her conic breasts, although their quivering firmness suggested no need of support. They were duly pert, but at the same time so ripe and heavy that they should hang: but they did not. The waist above a flat belly was a pencil, and her naked flesh showed deep indentations, as though she slept in a corset. Her skin was pearl white, and glowed with fragile translucence that belied the taut frame beneath, and the cruelty of her wide, disdainful lips.

'That's Henrietta Farle,' murmured Jess, 'she's third level. She could easily make fourth, and be a Sister Surveillant like Heckmondthwaite, but she prefers to stay here in barracks, as we call it. I think she just likes to lord it over the rest of us scrubbers. She's so proud of her body, the hag! All the treatment she's had . . . she can take the lyre, with those teats.'

Prue asked if all the adornments meant something specific, and was told no, nurses like Henrietta simply enjoyed certain tolerances. As for the lyre – well,

Prudence would soon know: it was the most hygienic of treatments, being at once stern discipline and subtle beautification.

'Watch out for Henrietta, she's easy with her affections when you least expect, then tight when you want her to be easy. Power like hers is not just rank, it is aura.'

Prue whispered mischievously that she supposed Henrietta had a tent-peg for her bumhole too; then asked Jess if she had ever been in Henrietta's power. Surprisingly, Jess blushed and looked down.

'Sometimes ... it is hard to resist naked power,' she whispered, then shivered and shifted on her commode.

As if summoned, Henrietta Farle stalked towards the two squatting nursemaids and glared haughtily down at them through the steam.

'Well, Jezebel,' she said, flicking her towel right against Jess's quim, 'I hear you have been up to tricks – corrupting a new nurse, and letting her bum smart for your naughtiness. Scarcely ladylike, my dear.'

She peered at Prudence, and then more specifically at her bare breasts, holding her gaze quite impudently on her nipples; Prue suddenly blushed.

'You're lucky, nursemaid, that it's only Heckmond-thwaite who's going to beat you. If it were me ... why, you'd be making commode standing up! And you couldn't bear the touch of your tunic against those teats for quite a while ...'

Suddenly she flicked her towel against Prue's nipples, very sharply. Both nursemaids watched the curl of Henrietta's ripe bare buttocks as she swaggered away.

'The vicious bitch!' Jess swore quietly. 'I'd like to tan her bum – and that Heckmondthwaite. Each wants Miss Bream and hates the other ... intrigues are like that here, Prue. But I promise you'll always have *my* affection.'

Solemnly, as though to demonstrate her sincerity, Jess

made a great fuss of wiping Prue's bottom for her, which made them both giggle. Then they showered hot, plunged into the icy pool, and scampered glistening and naked to their rooms to dress. Jess cheered her by saying she would be issued with further clothes in due course, once settled in – 'they may not pay much, but the kit is quite decent.'

Prue unfolded her new uniform, crisp and clean and starched. She had a white skirt, very short, like Nurse Heckmondthwaite's, and a pair of dark blue nylons, with matching rubber-soled 'sensible' shoes – evidently, the wearing of high heels was for the senior nurses only.

But she was pleased at the frilly blue bra, suspender belt and lacy nylon panties which were flimsy and almost see-through. Her blouse was white nylon, and her blue bra was quite daring and visible through it, as it pressed quite tightly against her breasts. Over that she had a thin blue cardigan which she allowed to hang open. Her ensemble was completed by a pretty blue starched bonnet. Jess said she looked tight, meaning it as a compliment, and said they really were good about kit: if a nurse did well, she could get oodles of nice things, silks and cottons and leather, and even latex, like Heckmondthwaite. Prue laughed, and said she already had such things, quite daring ones too, in her cases, and hoped she would get the chance to wear them. Meanwhile, she said she felt lovely in her tight things, the casing of her uniform like a shell, protecting her and at every move reminding her of her body.

They proceeded to breakfast in the refectory, a large hall with tables seating a dozen nurses at each, and with the meal served from trolleys by 'skivvies' as Jess called them: nurses who were purging some imperfection or other with this minor penance. There were perhaps fifty nurses; a dozen of them sat adorned in their fineries at high table above them. Jess said that the High Mistress of Hygiene rarely dined in hall, and in fact rarely appeared at all.

'What if no one has committed any imperfections?' asked Prue innocently. 'Who serves the food then?'

Jess's only reaction was to laugh and shake her head. They tucked into their breakfast of thin toast and margarine, plentiful tea, salami, and hard-boiled eggs, with pots of acrid rhubarb jam. Prue was assured this was very hygienic. Jess said the piquant salami was reindeer meat, 'from over there', gesturing across the North Sea.

'Much more humane than eating battery-farmed stuff,' she said between mouthfuls. 'The reindeer gets a jolly good life and plenty of reindeer snogging, before he pops his clogs. Not like our poor pigs and chickens, cooped up and tormented their whole miserable lives, as if they were human beings!'

After the meal, the nurses scurried off to their duties. Prue reported to Miss Bream, for her novices' examination, along with five other maids for their weekly irrigation.

The Matron was brisk and her smiles were brief as she ordered the nursemaids to strip and fold their uniforms neatly. Miss Bream paid especial attention to the neat removal of the girls' panties and bras, telling them not to tear them off hurriedly, but to slip them over thigh and breast with ladylike calm and precision. She first complimented Prue on how smart she looked in her new kit, and then Miss Bream unhooked her bra for her, and put her finger into the elastic of her panties, at the cleft of her bottom, to help her draw them down. Miss Bream said that the others should take their irrigations first, under the surveillance of her assistant, Miss Gageby, while she gave Prue her medical. Prue was asked to lie down on a sort of operating table, while in the bathroom she heard whooshes, gurgles and squeals of the girls at lavage. Matron prodded and poked her, inserted her rubber-gloved fingers into every orifice, pressing quite long and hard in her holes to establish that she was 'vaginally experienced'.

'But your bum is nice and tight, Prue,' she said, 'so I guess you are an anal virgin.'

Before Prue could react, she added that nurses were grown-up maids, and were free to organise their own affairs, as long as they observed hygienic principles. She felt Prue's breasts, squeezing her nipples quite thoroughly, as though she were a mere subject of scrutiny, to be handled like an animal, or naked slave girl. Miss Bream said that she had lovely firm teats and, with training, she might be privileged to take the lyre. Prue asked what that was, and Matron said it was a device for the enhancement of the breast, which caused considerable discomfort.

'The principles of the Hydro,' she said, 'say that the controlled pain of discipline is the cleanest beauty.'

Then it was time for Prue's irrigation. She was strapped to a small table which spread her arms and legs wide, with her furrow and buttocks stretched wide on a raised platform. The other nurses, their irrigations complete, were allowed to stand and observe. Matron inserted two rubber tubes into both her holes, and turned a jet of hot water whose pressure at the root of her anus made her buck fiercely. This was sucked out, then a new jet entered her hole, now of freezing cold water. As the irrigation went on, she no longer tensed her sphincter muscle in resistance, but relaxed to welcome the spurts which filled her to brimming.

The fillings grew longer and longer, and each time Prue was ordered to hold the liquid inside her before evacuating. She said she felt about to burst, but Matron said that after a while she would get used to it, and even enjoy it, and that she should enjoy, too, the privilege of being bound for treatment. On her nakedness were fastened the eyes of the sullenly beautiful Miss Gageby, who kept brushing an errant lock of hair from her brow as she manipulated the taps. The door opened and Nurse Heckmondthwaite entered, bearing a long knobbly cane with a splayed tip. Miss Bream sighed, and said that they came to the matter of Prudence's chastisement.

'It was Nurse Heckmondthwaite who reported your imperfection,' said Miss Bream, 'so it shall be she who administers correction. I have determined the sentence, of course, after consultation with the Mistress of Hygiene, who graciously conferred with me on this matter. She thinks it healthy, Prudence, that you should so soon experience public correction of your own person, as a first lesson in the harmony of hygiene and stern discipline, which we ourselves must welcome even as we administer it to our subjects. The sentence, Prudence Riding, is twenty-one strokes of the cane, on bare. Normally, for such an offence, you would be stripped and bridled, and led through Hydro to refectory to bend over the high table. However, as you are a novice, you shall be chastised before these nurses only. Instead of public bridling, I am going to apply an irrigation of chilled oil, and you will please hold it in for the duration of your chastisement.'

There was a ripple of laughter from the nurses as Prue squirmed on the rush of freezing liquid which spurted forcefully into both her holes. Trembling, she tightened her sphincter, so as not to let the slightest dribble escape her anus and slit. She heard Nurse Heckmondthwaite lift the cane and swish it twice through the air, and then suddenly the implement caught her squarely across her naked buttocks. She jumped, and her sphincter tightened involuntarily with the searing lash of pain on her bare flesh. Tears leapt to her eyes but she did not cry out.

She looked round helplessly as her head jerked in her pain; she saw the nurses smiling, or else pressing fingers to mouths agape; Miss Bream had one hand inside her Matron's tunic, as though scratching her breast-flesh, but her fingers seemed to linger on her noticeably swollen nipple; Nurse Heckmondthwaite's face was flushed, her eyes heavy and her lips twisted in a rictus of ardent pleasure. The caning was slow, clever agony, like a white-hot sword crushed into her naked flesh. The strokes took her expertly, at every part of her croup and tender furrow, the cane's tips stroking with cruel precision a hair's breadth from her quim lips. But she did not protest, not even when the terrible twenty-first stroke caught her cruelly on her anus bud.

'Good,' said Miss Bream.

Prue sighed in relief that her punishment was over, until Nurse Heckmondthwaite respectfully reminded Misses Bream and Gageby, unctuously careful to address them properly as 'Miss', in deference to their rank: the nursemaid Riding was previously sentenced to take four.

'Deliver four,' said Miss Bream. 'Tight ones . . .'

Four more strokes! The cruellest of her beating cracked on Prue's bare buttocks. Her insides full to bursting, she squealed through clenched teeth at each cut, while the other nurses giggled, and Heckmondthwaite grunted in cruel satisfaction, at the frantic wriggling of her buttocks and swollen belly. At last, she heard Matron's instruction to evacuate, and now she sighed long in relief as she let the freezing oil spurt from her holes. She was unbound, and stood trembling before her tormentor, her eyes misted with tears. She thanked Nurse Heckmondthwaite and Miss Bream for their thoughtful punishment, and declared herself truly cleansed. Nurse Heckmondthwaite seemed a little disappointed, but Miss Bream smiled, and told her in a brisk voice to shower and dress, as her tasks awaited.

'You have to assist in the treatment of two subjects today,' she said, 'one female and one male. As you already seem sympathetic to the matter of correction, Prudence, you might be permitted to do a little more than assist.'

4

Deepest Need

Mrs Shapiro's bare bottom was as smooth as an hourglass. Prue's job was to hose the squirming dark woman as she noisily took her irrigation.

'Oo!' she squealed. 'Oo, this is too much! You are not nurses, you are beasts!'

'You are paying for us to be beasts, Mrs Shapiro,' said Miss Gageby sulkily, manipulating her tubes, and brushing back her unruly lock of hair, as though it were itself Mrs Shapiro.

'How well I know. Oo! Oo . . .'

Mrs Shapiro was a petite woman with lustrous raven hair, and her olive-skinned body shaven all over like the nurses. She seemed very young to require treatment, and could not have been over twenty-five. Her lovely skin sparkled with jewels which, with her breasts, shook in agitation as she took the tubes in her two nether holes; the teats were squashed flat against the table but, even flattened, they were obviously huge, with the nipples cushioned underneath like soft dark saucers.

Prue had passed several 'hygienic chambers' on her way to this one, with nurses scurrying to and fro, ushering subjects along. Henrietta Farle, who was as striking in her nurse's uniform as out of it, said that subjects must be treated like the pond life they were, and with proper nurturing they might grow into something resembling a flower. Discipline was the only language they understood, and the sterner the better. Miss Gageby, the Assistant Matron, reminded Henrietta that discipline was for the subject's good, and the tall nurse agreed, without much sincerity.

The chamber in which Mrs Shapiro was tethered was pleasant and airy, with vases of flowers and a pergola of climbing plants. It smelt of the sea. The open window looked out on the billowing ocean; inside was a little bathing pool, quaintly dappled with lily pads, various tubs and baths, and an array of frames whose fastenings and straps indicated an obvious disciplinary purpose. Two pretty nurses, Helen and Angela, had Mrs Shapiro trussed to an irrigation machine painted with pretty swirling designs in leaf green, like wallpaper. The nurses were twins, identical in every detail save that one was blonde, the other auburn.

Mrs Shapiro's treatment was to be what Miss Gageby called a 'gamut', beginning with a seawater lavage. She said that Prue must always obey without question, as every detail of every treatment was meticulously planned. Some hygienic chambers were designed for those of a particular temperament, while some treatments were so special that the subject had a room designed just for herself – or himself. Henrietta snorted that such pampering was bad for these 'brats' and that they should be lined up in a draughty Nissen hut and flogged till they whimpered, then dowsed in freezing water and flogged some more, and that the more you abused them the better value they got, and the more they would pay. Miss Gageby yawned.

'O, Henrietta,' she said mildly. 'Anyone would think full treatment was somehow unavailable.'

'It's just that if you give them luxury,' said Henrietta, 'they compare it unfavourably with other luxury, like home, or the Ritz Hotel. But if you give them hardship, they revel in it, for they have no comparison at all. Look at boys' schools! Generation after generation pays for the privilege of being brutalised.'

'Girls' schools, too, Henrietta,' murmured Miss Gageby.

They contemplated the writhing bottom of Mrs Shapiro, whose squeals filled the chamber. Miss Gageby brushed her lock and said she thought Mrs Shapiro's situation was scarcely luxurious. Miss Gageby's voice was quiet and silky, and beneath her surliness there was a strength, emphasised by her wide northern face; her full lips and high cheekbones had something Scandinavian. A majestic figure swelled beneath her tight matron's tunic, and the torso was well encased in a very tight bra and corset above a croup which bobbed pert and closely sheathed against her skirt. Her hair was a pleasant natural chestnut with reddish overtone.

Miss Gageby signalled that Mrs Shapiro's lavage was at an end, and the svelte olive woman was released from her bonds. She stood up and brushed the suds from her thighs and buttocks, and said that it was scandalous to be charged good money to be treated in such a humiliating way. Miss Gageby smiled at Prue and said lazily in her soft northern tones that she quite agreed, but she only worked here, and a simple northern lass was ignorant of London refinements.

'Nurse Riding is a London girl,' she added suddenly, 'and I am sure she will sympathise with you, Mrs Shapiro.'

Mrs Shapiro gazed at Prue in wide-eyed appeal.

'I don't know,' Prue said. 'This all looks pretty cushy to me. I view Cloughton Wyke as a challenge, to instil a little discipline into these northerners. Flowers and lily pads, indeed! At least I am glad to see some proper instruments of correction.'

And indeed, on the wall hung an array of bushy birch rods, glinting in the bright light. Henrietta seemed to glower at Prue's boldness, but Miss Gageby smiled comfortably, as though at some private amusement.

'Hmm,' sighed Mrs Shapiro. 'Dennis said the sea air would do me good, and . . . the other things.'

She glanced resignedly at the birch rods.

'I suppose he knows best. I do want to please. When can I take the lyre, Miss Gageby? Surely my teats are ready?'

'Another couple of treatments, perhaps, Mrs Shapiro,' soothed Miss Gageby. 'Now into the pool with you.'

Mrs Shapiro sighed and squealed again as she slipped into the cold pool. She shivered and slapped herself as goose pimples appeared on her pretty breasts, whose nipples stiffened quite dramatically into lovely big plums. Her breasts were indeed large and jutted very proudly; such size had, wondrously, little need of support. She squatted in the pool up to her neck, and the other two maids began to remove their uniforms. Miss Gageby nodded to Prue that she should do the same, and when all three were naked, they climbed into the pool with Mrs Shapiro. The water was indeed icy, but imbued with scented oils which glistened on its surface. They plucked lily pads and began to rub Mrs Shapiro's feet, indicating that Prue should do the same to her breasts. She obeyed, and began to rub the soft leaves over the skin of Mrs Shapiro's teats.

'Sea-lilies ... most valuable,' said Miss Gageby vaguely. 'Essential oils: dihydro – something – oxin ... seawater has potassium, calcium, magnesium ... all those things with "um".'

Henrietta meanwhile busied herself with another machine, an arrangement of cups and pistons with an electric motor.

'Oo! That tickles!' cried Miss Shapiro, splashing in the water. 'So does that,' she said to Prue as she massaged her hard nipples, 'but I don't mind.'

She looked with wide dark eyes at Prue, and winked ever so slightly, then shut her eyes and moaned.

'Do you like my breasts?' she whispered.

'Why, yes, Ma'am,' said Prue truthfully.

'Like touching them ... rubbing them? Dennis does ... he has such gentle hands. He likes my feet, do you know that men love to suck a lady's feet? I suppose you do. He likes my bottom even more, says I must be supple for him, must have the juiciest bum in the world. A girl's bottom needs treatment, and I'm still a girl, aren't I?'

'I am sure you are a very naughty girl, Ma'am,' murmured Prue, glancing again at the birch rods.

Without being asked, she applied her sea-lilies to Mrs Shapiro's belly and thighs, and then to the dark bare space of her fount, where her pink lips gleamed blurred under the swirling water. She touched the lips with her lilies, found them distended in her subject's pleasure, and began to rub firmly, at the same time stroking and squeezing the nipples through the lilies. Mrs Shapiro's breath became agitated and she sighed quite rapidly, her belly seeming to twitch a little. Miss Gageby observed Prue's actions with a curious smile, and did not interrupt, even as the oily bath was enriched with oils from the subject's quim.

After twenty minutes of treatment, Mrs Shapiro was ordered to rise, and mount the machine which Henrietta held in readiness. The woman lay face down on a frame; again her wrists and ankles were clamped, as well as her waist, and her breasts fitted into two large cups which hung below the frame. Inside the cups were little rods like stubby cigars. A pad under her belly was moved by a lever at Henrietta's control, and it hummed, rising to stretch Mrs Shapiro's bare buttocks high in the air. Miss Gageby yawned again, and selected one of the birch flails from the wall. Prue and the others towelled themselves and resumed their uniforms – Mrs Shapiro's body was still glistening wet – and then one of the nurses was sent from the room.

'This treatment,' Miss Gageby said, 'aids both physical and moral coordination. According to Hydro's policy of cooperation amongst subjects, a male subject shall undergo therapy with Mrs Shapiro: she must learn submission to a female nurse, while herself accepting the obeisance of a male, and at the same time exercising her own control.'

Miss Gageby reached into her pocket and withdrew a paper bag, whence she extracted five packets of spearmint chewing gum sweets. She emptied all the packets into her palm, and then stepped towards Mrs Shapiro's upturned rump, while Henrietta parted the lips of Mrs Shapiro's exposed quim with her long fingernails.

Miss Gageby reached underneath and pushed her entire cargo of chewing gum deep inside Mrs Shapiro's quim. Mrs Shapiro moaned, perhaps in discomfort, but mostly, Prue guessed, in pleasure. Miss Gageby ordered her to 'start chewing' and told her that the gum must be well melded by the end of her treatment, and the sugar coating dissolved. Mr Dennis Shapiro was most insistent that his wife learn proper muscle control in her lady's place ... Mrs Shapiro's bare nates and thighs began to clench as she dutifully began her work of mashing the gum sweets inside her quim, and a dribble of liquid sugar moistened her thigh.

The nurse returned, leading by the hand a tall young man with a boyish shock of hair, and a firm, chiselled face that was almost female in its prettiness, save for the full silky 'handlebar' moustache that adorned his lip like petals. He was perhaps twenty years old, certainly not older than the bejewelled Mrs Shapiro, yet he wore a boy's school uniform, of grey flannel shorts, a striped tie and white shirt, and a dark maroon blazer with yellow piping. He grinned shamefacedly and hung his head.

'This is Mr Jeremy Pleasant,' said Miss Gageby with studied indifference. 'Only we don't call him that, we call him by his surname only, because he is nothing but a scruffy little schoolboy, isn't that right, Pleasant?'

'Yes, miss,' stammered the young man.

'You address me as Matron! That is one imperfection. And what do scruffy little schoolboys get when they are imperfect, Pleasant?'

'They . . . they get what for, Matron,' he mumbled.

'You may begin by making amends and serving this lady, Mrs Shapiro. I believe her feet need cleaning.'

Miss Gageby was handed a bucket by one of the nurses. The bucket brimmed with tiny seashells and pebbles, and Miss Gageby emptied it over Miss Shapiro's splayed feet. As though practised in this duty, Pleasant knelt before the naked woman and took her left foot into his mouth, then began to suck and lick her toes. Miss Gageby said that Mrs Shapiro must be sparkling clean, and if he let just one seashell mar the floor . . . She gently swished the birch in the air, and both Pleasant and Mrs Shapiro shuddered slightly.

The Assistant Matron yawned again, and positioned herself beside Mrs Shapiro's bare croup, which she absent-mindedly began to stroke, then nodded to Henrietta, who started her machine working. It hummed and throbbed and the suction cups began to vibrate powerfully on Mrs Shapiro's pinioned breasts. Miss Gageby allowed her fingertips to play lightly along Mrs Shapiro's furrow and stroke her anus bud and the glistening outer quim-lips. Mrs Shapiro moaned, this time in real anguish, and Prue gasped: the cups were sucking fiercely at her breasts, while the little cigar-rods or pistons pummelled and squeezed on her nipples, the whole effect being to widen, stretch and lengthen the breast-size. It was obviously very painful, and Mrs Shapiro's moans increased to a sharp squealing as Miss Gageby yawned again and casually lifted her birch to bring it smartly down on her subject's naked fesses, raising a pink flush.

Prue and the other nurses stood with their hands demurely clasped at their laps as the treatment progressed; the naked olive woman being simultaneously licked, breast-pumped, and flogged with a lazy but vicious birch, which soon had her olive rump mottled crimson. Helen explained that the treatment was to elongate and firm the breasts: the suction enlarged the mammary tissue, while the pistons toned the muscle beneath and pummelled the nipples into increased growth.

'Both the nervous system and the circulation of the subject,' Miss Gageby recited, 'are stimulated by correction with the birch. The buttocks are chosen because of the concentration of nerve ends in the adipose tissue of the gluteus. Males and females may react differently, as you shall see, Nurse Prudence, but each is morally stimulated by the lash on naked flesh, and the joy of submission to Nurse's will.'

She swished the birch casually on Mrs Shapiro's now squirming buttocks, but hard, and with unerring precision, so that the expanse of the fesses was becoming a tapestry of mottled crimson and purple. Mrs Shapiro moaned; her fount still writhed as she obediently 'chewed' her gum. Deep in her throat, she made shivering little sobs as her naked flesh trembled, but never quite cried out, as though her earlier squealing had been theatre, and now her discomfort was in earnest, severe enough to numb any ejaculation. Pleasant's mouth made little rattling slurps as he tongued Mrs Shapiro's feet. Helen and Angela were whispering mischievously, about boys, and clubs, and the 'top guns' from the air base at Goodenhall, and how rotten it was that their exits were so restricted.

'A flying officer!' said Helen dreamily.

'Specially a black one,' said Angela. 'They're so big!'

'Bet you haven't!' hissed Helen, delighted.

'Bet I have!' said Angela. 'All big and black and hot . . .'

'Bet we both have,' replied Helen, and they giggled.

Abruptly, Mrs Shapiro's treatment was pronounced over. Pleasant was ordered to rise, and he obeyed, showing Mrs Shapiro's bare feet gleaming clean, and with his mouth full of gritty pebbles and seashells. He was ordered to empty his mouth. Then Miss Gageby told Henrietta to retrieve the spearmint gum from Mrs Shapiro's fount, which was noticeably glistening with her secretions, as though chewing the gum, under beating, had excited her. The wad of glistening gum was promptly transferred to Pleasant's mouth, and his jaws clamped shut upon it, to the giggles of the watching nurses. Miss Gageby whisked her now tattered birch sharply across the young man's clothed bottom.

'I suppose you think you have done a good job, Pleasant?' she drawled.

Pleasant mumbled something eagerly but uncomfortably, and Miss Gageby swished him again, harder. Her lip curled.

'Talking with your mouth full!' she murmured, raising her eyebrows as though mildly astonished. 'My, what a slut you are! A scruffy little oik, who needs correction. Don't you?'

Pleasant, blushing in humiliation, nodded his assent, and was ordered to go to his chamber for his hygienic treatment. He was forbidden to empty his mouth, and was to await his nurses' arrival respectfully. Henrietta disengaged the suction device from Mrs Shapiro's breasts, and the subject was unbound and helped to her feet. She stood, alternately rubbing flogged bottom and pummelled breasts, and occasionally wiping a tear from her glistening cheek. In her trembling submission her body seemed to glow, and bit by bit a smile came to her face as she squeezed her enlarged breasts, which stood proud and jutting, showing the marks of their treatment.

'My, you do lay it on hard, Matron,' she murmured to Miss Gageby, kneading the purple skin of her bottom. 'It smarts so horribly! I'll have to take luncheon standing up, and all the other subjects will see me and know.'

She said this with some pride, and then anxiously begged that her breasts be measured. With a sigh, Miss Gageby ordered Henrietta to do so. At the result, Miss Gageby pronounced herself pleased, but that Mrs Shapiro was not quite ready for the lyre. Mrs Shapiro made a face.

'But you promised, miss! I mean, Matron!' she cried.

'A nurse makes no promises, Madam,' snapped Miss Gageby. 'A subject obeys, and that is all.'

She turned to Prue and the others.

'Now, nursemaids, it is time for the boy Pleasant's treatment. Some treatments are simpler than others, especially for males, who are by nature simple.'

She led the party down the corridor, and into another which was plush-carpeted with soft lights, and paintings of stern matrons on the wall. Miss Gageby opened an oak-panelled door, abruptly, without knocking, into a small chamber like a schoolboy's study. On the walls were photographs of football and cricket teams, and shelves held books, footballs, and cricket bats. There was a washstand, a desk, a small metal bed, a scruffy leather armchair, and a frame that looked like a gym horse. It smelt agreeably of leather and wax and linseed oil: a boyish smell. The umbrella stand held a selection of canes.

Pleasant knelt crouching in the corner, hands behind his back, his cheeks still bulging, and head bowed. He did not look up at their entrance, but caught his breath.

'Well, Master Pleasant,' said Miss Gageby, in a voice that was suddenly kind and gentle, 'let's see what treatment holds in store for you. Nurse Farle, will you please inspect the subject's chamber for any imperfections.'

With gleeful relish, Henrietta proceeded to poke the

immaculate bed, then rip covers and sheets from it, throwing them all to the floor; the tidy bookshelves and boy's paraphernalia received the same, until the room was thoroughly dishevelled. Pleasant emitted a rueful sigh.

'This boy's room is a disgrace, Matron,' said Henrietta.

Miss Gageby clicked her tongue, and shook her head sadly.

'Dear me, you are a mucky pup, Pleasant,' she said sombrely. 'I suppose this means I shall have to correct you. Why on earth do you insist on putting your nurses to this trouble? What? You have your mouth full? *Chewing gum?* Like some dreadful yob? Spit it out at once, boy, you know it is strictly forbidden. Why, this is imperfection on imperfection. We are quite at a loss how to deal with you. Aren't we, Nurses?'

All nodded, Henrietta in less surprise than the others; she murmured she had a very good idea how to deal with errant males.

'So I think it best if you decide your own treatment, Pleasant,' said Miss Gageby. 'What say you, boy?'

Pleasant nodded, his lips still glistening from the oils of Mrs Shapiro's gum wad, and mumbled something.

'What's that?' said Miss Gageby. 'Six of the best? Speak up, you wretched boy.'

'Let me deal with the scruffy oik, Matron,' blurted Henrietta. 'I'll tan his backside – strap him and gag him, with his mouth full of rocks and fill his bum with salt, and flog him till his bum's a blancmange!'

Miss Gageby smiled, and said she must agree with Nurse Farle, unless Pleasant could find a civil tongue.

'I deserve six, Matron – six on bare, if you please –' he looked up at the Matron's quizzical eyebrow '– no, a full set of a dozen is what I deserve. No! Nurse's discretion.'

Miss Gageby sighed, and said she supposed so.

'A full set at Nurse's discretion, Nurse Riding, means just that: the correction is without fixed limit. Pleasant, select a cane for your treatment, minding your manners.'

The young man crawled on his hands and knees to the umbrella stand, where he picked out a cane with his teeth and brought it back to Miss Gageby. She tut-tutted, and said the instrument was not half stout enough for such an errant backside, and he was to pick a more suitable one. Three times the boy repeated his errand, until Miss Gageby pronounced herself satisfied, with a yellow four-foot yew. She swished it against the armchair, where it made an alarming thump and raised a spurt of dust.

'What are you waiting for, boy?' she said, yawning. 'Do I have to do everything? Shoes and shorts off, please.'

Blushing, the young man stood, lowered his flannels and revealed a pair of shocking pink frilly knickers, where his manhood bulged quite prominently. Miss Gageby snorted that he was disgusting, to wear a lady's knickers like a smutty schoolboy. Pleasant whined that it was on Miss Bream's orders – as part of his *last* correction. Miss Gageby retorted that feeble excuses merited strong correction, and she had a mind to turn him to Miss Farle.

'No, Matron – Mistress – O, my cruel Mistress – do not, I beg you! I'll take your punishment, Mistress, on my bare, and for as long as you deem, without a squeak, I promise!'

Miss Gageby seemed pleased at being addressed as 'Mistress'; she stroked her chin and ordered him to get his knickers off and tie his shirt in a knot above his waist, then stretch himself over the gym horse. Prue and the nurses smiled. Pleasant stretched his belly on the padded top of the horse, his arms and legs splayed at each corner, and Miss Gageby signalled that the nurses were each to take a limb and hold him tightly by wrists and ankles. Prue caught an ankle, and pulled. She could glimpse the shaft of his naked manhood, a huge tube of flesh dangling gawkishly over the big flaccid sac that held the plums – let her gaze linger – and her face flushed.

Miss Gageby told Pleasant that his naughtiness distressed her, and his correction would hurt her more than him.

'The last day of treatment!' she murmured. 'You should have learnt manners by now, Pleasant.'

She touched the tip of his dangling organ with her cane, then tapped the balls, and Prue felt him shiver.

'At least you are not causing embarrassment before the new nursemaid,' she said. 'I remember the last time I corrected you. You stood up quite disgracefully.'

There was a whistle, and a sharp crack, and Pleasant's body jerked rigid as the cane took him full across his bare. He squealed and writhed so that it was an effort for the nurses to hold him down. Miss Gageby explained that it was good for the male to feel the restraint of female hands, as well as the kiss of a woman's cane, as it showed him the beauty of submission to woman. The cane whistled again.

'O! O! O! How it smarts. O, Mistress, I don't think I shall ever learn manners!' he cried.

Miss Gageby said he was an impudent boy, and stuffed the frilly knickers in his mouth. Thereafter he was silent, but at each stroke he jumped and trembled, and his whole body writhed in pain as his buttocks crimsoned. Miss Gageby said it was nice to see a captive, naked male with manners enough at least to accept a woman's cane in proper submission. After the tenth swish, Miss Gageby yawned, and said that she wanted to rest, and that another nurse could take over, since this boy evidently required a vivid memory of his treatment, to keep him in order when back at his duties.

'You, Nurse Riding. Let us see your work.'

Prue stood and received the cane with trembling fingers. Her place on the subject's body was taken by Henrietta, who now held two ankles. Miss Gageby plumped herself into the armchair, took out a packet of untipped cigarettes and lit one. She signalled that Prue should continue the beating until she said stop, and Prue lifted the heavy cane. With all her strength she lashed the male's bare bum, and as it jumped at her stroke, her quim began to flow strongly with the soft oils of her excitement. Behind her, there was a rustle of skirts as Miss Gageby shifted to be at ease, puffing blue plumes of fragrant smoke as she watched the beating.

Her blouse and panties damp with sweat, Prue flogged him fast and very hard, with Henrietta looking on jealously. Prue's quim and thighs and stocking tops became warmly moist with her fluid. She looked round at Miss Gageby for encouragement, and saw that she had fully raised her skirts and that she too wore frilly pink panties. Her bare white belly fluttered and shivered; her hand was deep inside her lady's place, caressing and frotting herself at the spectacle of the flogged male. Quite calmly and unconcernedly, Miss Gageby masturbated.

Prue dutifully continued the beating; the Assistant Matron had smoked three cigarettes before Prue heard her moan with a little 'mmm ... mmm ... mmm ...' and then, panting slightly, say that the correction was complete. Prue delivered a final slashing stroke for luck, and saw as she wiped the sweat from her eyes that Pleasant's manhood had somehow changed: the shaft of his organ was standing stiff as a telegraph pole, clutching the balls tightly beneath it. The young man was ungagged and released. He promptly knelt, whimpering, before Prue, and pressed his mouth to her shoes, licking and kissing her shoes and stockinged ankles like a lover's lips.

Brushing tears from his moist cheeks, he murmured,

72

'Thank you, Mistress, thank you for my correction, I have been naughty and deserved every cruel stroke of your cane.'

Miss Gageby briskly rose and threw her cigarette end on Pleasant's carpet, chiding him that the place looked like an ashtray and he was to lick it clean before his release from treatment. She smoothed down her skirts quite unconcernedly and accepted the male's homage to her own feet. Pleasant moaned with joy as he worshipped her feet, bunched prettily in their cream stockings with chocolate-brown seams. Miss Gageby noticed Pleasant's erect organ, and remarked drily that he was certainly ready for his final treatment, but that his impudent anticipation was a further imperfection.

'Perhaps Nurse Riding's discipline has been particularly cleansing,' she said. 'As an extra correction, you shall take the cannon as usual, and be buckled and bound for it.'

Pleasant moaned as though in protest, but his erection stiffened harder. The cannon was brought: a small pumping machine with a large perspex sheath attached by a rubber tube. Pleasant lay on his erect genitals, and clutched his ankles behind his back, like a crab. Henrietta fastened his ankles and wrists together in a bridled metal harness, so that he could not move, and then clamped the bridle part firmly between Pleasant's jaws, snapping it shut so that he was gagged and helpless once more, but without nurse's aid. Then he was ordered to roll on to his side. Henrietta pulled the sheath over his erect penis, then switched on the electric motor. There was a sucking noise as the cannon drew air from the sheath; to Prue's astonishment, Pleasant's organ leapt at least half as big again.

Miss Gageby ordered Helen and Angela to remain and attend Pleasant for an hour's treatment with the cannon, making sure that he licked up all the cigarette ends afterwards.

'A man with a small organ is a poor thing,' she said to the whimpering Pleasant, 'as all ladies will agree. The enhancement of vital organs such as breasts, croup and penis is the very essence of hygiene: for size of appendage is moral beauty. Why, boy, don't groan. Aren't you grateful?'

'Mmm! Mmm!' Pleasant agreed with fervent nods.

'And when you get back to your base this evening, Flight Lieutenant, you will be the envy of your squadron! Such a pity, with that lovely purple bum of yours, that you can't fly your planes standing up . . .'

She popped a piece of spearmint gum in her mouth and beckoned Nurse Prudence to follow her. Henrietta haughtily followed them, though it was Prue to whom Miss Gageby had beckoned, and it was Prue's hand and thigh that she brushed as they turned corners. They went to the refectory for luncheon, which was reindeer sausage and Yorkshire pudding with boiled greens, a grey confection that was eaten with great gusto by the nursemaids. Prue was hungry, and cleaned her plate, and attacked the spotted dick with watery custard with equal enthusiasm. When Jess sat down beside her and asked breezily how her bottom felt, Prue blushed and grinned and confessed she still glowed.

'You'll have to show me,' said Jess. 'Gosh! Did it hurt? The Heck is a frightfully keen whipper.'

Prue agreed that it had hurt very much, and Jess smiled and sighed, her eyes sparkling.

'May I touch?' she whispered.

'Certainly,' said Prue, 'when we are alone.'

'Mmm . . .' said Jess.

The afternoon was taken up with another colonic irrigation, of a male this time, who received no corporal chastisement. Then a female subject was given her balsamic vinegar bath, soaking in it for a whole hour while Prue was detailed to massage and tickle her feet, then rub them with pungent ointment. After her bath the subject – scarcely older than Prue herself – was lightly beaten on naked bottom, though with nothing more than a switch of stinging nettles, which Miss Gageby said contained more beneficial substances ending in '-um' and '-in'. After her bum-licking the nettles were applied to her feet, which Miss Gageby said was 'the bastinado', except that at Hydro they did not use cudgels. The bare woman squirmed and squeaked quite noisily at the tickling of the nettle leaves. Henrietta Farle said that, in the Tower of London, prisoners were tortured with nothing more than the tickling of their soles with feathers, or else having their feet licked by the rasping tongue of a tethered goat. Either of these supplices was enough to make a subject confess to anything.

'That was in the old days,' she said, with heavy regret.

Miss Gageby said that treatments were for the good of the *anima*, and not the same as supplices.

'The anima is what some call the soul,' she said, 'but the High Mistress of Hygiene prefers the anima. She is very wise, and hence very unseen.'

'Very unseen!' Prue exclaimed. 'You make her sound like a goddess, with us her priestesses.'

Miss Gageby smiled and said Prue had very nice feet.

'The feet are the mirror of the anima,' she said. 'So are the buttocks and teats, and, in the case of the male, the sceptre and jewels – the whole body, in fact. Our rigorous treatments make the subject *aware*. Most people ignore their body's potential. Extreme sensation leads to self-knowledge and to self-love, without which there is no love of others. Every subject must liberate her deepest needs.'

'And those deepest needs usually mean thrashing?' Prue said.

Miss Gageby smiled.

'The anima is a point of light trapped in a prison of flesh,' she said. 'Treatment dissolves the walls of the prison and allows the light to shine most brightly, at the point where pleasure and pain become one. In the dreadful solitude of the lash, Prue, is wisdom. Yes, our deepest need is thrashing.'

'*Our* deepest need?' said Prue.

Miss Gageby nodded, looking Prue full in the eyes, as her toes stroked Prue's foot, back and forth.

'*Our* deepest need, Prue,' she whispered.

5

Whipping Twins

At teatime, Prue and Jess were joined by the twins
Helen and Angela, who giggled a lot at the smallest
remark, and seemed to communicate privately with their
eyes. Prue asked if Jeremy Pleasant's treatment had
concluded satisfactorily.

'O, yes! We kept him in the cannon for more than an
hour. It is so scrumptious to see a male with his thing
all big and swollen, even when soft. And then when it
stands –'

They both burst into peals of laughter.

'It's almost as good as watching the lyre. Mrs Shapiro
will be ready soon. Henrietta is lyred weekly, attended
by some tame nurse. That's why she is so cocky.
Heckers is madly jealous, her titties are too small. But
sceptre is best! You'll see – you are coming out one
night, aren't you? Everyone does. You might see your
stud Pleasant.'

'He is not my stud!' cried Prue, blushing.

'He must be – his sceptre stood as you thrashed his
bum!'

Prue asked about permissions to stay out late, and
Jess said they could go into Cloughton, or even
Berwick, any time they wanted, duties permitting –
which was not often – but they must be back by
midnight.

'But the midnight curfew – well, Barker's on the gate

– you've seen her in her fur coat and rubber boots and nylons, haven't you? She wears nothing underneath, the cow! But do her a favour and she'll write you in as 11.59, no matter what time it is. We night hawks call ourselves the 11.59s. It's a sort of exclusive society.'

Prue asked how it was exclusive, if all revellers were marked in at 11.59, and Jess said that you had to do more than stay out late. It depended what you did in the time. If not up to scratch, you could be blackballed.

The twins shook with laughter. Prue asked what sort of favour Barker demanded, and Jess smiled.

'Now *that*'s a silly question,' she said. 'You've been at Hydro a whole day, Prue . . .'

Prue amused herself in the evening by reading, and watching a little TV in the common room, which quickly bored her. Here in Northumberland, the programmes seemed so metropolitan and distant. She finally took a walk, alone, around the grounds. The sky was starry and the moon clear, and Prue filled her lungs with the soft sea air. She saw flower gardens and orchards and lakes stocked with bright fish. Prue went further and further into the groves dappled with moonlight and still smelling sweetly of the waning Northumberland summer. The night air was pleasantly warm, and when she came to a large flat lake, bubbling with tiny fish, she threw her arms up towards the sky, and sang to herself. She stripped and let fall her uniform clothing, then folded it neatly on the shore, under a rock.

Nude, Prue slipped delicately into the soft water and began to swim. The water was delicious on her bare skin, and soothed the still tender flesh of her whipped bottom, and as she parted her legs she felt the cool fluid in her crevices, and said 'mmm' to herself. There were many lily pads; she swam amongst them, letting the leaves slither along her nipples and quim-lips. She swam long and far, and when she finally emerged dripping on the grass, she picked up her uniform – and discovered it was not hers. The stockings and garters were cream-coloured.

Nearby, she heard a strange music. It seemed to come from a grove of pear trees. Straining her eyes in the shade, she made out her own clothing – on the far side of the lake. She was going to swim across to it, but something about the music made her halt. It was accompanied by a woman's sighing, and by little squeals and moans. Prue approached.

'Tighter! Tighter! Ooo ... O!' she heard, in an anguished woman's whisper.

There was a swish, like the breaking of a wave, and the strange, tinkling music jangled more loudly.

'Such fine titties,' sneered another woman's voice. 'It must be hell to keep them squeezed in that corset all day, and to release them, only to take *this*!'

There was another swish, harder, and a tinkle of chords.

'I can scarcely stand it,' sobbed the woman.

'But you love it,' whispered her tormentor.

'Yes. O! O ...!'

Prue positioned herself in the bushes on the orchard's rim, to peep. In a clearing, under the browning leaves, squatted a woman, nude, in a position of extreme supplice. Her body leant forward, supported by her outstretched arms, whose wrists were roped to the swaying branches. Her torso was three or so feet off the ground, and her legs were folded up as a contortionist, so that her feet met behind her head, held in place by a thick chain necklace. Her bare thighs dangled above a tree stump: two carved, striated shafts of wood, polished and resembling male organs, were firmly embedded in her fount and anus, serving both as support and as torment.

The woman balanced herself on these shafts as her tormentor strutted around her radiating the satisfied contempt of a female who has another utterly in her power. The victim's cries were enfeebled by a nylon stocking which entirely sheathed her head. The tormentor wore black boots with pointed heels, very high, and sharp toes, which gleamed dully in the moonlight. She carried a short bouquet of birch rods; otherwise, she wore only tight black panties, which left her buttocks almost naked, a very tight satin corset and a metal brassiere of two conical points which held her breasts firmly out, almost grotesquely, like the two guns of a battleship. Her flesh, where it was bare, was twinkling with studs and looped golden chains. From time to time the tall woman would lash her victim across the shoulders with the birch, or else reach down and whip the upper buttocks, which were already glowing dark red. The tall woman turned: it was Henrietta Farle.

Her victim had her breasts trapped in a machine like a carpenter's vice. Her teats were very long and full, with the nipples squeezed big as pears. The device was a simple plank, or tablette, suspended from the victim's neck-chain by a series of wires, the two most prominent being clamped to wide nipple rings pierced through the nipples themselves. At each stroke of the birch to croup or shoulders, the wires jangled, like strings of a guitar. Her breasts rested upon the tablette as though served on a platter, but were secured to it by a crossbar over their tops; in the middle of the tablette a tiny screw-vice tightened the bar so that the tips of the breasts were forced to stand upright, with the nipples facing her chin.

The swollen breasts bulged like vast udders about to burst, the veins purple in the distended skin. From the nipples, another lattice of wires snaked across her belly, to the lips of her fount, which were clamped wide open – 'pegged' – by a metal bar which indeed looked like a tent-peg. Rings pierced her quim lips, and the wires across her belly sang too at every whip-stroke. Henrietta Farle smoked a fragrant cigarette, keeping it between her lips like a man, and tongue-flicking ash on her victim's breasts. Fierce strokes rained on her, the tips of the birch landing cruelly on the woman's distended nipples and causing her to cry and convulse in shudders. The glade rang to jangling strings. Prue watched and felt her belly flutter; there was a tingling in her lady's place, and she felt the beginning of a seep as her quim lips moistened. The wooden shafts glistened with the woman's love-juices.

'Long enough?' drawled Henrietta.

'O ... no ... more, please,' mewled the trussed woman.

Henrietta reached down and tightened the vice, so that the swollen, stretched breasts bulged to bursting. Now Henrietta began to flog the teats more severely, and their mottling colour darkened livid from the birch's stroke. After a shuddering interval of dry, crackling swishes to the naked breasts, accurately touching the nipples with the birch-tips, Henrietta moved to beat the stretched bare nates. The metal strings filled the glade with their tortured music as the victim bounced up and down, in writhing agony at each cut of the birch to her bum-flesh, the birch stroking her furrow, her anus, and reaching through her thighs to the swollen quim lips.

At each stroke, Henrietta urged her charge to bounce and make music, and now the flogged woman, hanging to her suspending branches, was panting hoarsely with little whimpering cries in her throat. The shafts that plunged in and out of her nether holes were shining bright with her cascade of love-juices, and as Henrietta flogged her, the nylon stocking became distorted as the woman frantically chewed it in the extremity of her sensation. Prue wondered what pain and pleasure must flood her body, and longed to know for herself; she put her hand to her own naked, shaven fount, and gasped: she was gushing with love-oil. Suddenly, Henrietta ceased flogging and bent down by the nylon stocking on the head, to take the bare feet in her mouth, one after the other. She sucked and bit the feet, licking and biting, for some minutes, and doing so began to frig herself through her panties. Her subject moaned in pleasure.

Henrietta lit another cigarette and her fingers were trembling. She stuck the cigarette in her mouth and resumed the flogging, but now her fingers were dancing across her own quim, through the tight nylon of her panties which gleamed wetly in the moonlight. Prue was now masturbating too as the flogged woman writhed on her twin impaling shafts. Henrietta, gleaming like a metal goddess, frigged with shameless exuberance as she flogged the quivering body.

'You love it, Nurse, don't you?' cried Henrietta.

'Yes, I love treatment, just as you do, Henrietta.'

Henrietta spat.

'*I* do it for my pride and beauty! Not for humiliation.'

'Your beauty, like mine, is to submit to the supplice, Henrietta,' was the whimpered reply.

'I'll give you supplice! I hate you! You have a thing for the new bitch! Don't deny it!'

Henrietta's snarl begged for denial; yet there was only silence as she continued the whipping, and then moans, louder and louder, of 'yes ... yes ... do it to me ...'

Plumes of smoke eddied from Henrietta's grimacing lips, until her victim cried loud and long in a fierce spasm of pleasure. Her hair peeped from the twisted nylon stocking as she chewed it, and the hairs were auburn tinged with red. The nylon sheath, torn, was half off, revealing the subject's lower face and the lips twisted in sobbing joy. Henrietta grunted in low, despairing spasms as she frigged herself through her knicker cloth and brought her own pleasure. Prue gave way to her own spasm, as the music of the strings echoed in maddened accompaniment. And when her gasping had eased, she padded away, satisfied that she had seen Miss Gageby taking the lyre.

As she entered the lake, to swim back for her own uniform, Prue tore a lily pad to a scalloped edge, and mischievously put one half on Miss Gageby's clothing, keeping the other half. She swam to where she had left her own uniform, and found it gone. There was the rock, and the flattened grass, but no uniform. Glumly, Prue picked some more lily pads and fashioned an apron, which she had to hold against herself, and left her buttocks bare. There was rustling on the far lakeside, as Henrietta emerged with Miss Gageby, the Assistant Matron heading for her own clothes on all fours, tethered, and with the imperious Miss Farle riding on her back, and lashing her naked buttocks with the birch, as one final degradation. Prue fled the scene, and headed gloomily back to certain disgrace at Hydro. The night air was cold, now, on her pimpled skin, and she fancied she heard peals of girlish laughter, as from twins.

'Immodesty!' cried Nurse Heckmondthwaite.

Nude, Prue looked down at her tell-tale trail of water droplets. She blurted her explanation, leaving out Miss Gageby and Henrietta Farle. Nurse Heckmondthwaite leered.

'Only your first day here – already a whipping – and now, certainly, another!'

'But what harm did I do?' Prue demanded. 'Surely the imperfection is with the girl –' she recalled the mocking peals of distant laughter '– or girls, who took my things?'

'Insolence upon imperfection! It is true that a naked swim, even alone, may be ascribed to hygienic impulse. But carelessness over your nurse's uniform – that is unforgiveable. I shall see Miss Bream in the morning.'

Prue continued to her room, and went to bed miserable at the thought, not of Miss Bream's beating, but of her displeasure. Much later, she awoke with a start. Her room was bathed in moonlight; she discerned two shadowy shapes in her room.

'Shhh!' hissed a voice. 'You'll wake her!'

'Surely we are supposed to wake her?' said the other.

'I want to peek at her things first! I bet she has some gorgeous things, from London!'

Prue said drowsily that she was already awake, and that they were free to peek at her things, if it would give them pleasure. She rubbed her eyes and recognised the twins, Angela and Helen, their hair bobbing with excitement, one blonde, the other auburn.

'What is it you want?' she said.

Helen held out a bundle.

'We brought your uniform back,' she said. 'We're awfully sorry, we didn't mean to get you into trouble.'

'It was just a prank,' said Angela.

Prue sat up and tugged up the straps of her nightie.

'It was a jolly tasteless prank,' she said crossly.

The twins sat on the bed, and Helen put her arm around Prue's shoulder.

'All new squids get a bit of a ribbing,' she murmured. 'it is just to show we like you. But if you are cross with us, I suppose we'd better make amends somehow.'

'I'll have to go before Miss Bream. I don't quite see . . .'

'A spanking, of course,' said Angela gaily. 'You can spank our bums until we moan and squeal and get terribly red and sore, and then you'll know that whatever you take from the Breamer, you've doled it out too!'

As one, the twins positioned themselves on the floor, lifted their skirts and unfastened their garter straps. Their stockings and knickers were rolled to their ankles, and they stood splayed, the knicker cloth stretched like tightropes as their bare bums gleamed, awaiting punishment. Prue smiled, despite her irritation. She got out of bed and went to her wardrobe.

'Are you sure spanking is enough?' she said quietly, taking out two braided leather riding crops of Miss Macardle's.

The twins looked up nervously, then their eyes strayed to the treasures inside the wardrobe.

'I don't think it's enough,' Prue continued. 'I think you are a pair of naughty fillies who need your cruppers tanned.'

'May we try on your things, Nurse, afterwards?' cried the twins in unison. 'Please say yes!'

'Certainly, if you can stand the slightest touch of silk on bare skin, for I'm going to whip you fillies very hard.'

'Oo . . .' moaned the twins, and then cried 'Ooo!' as the two crops lashed firmly across their bare buttocks, making them quiver like lovely pink jellies.

Prue's nightie swished against her thighs and belly, and her breasts bobbed so that they almost popped out at her exertion. But she kept up a rhythmic double flogging, placing neat, hard strokes across the nurses' bums until a pleasing blush had been raised on each croup. From time to time one or other of the twins would moan, or squeak when the moan was rewarded with two extra-rapid cuts. Prue smiled. The twins began to tremble and shudder quite severely as the flogging progressed. One of them had the temerity to ask in a whimper how many strokes they were to take, and Prue barked that they added insolence to imperfection, and that their beating would be 'Nurse's Discretion' – as many strokes as she cared to deliver.

She ordered them to splay their bums wider, so that she could stroke their furrows and bumholes, and trembled herself at the awesome surge of power she felt as the twins, straining, obeyed. Prue was rewarded with a delicious view of the cracks of their bums, and noticed that the twins were not perfectly shaved: a few downy hairs glistened around their pert wrinkled bum-buds, and to her surprise they were neither auburn nor bright blonde, but dark honey. Not one, but both of the twins, dyed their heads.

Each bottom had taken at least sixty strokes of the crop by the time Prue ended the beating. Her nightie was soaked in sweat, and the bare buttocks before her glowed prettily in the moonlight, a patchwork of crimson and purple with very strong markings where Prue's lash had caught their furrows and soft inner thighs. The twins were allowed to rub their bottoms – which they did, whistling that Prue whipped awfully tight – but not to stand before explaining the mystery of their coiffures. At this, they did stand, and each gleefully swept her hair from her head, revealing an entirely shaven skull. Not dyed, but bewigged! The twins' scalps gleamed as white as their bare bottoms gleamed dark. Both giggled at Prue's astonishment.

'Haven't you ever seen a clean girl before?' said Helen.

Prue confessed she had not.

'It's super,' said Angela. 'It means we can be each other if we want, and can get away with all sorts of mischief.'

Prue reached out and stroked Angela's head, then Helen's. She shivered: there was an uncanny beauty in the smoothness of the skin, and the bones of the skull felt clearly beneath, as though the women really were naked, their femininity more powerful for its lack of adornment. She told them it was very nice, and slyly added that she wondered what sort of mischief they got up to.

'Well, you know . . . the 11.59 club. O, I suppose you don't. You must join, Nurse, we have such fun.'

Prudence said that she was sure she could manage to return late from her evenings out.

'That's not enough,' cried Angela. 'You have to do a special deed, something really outrageous . . .'

'Or lots of them,' added Angela. 'Being permitted to take the lyre, for example – that might get you in.'

Quite brazenly, she put her hand on Prue's left teat and began to squeeze it, rubbing the nipple between her fingers so that Prue felt herself involuntarily stiffen.

'You should manage it,' she said. 'You have such lovely big teats, full and long and everything. We don't – little firm titties – so we must be extra naughty for the 11.59s.'

'Like going with a lovely big black man.'

'Two black men! Or three!'

'Black is best,' said Helen thoughtfully. 'Why, there is nothing like it. Filled in both holes ... yummy! And such a lovely smoky smell! Especially when you plate him with your tongue, and squeeze his bollocks and suck all the spunk from him. They are such heavy spunkers! It is much better than diddling. Not that diddling isn't super, too. You've made my bum smart so, and that always makes me hot to frig. Doesn't it you, Nurse?'

'I ... well!' stammered Prue.

In truth, her quim was wet at the sight of her new friends' whipped bums, and she shivered a little as the pair began to rummage through her carefully hung underthings and skirts, squealing with delight. They picked out corsets and jarretières and blouses and knickers, holding them against their bodies, their own panties still rather comically round their ankles. But in no time panties and garter belts and skirts and bras had come off, and Helen and Angela stood naked, feverishly squabbling over this or that silky undergarment.

They tried them, discarded them, matched colours in strange combinations that made them giggle, and when they got to Prue's selection of rubber and leather things they grinned and said that Prue's stuff was brilliant, and that, with a tight rubber petticoat and conical bra, the males would not be able to keep their hands off her.

Quite casually, as they touched the garments, each twin's fingers crept to her shaven fount, and Prue saw that each was gaily frotting herself, with cosy little sighs and moans. A woman's body was such lovely sweetness, now garlanded in a rainbow of petals, in silks and satins and bright colours; now sheathed in a stern hide or uniform – the carapace of a Mistress.

'Such lovely things . . .' mewed Helen. 'O, I'm going to come just looking at them . . . feeling them against me. Don't you want to come, with all these lovely things, Prue? I mean, you know . . . rub your clitty to spasm.'

She began to play with some of the more exotic of Prue's footwear; high lace-up bootees with teetering heels, shoes of gleaming patent leather and rubber and slippers of satin, with curled oriental toes, even a pair of thigh-boots with spur-rings, that might have graced Henrietta Farle. Helen began to rub the boots against her open quim, and moaned. Angela did the same with stockings, in a rainbow of hues and fabrics, some daringly translucent, some in fishnet or with the seams gashed at the back. Angela rubbed a pair of these back and forth between her thighs, wetting them profusely and stroking her clitty; she said, giggling and gasping, that seamed stockings pleased men because the seams were like roadsigns pointing to the essential, the warm oily pond where men had to bathe their cocks and spurt cream.

Prue was wet – she lifted her nightie over her breasts and joined in the game, as all three girls stood facing each other and played with themselves, quim lips expertly parted to reveal stiff little nubbins all glistening and pink. Helen and Angela twisted their wrists, inserting a full hand right inside their quims, while thumb-frotting their damsels. Prue did likewise, swooning with the pleasure of fist-frigging her pouring wet slit.

'That isn't your only hole, girl!' murmured Helen.

Unbidden, Prue shook her nightie right off and was naked. As Angela began to tongue her erect nipples, Helen gently parted her thighs and slid her fingers into Prue's furrow, to tickle her anus bud, which made Prue jump with a new and giddy pleasure. She licked Helen's baby-soft shaven head.

'O!' she cried. 'My bumhole . . . that is naughty.'

'Not as naughty as this,' said Angela.

Prue was turned, her cheeks spread, and Angela put a finger inside her bumhole itself, waggling it round to make Prue's sphincter relax. Then she had two fingers in, and then she was joined by two fingers of her twin, until Prue's bumhole was stretched to its limit and she felt she would burst, just like taking her lavage.

'Just think of a black man's cock inside your bum,' whispered Helen. 'They love it, they call it cornholing.'

'And one in your slit,' said Helen. 'At the same time!'

The fingers sank into her bumhole to the hilt while two thumbs flicked at her tingling damsel and she felt teeth chewing her nipples with thrilling roughness. Her body was skilfully twisted, as though in a clamp, and her own hands were put to work on two hard trembling clitties, awash in the oils of two swollen quims.

It was not long before she felt the spasm well up in her belly, she shivered and trembled and clasped the shaven heads to her, stroking and kissing them like hard bare breasts – and then she cried out in a glorious spasm that flooded her with pleasure, which she knew would forever be linked to that insidious, gorgeous tweaking of the thrusting fingers in her bumhole. She was aware that the twins cried out too, in their own spasms, and she smelt the rustling silks and rubbers and leathers as three bodies writhed.

In the morning, Prudence was awakened by Nurse Heckmondthwaite and told to report directly to Matron, in her nightie. Prue had time for privy; Heckmondthwaite watched, gloating, as she squatted, and said her bum would soon be too sore to squat. Defiantly, Prue took a long and rather showy time wiping herself.

'Well, Nurse Prudence,' said Miss Bream, 'you have been a busy nursemaid. Another imperfection, and so soon! Thanks to the sterling detective work of Nurse Heckmondthwaite.'

Her tone was not without irony, and Heckmondthwaite's beam turned to a puzzled frown.

'Matron,' said Prue, 'I submit that I was not doing anything wrong. A naked swim – surely that is hygienic, and as for returning to Hydro in ... in Nature's knickers, why, that is surely not immodest. And no one saw – no one *else*.'

The Matron chuckled.

'Nature's knickers! I like it. Except that you had only partial knickers, Nurse, for your buttocks were visible. Only *half* a lily pad around your lady's place.'

Miss Gageby stared for an instant at Prue, then pursed her lips in a wry smile, winked, and looked away.

'This is interesting,' Matron continued. 'You have been caught, but no one is quite sure what you have been caught *for*. Perhaps your imperfection is like the "keep off the grass" signs – walking on the grass is not wrong in itself, but we cannot have everybody doing it.'

Prue bowed her head and said that she would take Matron's treatment.

'I could order you to take a hard twenty-one with the cane,' said Matron thoughtfully. 'But still – is it an offence or isn't it? I think we shall let the nurses decide. In the old days, miscreants were put in the pillory to be pelted, and if the public did not disapprove of them, they would be pelted with flowers. So your sentence, Nurse Prudence, is to spend the day dressed only in your undergarments, and go about your business with a sign indicating that any nurse may visit her own corporal punishment on your person.'

'Matron,' said Prue, her heart thumping at the daring of her untruth, 'I ... I haven't my uniform nor underthings.'

'Well, until you get new ones, wear what you came in,' snapped Miss Bream.

Prue dressed herself in the mauve underthings she had from Miss Macardle; a lovely tight corset which thrust her breasts high and almost painfully forward; high-cut panties with a scalloped front, like the scales of a fish or a cascade of flowers over her fount, but with only a string at the back, so that her buttocks were almost nude; stockings to match, of gleaming mauve nylon; and dark purple shoes with the highest, most teetering heels. At the small of her back she carried a card saying simply 'Naughty Nurse, Spank Me' and thus attired she went about the daily business of a nurse, swelling with pride at the attention and envy her underthings aroused. After tea, she reported back to Miss Bream, who inspected her bottom and remarked approvingly that there was fresh crimson, but not deep.

'Didn't Henrietta Farle take advantage, Nurse?' she asked mildly. 'I would have thought ...'

'She disdained, Matron,' said Prue; 'said she had better than spanking in store. I took a set from Nurse Rise of fifty spanks – she said she didn't want me to feel neglected – and fifty spanks each from the twins, Nurses Helen and Angela.'

When Prue was dismissed, assured by Matron that she was free to go clubbing, Miss Gageby took her aside, hissing that she wanted urgent words. Prue gulped. The lily pad! How silly she had been! Miss Gageby knew she had been espied, and now would be Prue's enemy! Prue began to stammer that she would keep mum, but Miss Gageby told her to hush.

'Those mauve undies of yours – they are to dream of! I must borrow them to go out in – I'm sure you have plenty – a London girl – please, please say yes!'

Prue concealed her relief, and her excitement too at finding Miss Gageby in her power.

'You want to borrow my skins?' she said thoughtfully.

Coolly, she placed her hands on Miss Gageby's breasts, now tightly corseted beneath her uniform. Prue found the nipples and squeezed ever so gently, making the Assistant Matron catch her breath. Prue shivered with desire, remembering Henrietta's cruel birching in the glade.

'You have lovely breasts, Miss Gageby,' she murmured, 'fit for the lyre . . .'

'And you a lovely arse, Nurse Riding, fit to bare for a lady's cane. Now, may I borrow your things? Please?'

'I don't see why not,' Prue said. 'It will be amusing to know you are dressed as me. But I reserve the right to reclaim my property at any time after 11.59 . . .'

6

Cupped and Stretched

Prue's days were busy: after her own bottom's stern initiation into the disciplinary ways of nursing, she was often called upon to administer treatment to the bottoms of her subjects. Her expertise, born of enthusiasm for the flagellant rods, was evident, and she knew she was gaining favour; as the treatments she learnt seemed more and more wondrous, she never lost her excitement at their intricate and daring subtlety. No limb nor orifice of the body was deemed unworthy of treatment, or cleansing, and especial attention was paid to anal and vaginal hygiene, as well as the development of breast and buttock: 'bumps and sumps', as Jess rather crudely put it. And the nurses must practise what they preached, taking full treatments themselves, in private session; Miss Gageby explained that it was the same military principle whereby a parachute instructor, say, had to show himself superior to his charges.

This was the occasion of Prue's introduction to Nurse Crennet, who was a pretty woman about Miss Gageby's age, with a face of pale, translucent beauty, unadorned, and a very slim body that was almost boyish in its litheness. She wore her raven hair very long and combed flat, as though this startling femininity would counteract her boyish grace. The taut muscles of her body moved with casual ease against her tight nurse's uniform, making it seem almost like military attire. The only strikingly feminine thing, apart from her hair, was her croup, a pleasing swelling of great muscular power which, though large, still fitted perfectly with her gamine frame, as though it were an accessory thoughtfully made to order. By the same token, whenever her tight skirt brushed her fount, or became notched between her thighs, the mons suddenly appeared as a very large swelling, almost like a small breast worn between the thighs.

There was no panty line to mar the smoothness of her bottom, but the sumptuous mound that swelled at her lady's place hinted at a mink of tight and luxuriant curls. Nurse Crennet was a reputed expert in advanced herbal remedies. Prue noticed that Miss Gageby deferred quite politely to her, yet Henrietta Farle adopted one of her now-familiar sulks and pouted, as though the splendour of her much-pierced and bejewelled form was in some way threatened by Nurse Crennet's elfin *minceur*.

'There are no advanced herbal remedies,' chided Nurse Crennet in a soft fluting Welsh voice, 'for everything is a herb, therefore everything is remedy. Water is a herb,' she added firmly, as if to settle the matter.

Nurse Crennet's definition of herbal seemed enchantingly elastic, just like her lilting accent. Everything, it seemed, was a herb: a corset, a dildo, a pair of panties or stockings, a stout whip.

'It is all in the arrangement of *molecules*,' she explained, stretching the word into five musical syllables. 'When our flesh touches flesh, or a flower, or water, or a whip or knickers, then molecules are exchanged. And when we look at each other here –' she looked suddenly into Prue's eyes '– then knowledge is exchanged, and knowledge is made of spiritual molecules. Every touch teaches.'

Prue, a little charmed by the frankness of Nurse

94

Crennet's gaze, settled down to learn about molecules and their uses. This treatment chamber looked out over the dunes and sea, whose bare rippling majesty was in quaint contrast to the fussy clutter of the hygienic apparatus, rather like a Victorian lady's boudoir. There were jars of leaves and dried fish and berries and all sorts of herbs; devices of restraint and hygiene – a frame that could only be for flogging the subject, for example, and, moreover, a subject knotted into the most uncomfortable contortion.

Helen and Angela – it seemed accepted at Hydro that the twins did everything together – introduced their subject, a pleasant female of about thirty years old, in (to Prue) quite wonderful shape, and glowing with health. This was Mrs Araval, another handsome female avid to achieve the perfect bosom and croup, the perfect quim, the perfect combination of 'bump and sump'! Certainly, when she disrobed from her smart grey business suit, her body, in a one-piece teddy or corselage of blue silk, with matching straps and stockings, seemed already harmonious in bosom and nates, though her breasts did not seem quite full enough for the lyre; by the way Mrs Araval unconsciously kneaded her own teats and nipples through the teddy, this seemed a matter of concern to her. Certainly, when Nurse Crennet ordered her to strip naked, she put up a show of girly modesty, protesting rather feebly, with a delightful blush, as she slowly unstrapped her stockings and peeled them down superbly gleaming thighs.

'I'll never get used to stripping like this,' she murmured. 'It seems so shameful and immodest.'

'Everything off, Mrs Araval, you lazy girl,' said Nurse Crennet, as though playing her part in an accepted drama.

'My boobs,' cried Mrs Araval – 'I'm so embarrassed to show them. They are so tiny, like fried eggs. Do make them bigger, Nurse!'

She lowered the top of her teddy and one breast peeked shyly out. Prue thought it perfectly well formed, quite large and pleasingly pert, standing up quite unaided by support, and with the rubbed nipple very big like a lovely gooseberry. Nurse Crennet said that Mrs Araval was improving, and might possibly take the lyre soon. At this, the other breast appeared. Then the teddy began to slink down the subject's flat belly, riding over the hips until the top of the mons could be seen, hairless. Mrs Araval too shaved herself, or was shaved.

'Give me a good four-thonged whisk, and I'll make those fried eggs of hers into a soufflé,' whispered Henrietta.

'I want you nude, Madam,' said Nurse Crennet crisply, 'naked as a lily pad.'

Mrs Araval shuddered with pleasure.

'I feel so frightened and helpless,' she said, relishing her submissive pleading. 'I know I shouldn't – as though I am being ravished by your eyes.'

The teddy came off, and she stood naked, with her hands behind her back, nestling at the top of her bum-cleft, and head bowed. Her fount was already shaven, and revealed a pair of quim lips that stood very thick and swelling between her soft thighs, as though already engorged; between them glistened a clitty as stiff as the downy berries of her nipples. The whole mound was as delicious an accessory as Nurse Crennet's full bottom was to her own body. Mrs Araval was already tensed with excitement, and there was even a tell-tale glistening on her thigh skin; the quim lips were full and swelling, like juicy fat oysters, quaintly matching the clamlike tautness of her pert bare breasts. The trim croup now bore faint crimson, meaning Mrs Araval's herbal treatments did not preclude the whip. And indeed, Nurse Crennet now picked a thick braided riding-crop from her case, and cracked it casually against her own thigh.

Miss Gageby trembled slightly, and flushed; she looked down at her stockings and scratched herself between the thighs, letting her skirt ride up to show the cream fabric and chocolate seam; suddenly, Prue whispered to Miss Gageby that she could have her mauve undies for going out, but only if she would swap her stockings. Miss Gageby, distracted by the nudity of her trembling subject, said yes.

'And panties too?' said Prue, pursuing her advantage.

'Yes, yes,' snorted Miss Gageby, 'take the whole uniform if you want. Now, Nurse, pay attention to the treatment.'

Nurse Crennet consulted her notes, and said she thought it was time for a partial gamut. Mrs Araval asked nervously if that meant she was to take a formal beating; Nurse Crennet smiled fleetingly and answered in her melodious lilt, only if Mrs Araval were *rebarbative*. Casually, she popped a wad of chewing gum in her mouth and started to masticate, letting the juice dribble down her chin.

'But you always say I am rebarbative, Nurse!' wailed Mrs Araval. 'And I still don't understand it. Why, last treatment, Nurse Heckmondthwaite didn't lace me at all.'

'Then,' said Miss Gageby, 'you shall get a double portion today, madam. Note that, Nurse Crennet. I shall have to speak to Nurse Heckmondthwaite.'

Abruptly, she reached out and stroked Mrs Araval's bare bottom, which made the woman shiver and smile.

'Such globes may not go untreated,' said Miss Gageby, allowing her palm to linger on the goose-pimpled flesh.

Mrs Araval was invited to position herself on a mat, and squat, as though for commode. She was to hold still in this uncomfortable position, and did so, her palms on her buttocks, and her feet on tiptoe. She trembled, but balanced herself with skill; a silver chafing dish was placed under her spread thighs, directly at her bulbous quim lips. Nurse Crennet laid aside her crop after giving a single carefree but hearty stroke to the tops of Mrs Araval's buttocks, which made her jump but not lose her balance. The nurse smiled but said nothing, and then ordered Henrietta to apply the quinine bark. This was a shaft of dark wood, rather rough, and with new leaves sprouting from it. Nurse Crennet said to Prue that quinine was a most valuable molecule, particularly when applied to the female places, and then gave her another unnerving stare. At her signal, Mrs Araval pulled very hard on her bum-cheeks, spreading them very wide so that the crinkly blossom of her anus was fully exposed, and, to Prue's amazement, the folds of her bud were large, like her quim lips, in the shape of a lovely curly rose.

Henrietta began to rub the quinine leaves gently across the open hole of her anus, and Mrs Araval began to moan and shiver, with a little giggle. Her anus hole began to contract and tremble as the leaves tickled her, and gradually her moans became softer, yet deeper, as she sighed to the tickling. The silver dish beneath her quim spattered with little gleaming droplets, which fell like dewdrops from Mrs Araval's open quim. The lips of her fount were now truly distended, swollen and shiny pink as the arse tickling evidently excited her, and Prue saw the damsel swell to a wonderful hardness, almost like a little penis. Her quim juice began to drop hard and fast into the dish, and gradually filled it to the depth of half an inch.

'Mrs Araval is a heavy juicer,' murmured Nurse Crennet approvingly as she watched the woman's buttocks wriggle at her arse-tickle, and occasionally, as though for private amusement, flicked the crop quite hard across the tops of her buttocks, leaving vivid pink lines. This made Mrs Araval's bottom wriggle even more prettily, and her juice spatter faster.

At each flick of crop to bum, Nurse Crennet urged her subject to hold her anus bud wider. Chewing her gum vigorously, she drawled from the corner of her mouth, 'Doesn't she widen for Mr Araval, when he chooses to poke you there? He must have a big fat cock, to pleasure a lazy slut like you, madam, and a bumhole that tiny would never admit a real man.'

'What . . .?' cried Mrs Araval. 'Well, really, Nurse!'

'You are under treatment, madam,' said Nurse Crennet, 'and a subject is obliged to speak truth. Be lucky you are not a nurse! At our truth games, we must speak truth on pain of severe discipline – flogging, and not just on croup.'

'If you must know, yes,' stammered Mrs Araval. 'He pokes me there quite a lot. Mr Araval is a real man, and his cock leaves nothing to be desired, especially when he – excuse my language – when he arse-fucks me, as he puts it, and spurts his spunk right at my root. My anus gives, and takes, quite a lot of pleasure in being arse-fucked. But, Nurse, you are wicked: I have confessed this before.'

All the nurses grinned, licking their lips.

'And you enjoy it there? Being . . . arse-fucked?' said Nurse Crennet.

'It is different . . .'

Crack! The crop lashed her fesses very hard.

'Yes . . .' moaned Mrs Araval, 'I enjoy it. I love it, love my bumhole filled by my man's big cock! He loves to poke me there, says my bum-flower feels like roses caressing his balls as he thrusts. So there! But,' she gasped, 'you know that too. O, you do take your pound of flesh, you nurses.'

Prue whispered suddenly to Miss Gageby that she had an idea; what if a device existed to peg a subject's bumhole, as well as her quim? Or perhaps both at the same time? Miss Gageby smiled and said that would be a device indeed, and more of a scaffolding than an appliance.

Now the twins lifted the chafing dish from beneath Mrs Araval's dripping quim, and replaced it with an empty one. Prue was given a sponge, and followed the twins' example; together they soaked their sponges in the oily love-fluid, and began to bathe Mrs Araval's body with her own secretion, all over, including face, breasts, and the very quim from which the secretion had flowed. Nurse Crennet explained that the female body must bathe in its own sea. Prue marvelled at the tautness of the quim lips, when she had a chance to rub them, and allowed her bare fingers to stray over the sponge's top; the quim lips, like the pert stiff nipples, were as hard and full as foam rubber.

Henrietta stopped rubbing with the quinine bark, and set it propped standing up, underneath Mrs Araval's bottom, so that the leaves still touched her anus bud. Mrs Araval sighed, and Nurse Crennet said it was time to hop, and the subject at once obeyed. She began to jerk her hips back and forward so that the quinine leaves continued to tickle her bud, and now the drops of secretion from her quim flew on all sides of the dish with the intensity of her motions, which seemed to Prue more and more lustful.

'Yes,' said Nurse Crennet, flicking the crop twice, rapidly, against the bare twitching fesses, 'imagine it is Mr Araval's helmet tickling you. He is making you wait – an agony of longing! – till he plunges his cock right into your bum, Mrs Araval. And you'll love to take it there, won't you? A dirty girl, getting what she really wants, a hot cock to cleave her anus and fill her belly to bursting as she screams and squirms and begs him to spunk in her.'

'O! Mmm . . . O!' Mrs Araval nodded frantically.

'Then he'll probably spank you while he's poking,' said Nurse Crennet; 'men like that . . . or even whip your bare bum, like *this*.'

She delivered three quickfire strokes to Mrs Araval's reddening croup. Prue's quim tingled, as the treatment of this naked subject became ever more lustful. She continued to rub the oily secretion over Mrs Araval's now glistening bare body, without any pretence to hide her caress of the stiff, throbbing damsel and nipples. She felt her own body respond in sympathy, as Mrs Araval's moans became a deep sighing rhythm. Then she heard her moan more deeply, strain herself, and, looking down at the woman's red buttocks, she saw the anus distend still further, sink over the quinine bark, and draw the wooden shaft into the bumhole itself. Mrs Araval's buttocks squirmed; a trickle of oily sweat ran down her back and furrow, making the bark shine, as it disappeared inch by inch into the pink folds of her anus. Prue stopped rubbing, mesmerised by the spectacle; the bark disappeared entirely into the woman's fundament, and then began to pop in and out: a couple of inches would protrude, then be sucked back inside the anus.

The process continued, and the flow of love-juice from Mrs Araval's fount became a gush. Twice, Prue and the twins had to change the dish, and now simply emptied the contents over the subject's heaving teats and belly, until she was a gleaming ocean of her own secretions. Prue concentrated her fingers on Mrs Araval's stiff clitty, while each twin had a nipple between her teeth. A deep growl grew in Mrs Araval's throat; her belly twitched and shook as she cried out in a spasm, the shaft thrusting in and out of her squirming anus as though powered by its own demon. A murmur of approval rose from the nurses, and Nurse Crennet said that the subject had demonstrated correct control.

'You have poked yourself well, Mrs Araval,' she said, 'showing that a woman is contained within herself; laved by her own juices, poked by the strength of her own hole. On your next treatment, it shall be the birchwood in quim . . . But now, you shall complete this phase by punishing yourself for your indulgence. You naughty, lazy girl! Whip yourself.'

Prue was ordered with the twins to continue their massage as Mrs Araval took the crop with trembling fingers and began to flog her own bottom! Nurse Crennet gave prim directions – a little more to the left, up a bit, now straight in the furrow, bite the arse-bud with the tip of the crop, and always exhorting: harder, harder! The squirming subject moaned, now, in real discomfort, and belaboured her own fesses so obediently and so hard that her whipping arm was almost a blur. Prue and the twins were ordered to step back – Prue could tell from their flushed faces that their own founts were as wet as hers, and they permitted each other guilty smiles, not unnoticed by Miss Gageby.

Meanwhile the hapless Mrs Araval was ordered, or rather 'invited', to apply the crop to her naked breasts. She obeyed, letting out a long moan of anguish as the vicious leather flogged the pert bobbins of her nipples. At each crack, the nipples seemed to stiffen harder, and now Mrs Araval's fingers crept to her own damsel, whose stiff protruberance she twitched as frantically as the whip cascaded on her bare teats. Her thighs were awash with glistening rivulets, and the dish brimmed.

At last, the sobbing woman was told to attend to her softest part. Mrs Araval was ordered to lean her wrist on the floor, her fingers clutching the crop, and flick it up towards her fount without letting her wrist leave the floor. She did so, squealing loud as the crop flicked against the engorged lips of her quim. She continued to whip her precious fount-lips until Nurse Crennet suddenly ordered the beating to stop. Moaning, and rubbing her sore gash, Mrs Araval threw down the crop and began to sob. Henrietta helped her somewhat roughly to her feet, and Nurse Crennet placed her hand on the woman's inflamed fount, allowing her fingers to slip right inside the slit.

She grasped Mrs Araval by her pubic bone and squeezed hard, making the subject yelp. She stroked the mottled crimson tissue of her raw bottom, and pronounced herself satisfied. The treatment proceeded at once to the next stage. The surprisingly docile subject lay down on a trestle, like a horse, with a saddle to cup the small of her back, from which hung wide, laced flaps of black rubber. Her face was eager, and she smiled through her tears. She stretched her limbs straight out and Henrietta raised the rubber flaps, then wrapped her belly in the sinister corset, its straps attached to an appliance like a carpenter's vice.

Mrs Araval's belly was strapped very tightly in this corset until she panted and exclaimed little cries of 'O! O!' Her breasts were forced upwards and protruded very sharply. The twins took her ankles, then slowly raised them, bending them straight back until the feet clasped behind Mrs Araval's neck. Then they took her wrists and fastened wrists and ankles together into the pocket of a black leather harness with shiny buckles which they snapped tight, so that Mrs Araval could not move: only the restraint of the corset held her balanced on the saddle.

The subject's bare white thighs, buttocks and quim, cruelly exposed, glistened in the sunlight that illumined the scene. Far away there was a hiss of the sea. Henrietta began to turn the wheel of the vice, and Mrs Araval moaned anew, for the vice tightened her corset still further, causing her breasts to swell and thrust as though they would pop from her body. Her waist narrowed to pencil thinness under the relentless constricting of the corset.

'Yes . . . more . . .' groaned Mrs Araval. 'Squeeze me!'

Nurse Crennet busied herself with a gleaming machine which resembled the one used on Mrs Shapiro's breasts and Jeremy Pleasant's erect manhood, except that this one seemed slightly more complex. There were the same perspex chambers, or suction tubes, which the nurses now positioned over their subject's breasts, fount and anus bud as well, one cup for each extremity. Nurse Crennet fetched two large handfuls of a crinkly purple substance, leaves of some sort, or dried seaweed. As Henrietta continued to tighten the wicked rubber corset, Nurse Crennet calmly thrust the weed into both anus and fount of her subject, forcing it firmly in until Mrs Araval groaned in this new discomfort.

'Dulse,' she said to Prue, 'a great delicacy in these parts. It is dried seaweed, and rich in potassium and other good nutrients, which are most effectively absorbed by the mucus membranes Nature has thoughtfully provided at a lady's most intimate places. Taste it.'

Prue did, and said that it tasted nice, like fish. Nurse Crennet smiled, and said that dulse was best matured in a number of ladies' founts, and a connoisseur could tell which ladies had held the portion they were eating. Prue looked her in the eye and chewed, swallowing every last bit, then said it was truly delicious.

'This portion was in *my* fount,' murmured Nurse Crennet.

Calmly, she removed the shapeless wad of glistening chewing gum from her mouth, and divided it in two. One half she shaped into a finger, and poked it into Mrs Araval's anus until it disappeared, locking the healthful dulse in place. She did the same to Mrs Araval's gash, playfully sticking her quim lips firmly together so that they bulged like the pouting lips of a mouth.

'Now this Madam is ready for her enlargement,' she said.

The suction tubes were locked on Mrs Araval's breasts and nether holes, and Henrietta started the motor. At once, the fount-lips, breasts and the rose of the anus leapt into startling prominence as the vacuum was formed. Nurse Crennet explained that the dulse, as well as being nutritious, was a test of muscle control, for not one scrap of dulse nor chewing gum plug must escape the subject's holes to appear in the 'expansion cup', or there was the promise of her severe displeasure. Prue watched in awe as the nipples and fount-lips blossomed like flowers, and the folds of the anus bud swelled up like a luxuriant rose. Nurse Crennet said that Mrs Araval was not ready for the lyre, but that this was 'moulding therapy' according to the principles of harmony established by an ancient shaman of Lapland. According to the golden proportions of the hexagon, quim lips, nipples, navel and anus bud should strive to be equal in dimension.

'It is not often that the sacred harmony is precisely achieved,' she said, 'but Mrs Araval has quite a prominent navel, and . . . well, we shall see.'

The truncation of the waist, as Mrs Araval groaned in her ever-tightening corset, also served a geometric principle, the balance of waist, breast, buttock and calves, and Nurse Crennet said that the human body was like a crystal: no two were exactly the same, but all obeyed the same principles of harmonious symmetry.

Miss Gageby was supervising the other nurses at their moaning subject, and Nurse Crennet looked at Prue once more.

'I sense harmony in you, Nurse Riding,' she said. 'I saw your curiosity as to my person.'

She gestured towards her skirt, and the intriguing bulge of her mons. Swiftly, without letting the others see, she raised her skirt for an instant and revealed her naked mound to Prue's eyes alone. Prue gasped.

'I . . . You are beautiful, Nurse!' she blurted.

Nurse Crennet's mound was of a size with her breast, as though sculpted thus. And it was indeed not shaven; instead, her mink was the lushest Prue had ever seen, or could imagine, a veritable forest of shiny black silk that seemed to extend up almost to the navel, and droop inches down the firm white thighs, as though some great black daw had nested at the woman's fount. Moreover, the hairs were absolutely straight, and combed flat, in a mirror image of the hairs on her head.

'You see?' said Nurse Crennet with a little smile. 'The beauty of symmetry. And now, I think Miss Gageby will wish us to attend our next subject.'

Miss Gageby said that it was so, and nonchalantly gathered her things.

'You are not leaving me like this?' wailed Mrs Araval.

'O, I can't be bothered to undo such a fussy little squit just now,' said Miss Gageby, yawning and flicking back her kiss-curl. 'We'll leave you here until I choose to come back for you. If I choose. If I don't, why, your quim and your arse-bud will be bigger than your head, and we'll all have a good laugh.'

'I'll scream for help!' cried Mrs Araval.

'No you won't,' retorted Miss Gageby, and took a leather gag from Nurse Crennet's store, then swiftly fastened it around the subject's mouth, the heavy grey cast-iron ball on the spiked strap preventing her from doing more than grunt in anguish.

Nurse Crennet nodded in approval, saying that iron molecules were very good for firming the organism. The spikes on the gag-strap were placed inward. Mrs Araval's feet feebly wriggled against her wrists, even though pinioned at the back of her head. The sinews of her bare thigh-backs and marked buttocks seemed stretched to breaking point as they cradled the sucking, humming expansion cups working on her tender engorged parts. Miss Gageby said that utter stillness was required and that the treatment must not be spoiled by any wriggling or any movement at all. Taking a coil of wire, she bound Mrs Araval's naked feet, winding the wire round and round several times very tightly until only the toes bulged from their metal prison. Then she produced a box of iron thimbles and with careful selection, or pretending, she clamped one on each of

Mrs Araval's toes. Each thimble was fastened to a wire which was looped to the studs in the woman's gag, and stretched taut.

'There!' said Miss Gageby. 'I bet that hurts. Not the lyre proper, but a girly's lyre, eh? Move your tootsies and you'll be very uncomfortable. Just think, Mrs Araval, you will hear the door clang shut, and you'll be all alone in this dungeon ... helpless, bound and gagged, your bum smarting and your holes crammed full, with nobody to hear or rescue you. I wouldn't like to be you, or your holes!'

'Mmm! Mmm!' Mrs Araval squealed, and squirmed frantically, but she did not drop any of the precious dulse from her fount or anus.

'And just to remind you to keep *absolutely* quiet and *absolutely* still . . .' said Miss Gageby.

She lifted the crop again and positioned herself beside the trussed naked body like an inspector in a meat plant. Very coolly she began to lash the stretched thighs, passing right down to the already reddened buttocks, whose flesh rapidly seared to deep purple as the cruel Assistant Matron pitilessly flogged her subject. She attended each side of the captive in turn, until the tethered body glowed with the lash's caress in a kind of tormented symmetry that Prue found beautiful. Miss Gageby repeated, as she whipped the woman, that Mrs Araval should be glad she was not getting a proper beating: this was just a stimulant, to ginger up her circulation, hygienically . . .

Tears streamed down Mrs Araval's red cheeks. But Prue saw that, as the door clanged shut leaving her alone, she was smiling blissfully behind her gag, and when they listened at the door, her moans were moans of unutterable contentment. Miss Gageby grinned. She ordered the twins to stand guard and observe the subject through the peephole, then after an hour had passed, to release her.

'Is she to be whipped, Matron?' said Helen.

'Is she, Matron? Whipped bound and bare? O, please! Pretty please!' added Angela.

'Yes,' said Miss Gageby, po-faced, 'I don't recall Mrs Araval has taken her proper thrashing yet. Of course she is to be whipped, bound and bare. What other way is there?'

As they proceeded along the corridor, she said to Prue, 'You see, Nurse Riding? The best treatments are like the best knickers – tailored exactly to the individual . . .'

7

Rubber Wrapped

'Health, Nurse Riding,' said Miss Gageby, 'is submission. And submission is freedom from stress, the greatest cause of ill-health. What causes stress? Responsibilities! The constant nagging demands of *things*, and things include other people. At Hydro, our subjects submit to health, and enjoy blissful freedom from choice: the right things to wear or eat, the right places to live and work and be seen. The subject has no decisions to make at all. Think of dear Jeremy Pleasant, frowning as he pilots his planes with all their flashing lights and whines and beeps . . . nagged by things! Here, he is a simple mucky schoolboy, his bum bare for the cane, his tongue worshipping a lady's feet, his cock caressed by the expansion tube . . . His world becomes gorgeously simple, and he returns cleansed to his duties.'

'The same for Mrs Shapiro and Mrs Araval?' said Prue.

'The same. They return to their complicated lives snug with their memories of freedom; here, they have been a body, flesh with holes to be tickled and filled and whipped, used with total disdain and abandon, and powerless. They may spend their lives enslaved by objects, but at Hydro they enjoy the glorious luxury of being one. Miss Delahaye, whom you shall now meet, is a most interesting subject. She is one of our snowbirds, from abroad, who can only visit rarely, and when they do, they pay handsomely for total treatment – a gamut, and more.'

'Then I shall be able to see, or administer, the lyre,' said Prue mischievously.

'In time, perhaps,' said Miss Gageby, with raised eyebrow. 'I should enjoy putting you under the lyre, Nurse.'

'Or helping Nurse Farle do it?' said Prue.

They entered another 'personal' treatment chamber, and this one reminded Prue of Jeremy Pleasant's schoolboy room, except that it obviously contained a female. The decor was bright, in pinks and baby blues, the wall was festooned with pinups of garish young men, the tables a litter of potions and perfumes, fluffy toys, underthings and carelessly discarded clothing. However, certain items of furniture, beneath cloth drapes of bunnies and teddy bears, hinted at a sternly hygienic purpose. There were footsteps behind them, and Nurse Heckmondthwaite arrived with Jess in tow, adjusting her nurse's bonnet. In the centre of the room stood a female of impressive height – like Henrietta Farle – and with corn-blonde tresses braided in two pigtails. Her posture was meek, with head bowed and hands clasped decorously at her fount. Beneath her clothing, her body – the breasts in particular – hinted at a splendour to equal Miss Gageby's or even Henrietta's, while the long coltish legs led to a croup that swelled with girlish and almost insolent grace behind her tight little skirt.

Although about thirty years of age, Miss Delahaye was dressed as a schoolgirl. She wore a crisp white blouse which showed clearly her swelling black bra beneath; a striped tie; grey pleated skirt, very short so that her stocking tops of black lace, and the straps to her garter belt, were fully visible, as was a triangle of black shiny panty at her crotch. The only jarring note was her shoes, sumptuous and high-heeled.

'Well, miss,' drawled Miss Gageby, 'you are a little slut, aren't you? Black undies, indeed – you know that's forbidden – and just look at the state of your room. You shall have to pay for that before we even begin your treatment. I think you know what to expect, and for your sluttishness, you shall have the humiliation of a trainee nurse attending you. Fetch the whippiest cane from your cupboard, miss!'

The room was indeed very untidy, with papers and things strewn higgledy-piggledy on the floor, as though on purpose.

'O, no!' cried Miss Delahaye, making saucer eyes and with mauve-lacquered fingers flying to her mouth. 'Not the cane, Miss! I know I'm naughty, but the cane will tear my new panties to shreds.'

Nevertheless, she moved to the cupboard and selected a long whippy cane, with crook handle and forked tip, which she proffered nervously to the Assistant Matron. Miss Gageby handed it to Prue.

'Don't worry, miss, your panties shan't suffer, because you'll take it bare. Now bend over, raise your skirt, and touch toes. Thighs well apart – you know the drill.'

'On the bare!' wailed Miss Delahaye. 'You are cruel, miss! O, my poor bum! How she'll smart!'

She obeyed rapidly, mewling to herself, and Prue was presented with superb orbs of her fesses, the tight black silk of the high skimpy knickers clinging to the flesh like the skin of a nectarine. She reached forward and hooked her finger into the panty silk, then began to pull the panties down, very slowly, relishing the girl's dismay as her firm white flesh was revealed. She pulled the panties down to the knees, where they hung stretched like a drawbridge above the sleek muscled calves, revealing the baby-smooth moons of her croup.

'And in front of these nurses!' cried Miss Delahaye. 'If I'm to be bare, may it not be in private?'

'Certainly not!' barked Miss Gageby. 'We nurses shall watch as your naughty white bum reddens, miss, and smile as you wriggle under the cane. Yes, that will be fun.'

'Such cruel fun! O! I'm never coming to this horrid place again!'

Miss Gageby snorted that for cheek, she was now forbidden to squirm or wriggle; she must take her dozen standing quite still, without the least hint of a tremble, or else Nurse Riding would be instructed to give her the set again.

'A whole dozen! Bare, and not squirm!' squealed the subject, her pigtails dancing in agitation.

'And one for luck,' added Miss Gageby, nodding to Prue.

Prue lifted the heavy yellow cane and swished it, testing, in the air. It made a delicious, terrifying whistle, and Miss Delahaye groaned. She was indeed shivering, and abruptly Prue lashed her naked bottom very hard, right across the white pale skin at the centre. She was satisfied to see pink instantly flush across the pale fesses, and that Miss Delahaye had to stifle a cry of anguish. Her own tight uniform caressed her breasts and fount, as though her clothing were an accomplice in the flogging. She caned Miss Delahaye quite rapidly, making sure her whole bottom was coloured, with a couple of subtle strokes to the thigh-backs, and two directly in the furrow, stroking the bumhole which nestled inviting and pink between the two mounds of taut flesh; though Prue was pleased at the involuntary jerk of the arse-globes after each cut.

Behind her, Miss Gageby counted the strokes, and when she reached twelve, suddenly Miss Delahaye's buttocks erupted in a veritable passion of squirming, and the bum wriggled and danced in maddened humiliation.

'Squirming,' murmured Miss Gageby. 'One stroke to

go, and you blub, you horrid girl, you take the set all over again.'

This time there was no ban on wriggling; at the dance of the bare buttocks under Prue's cane, the pink turned to crimson, then darkened to purple, delicious against the white straining skin of the back and thighs. She dealt the thirteenth stroke of the second whipping, and, panting, lowered her cane. Gently, she reached out to lift the sobbing Miss Delahaye's panties up over her bottom again. The panties were soaking wet: Miss Delahaye's quim had seeped through the beating, and her striped inner thighs glistened too. She rose to her feet, rubbing her pantied bottom before smoothing down her skirt, and said she had never been so hurt and humiliated.

'For a trainee, miss, you cane pretty tight,' she said shyly to Prue.

Miss Gageby rapped that Nurse Riding was to be addressed properly.

Miss Delahaye smiled, and her tear-stained eyes shone.

'You cane very tightly, Nurse Riding,' she whispered, 'and I hope your name meets its promise.'

'I heard that,' said Miss Gageby in a mild tone. 'Such sauce! I believe this subject requires a long period of correction before the treatment proper begins, so I arranged to have our luncheon delivered later.'

'You knew she would be cheeky, then,' said Prue.

Miss Gageby took the cane and touched Miss Delahaye's lips with its tip, then ran the tip down her breasts and belly to rest between her thighs, on her mound.

'I guessed,' she said, raising an eyebrow.

Miss Delahaye said, 'Mmm . . .'

Miss Delahaye was to be allowed no respite in her correction, before 'treatment proper'. She was invited to strip herself completely, and she obeyed, trembling as

113

she eased off her shoes, then unfastened her garter straps, with tiny little clicks, almost electric in the stillness of the room. Salt air washed them through the open window and, outside, the dunes were oblivious to the drama of submission unfolding within. High in the air, Prue saw the lazy vapour trail of a jet plane. Miss Delahaye peeled off her stockings one by one, as though sad at the departure of friends, yet somehow relishing the teasing slowness of her disrobing.

Then she slowly unbuttoned her blouse from the bottom up, revealing a flat, downy belly with a big whorled navel and, with something of a flourish, unbuttoned the last button to open her generous cleavage; her black scalloped bra spilled out, the breasts scarcely contained by the lacy thin fabric, and the wide saucers of her nipples clearly visible. Next, the skirt was unfastened at the rear, and it took Miss Delahaye some time of fumbling before it slid down, the garment being a one-piece wraparound which revealed a slice of thigh at the back, immodestly for a schoolgirl . . .

The subject stood in panties and bra, both garments of the same translucent silky fabric, and the bulge of the fount, with its thick curly mink, was seen clearly swelling through the skimpy black triangle of cloth. Miss Delahaye suddenly looked up and smiled shyly, yet with a dangerous glint in her eye. She turned and showed them her firm white fesses, the vivid crimson and purple of her caning rising above and below the high panty line. She rubbed herself again and said how horrid the smarting was, before hooking the waist elastic and beginning to slide the panties down over her mottled buttocks, very, very slowly: Prue felt herself moistening at the teasing promise.

Miss Gageby clapped her hands to hurry proceedings, but Miss Delahaye would not be hurried, and her grin broadened. She, the submissive one, seemed somehow in control of her own submission! At last the panties

114

dangled between her thighs, and the true luxuriance of her mink was apparent. It was a jungle of thick curly russet, neatly trimmed into a heart shape. Not a single strand hung down to mar the alabaster perfection of her soft inner thigh. At last Miss Delahaye's fingers moved behind her back, and the bra fastener slithered open. The bra drooped and hung around her breasts, suspended from the big dappled areolae of the nipples, and she stood with her hands on hips, the panties strung between her thighs and the bra drooping from her pendulous teats.

Miss Delahaye began to jerk her upper body, twirling the bra on her breasts, as if in mockery. Her breasts were tulip-shaped, big and seemingly floppy, yet by their twirling revealed that there were slabs of powerful controlling muscle behind. Prue stepped forward, unbidden, and asked if she might help. Miss Gageby did not stop her; she bent down and slid the panties down to the woman's ankles, and Miss Delahaye stepped out of them and stood in bare feet. In doing so, Prue brushed the woman's mink with her nose, and her fingers rested on the varnished toes. The mink smelled of strange flowers. She felt Miss Delahaye shiver.

Then she rose and took the bra from the breasts, leaving them bare, and her palm brushed the big nipples, which she sensed were already stiff, as if Miss Delahaye's stripping had excited her. Prue took the garments and folded them carefully on the table, on top of the stockings, and she noticed that the crotch of the panties was sopping. She looked at the filmy gauze of the stockings, and wondered that such an inoffensive strip of cloth could, on sheathing a woman's legs, become so beguiling. She longed suddenly to put those stockings on there and then.

'You have let your mink grow,' Miss Gageby observed coolly. 'Another imperfection.'

'I mean to shave, but I am so busy.'

'Shaving won't be enough, Miss Delahaye. When we have you restrained, we shall attend to your disgusting hairiness.'

The naked Miss Delahaye padded to the corner of the room, which led into a privy. From the privy she wheeled a long trolley on metal wheels, covered in a cloth with a merry design of owls and pussycats. When the trolley was in the centre of the room, she bent down decorously at the knees – but showing her arse-furrow stretch mischievously – and folded the wheels up so that the trolley stood firm. Then she pulled off the cloth and revealed a tubular frame of gleaming steel, with pulleys, levers and struts.

Miss Delahaye lay down on her back, on a cushioned pad of white leather in the centre of the frame, and splayed her arms and legs out like a starfish. Henrietta stationed herself by the controls and began to manipulate levers, so that the subject's limbs were raised, then lowered, now her arms, now her legs. Satisfied that the appliance was in order, Miss Gageby sent Jess to the privy; she returned with two great rolls of white tubing, like a garden hose. Nurse Heckmond-thwaite, meanwhile, had removed another jolly tapestry – a sort of Peter Pan motif – to reveal an arrangement of curious planks, boards and metal bolts. Jess indicated to Prue that she should follow her; Miss Gageby smiled and lit one of her fragrant cigarettes.

Jess unwrapped the tubing: it was not tubing, but a long flat strip of white rubber, and she began to wrap the gleaming latex around Miss Delahaye's left hand. Prue obediently began on the right, following Jess exactly. When the hands were swaddled, they moved to the wrists, then the forearms, wrapping the limbs to several thicknesses of this curious bandage, and very tightly, so that Miss Delahaye began to shift uncomfortably. The bandaging continued across her shoulders and neck, and then Jess indicated that Prue

116

should start on her leg, while Jess proceeded to wrap the woman's head entirely in the white rubber, leaving only holes for lips and nose. Miss Delahaye was thus blindfold as her wrapping continued across her breast and belly and thighs; she groaned as the swaddling bit tightly and thickly layered across her belly, narrowing it sharply like a wasp rubber corset. Prue swaddled her feet tightly on Miss Gageby's orders, then continued the binding up the calf to the thigh.

Soon Miss Delahaye was swathed from head to foot in the tight shiny rubber, the only bare spaces being her mouth and nose, her breasts, and her fount and buttocks. Nurse Heckmondthwaite produced a thin flat plank, precisely the length of an arm, and positioned Miss Delahaye's arm above it. Then she put a semi-circle of iron across her wrist, and fastened it to the board with large screws, secured by nuts. The same was done to her other arm, and then to both her legs, her ankles being clamped tight. Then Henrietta moved her lever, and the straightened limbs bent up slightly, to allow Nurse Heckmondthwaite access to the back. This too was secured and screwed to a slightly wider plank, or splint as Prue supposed it to be. A large iron band was clamped cruelly tight across Miss Delahaye's waist, tighter even than her rubber corsing, and fixing her back ramrod straight to the backing splint; the same under her armpits, biting them severely, and across her collarbones, thrusting her squashed breasts up.

Miss Gageby said something about the therapeutic properties of rubber on the skin, and straightness of the limbs – bone structure – posture – molecules again. For this treatment, it was necessary that the subject be completely bound and still. She was awed by the swaddled figure before her, strapped and screwed and splinted, completely at the mercy of her nurses, and with her tenderest parts exposed to their attentions, like a living rubber puppet. Miss Gageby threw her cigarette end on the floor, and fetched a large pair of tweezers, and what looked like an electric hair-dryer.

Now, Nurse Heckmondthwaite drew from the ceiling six copper chains, on pulleys, with clamps on the ends; these were fixed to the wrist and ankle shackles which tethered the subject, and to the clamp at waist and breastbone; Henrietta manipulated her levers until they were drawn tight, lifting Miss Delahaye's legs and torso at a slight angle from the leather cushion at the small of her back. Two further, heavier chains were lowered, and each bifurcated into two heavy clamps. Henrietta and Nurse Heckmondthwaite together fastened each clamp to each nipple and each quim lip. Miss Delahaye shuddered; the padded clamps were tight on her tender places.

When the clamps were fixed fast, the chains were tightened; Henrietta moved another lever, and the back-cushion sank abruptly away from Miss Delahaye, leaving her suspended in mid-air, entirely supported by the chains, the tightest being those clamped to her teats and quim! The nipples and breasts were stretched to an alarming size, and the quim lips were distended and pulled up so that they became like gloves; it was as though the entire body of the woman were hanging by her tortured quim and teats alone – though the chains at wrists and ankles supported her too. Miss Delahaye shivered and moaned beneath her swaddling, but could not move or squirm in her anguish, without increasing the pulling of those cruel clamps to her nipples and quim. She was utterly helpless in her rubber cocoon.

Jess fetched another device from the seemingly inexhaustible privy, and suddenly Prue asked to go. Permission was granted; she entered the dark bathroom and squatted on the commode, lifting her skirt high and lowering her knickers but not bothering to shut the door, as she was too anxious to follow what was happening. Miss Gageby was busy with the hair-dryer,

Nurse Heckmondthwaite between Miss Delahaye's thighs, while Henrietta cranked her pulleys to raise and separate the subject's legs, and reveal her naked lady's place. All the nurses took time to peep at Prue's shaven fount as she made blissful and noisy evacuation.

She wiped herself hurriedly with lavender-scented blue paper, and returned to find that a massive double dildo had been placed halfway inside Miss Delahaye's holes, and that Nurse Heckmondthwaite was in the process of pushing the great striated prongs right up her as far as they would go. Miss Delahaye's body writhed in gentle agony, making her suspension chains twang. The dildo was pushed in right to the hilt, and now the woman's groans were unabated. Miss Gageby ordered her to hold the prongs firmly inside her, on pain of further correction before her treatment began, and Miss Delahaye's moan became a wail. Henrietta looked eagerly at Miss Gageby.

'May I?' she whispered. 'A hygienic queen?'

Miss Gageby nodded.

'If she is going to squall so,' she said. 'But be careful, Nurse Farle.'

'Am I not always, Assistant Matron?' said Henrietta.

Miss Gageby brushed her kiss curl two or three times, then turned on the hair-dryer to full power, and on cold, so that an icy blast of air swept Miss Delahaye's mink, the curly hairs promptly standing up. The helpless woman's head hung at waist height; Henrietta positioned herself beside Miss Delahaye's lips, and then lifted her skirt. Swiftly, she let her knickers fall to the floor and stepped out of them, then lifted one long leg and swung it over Miss Delahaye's head so that her quim was above her mouth as she straddled her. Smiling grimly, Henrietta lowered her naked quim squarely on to the trussed woman's mouth and her anus pressed the nose. Her legs were straight, her weight only slightly on the subject, but she continued to squat, placing more and more weight on the subject and making the chains twang in protest. Miss Delahaye's nipples and quim lips seemed ready to burst, distended so by Henrietta's weight.

'Careful, Henrietta,' said Miss Gageby, and suddenly Henrietta, with balletic grace, looped both her legs up in the air and brought them together so that her feet were resting on the woman's breasts, the full weight of the nurse's fount and buttocks pressed to the woman's face.

Miss Delahaye jumped violently, and squealed deep in her throat, and when Miss Gageby said that was too much, Henrietta slowly uncurled her gorgeous legs, balanced for a moment with only her quim and anus supporting her on Miss Delahaye's moaning face, then placed her feet back on the ground. She continued to 'queen' Miss Delahaye, her legs slightly bent so that some, but not all of her weight was on the blindfolded woman, and the squeal abated into an exhausted sobbing. Miss Gageby, meanwhile, began to pluck the hairs from her mink, one by one, with her tweezers.

As each hair came out, Miss Delahaye jumped and squealed, and the bare skin left was soon goose-pimpled from the icy air. Her moans were shortly joined by Henrietta, who was still queening the subject, and with her eyes shut and a shy smile on her face, was gently crooning, and rubbing her quim against Miss Delahaye's lips. Prue saw that Miss Delahaye's tongue was busy at Henrietta's glorious stubby damsel: she was gamahuching her tormentor, and a slither of Henrietta's love juices was glistening on her subject's chin. Miss Gageby seemed not to notice, or not to mind.

Prue asked what the hygienic purpose of the double dildo was, and Miss Gageby, attentive to her plucking, and carefully placing each plucked mink-hair on a metal dish, replied that this dildo was corrective, as could be seen from the painful nodules and striations that adorned it. Miss Delahaye's thighs were widened and her furrow spread, the buttocks shining in the pale sea-light. Miss Gageby proceeded to pluck every single hair from the blonde cluster at her anus and bum-crack. The subject sobbed, and begged to be released, promising to be a good clean girl in future.

'I beg for my freedom, you cruellest of ladies!' she cried dramatically.

'Tut! You have quite enough freedom in Switzerland. Only here in Northumberland may you enjoy the glorious freedom of being disciplined, Miss Delahaye,' said Miss Gageby, in a motherly voice, plucking the final hair from Miss Delahaye's now gleaming lady's place. 'There! Now I think it is time for lunch, before her treatment proper.'

Luncheon was brought: a tureen of soup, and a dish of chicken wings, and even a carafe of wine. These were placed on Miss Delahaye's bound belly, and the woman was ordered to remain perfectly still, or merit further correction. The nurses ate merrily, throwing the scraps of bone and skin on the floor, and wiping their greasy fingers on Miss Delahaye's breasts and quim. Soon, her naked flesh was gleaming with grease, but her quim lips were glistening with more than food slops: as each nurse wiped her fingers, she playfully brushed the woman's pink damsel, which was now standing pert and stiff amid the rich folds of her quim lips, and Miss Delahaye's slit was seeping. Prue joined in, exciting herself at the stiffness of the nubbin which increasingly matched her own. For a moment, she longed for her own body to be bound, for the other nurses to eat off her, and whip her bare, and queen her, making her taste and swallow cascades of sweet juices . . .

The wine made them merry, and they debated how to proceed with the naughty Swiss slut's correction. There was some soup left; in a trice, the dildos were pulled roughly from the woman's distended holes, making a plopping squelchy sound, and Henrietta worked her levers to upend the legs. Nurse Heckmondthwaite, giggling, parted the quim lips with thumb and forefinger and poured the soup straight into Miss Delahaye's slit! Prue and Jess found themselves quite naturally holding hands, then touching each other's tensed thighs, and it was not long before their fingers strayed beneath their skirts. Prue thought Miss Gageby winked.

The Assistant Matron lit a cigarette and invited the nurses to test Miss Delahaye's powers of muscle control. Each nurse in turn positioned herself between the fleshy buttocks, her tongue below the slit, and was rewarded with a spurt of brown soup from the pumping quim! Miss Delahaye grunted – her voice nameless and her body bound in utter submission to her carers' will. Wine brought joy; Jess said they should all have a chance to queen the slut, and Miss Gageby, lighting another cigarette, agreed, except that they were to keep their panties on, for decorum. Prue went first, and giggled at the woman's tongue lapping at her wet panties, like some blind polyp in the sea, as she let the full weight of her buttocks squash the mewling face helpless beneath her. Then it was Jess's turn, and she writhed enthusiastically, her knickers pulled up as tight as she could, and her thighs pincers as Miss Delahaye's mouth and nose became fleshy instruments of her frotting. Then, it was Nurse Heckmondthwaite's turn, and she protested that if Nurse Farle were permitted bare quim, so she should too.

'Nurse Farle is in charge of restraint,' said Miss Gageby, blowing smoke at Nurse Heckmondthwaite.

Wine-flushed, Nurse Heckmondthwaite pouted, and defiantly ripped off her panties, then squatted with her full weight on the woman's face, writhing as the tongue flickered on her naked gash and clit; her fount shone with juices that tumbled across Miss Delahaye's chin and sucking lips. Miss Gageby sat back and watched, smoking and openly fingering her own panties, with her skirt riding up and a delicious wet patch on her cream silk knickers. Prue and Jess had no hesitation in diddling each other, hands feverish in their panties against their naked quims. Henrietta placed herself behind Miss Gageby and, still smiling like a sphinx, plunged her hands into the Matron's bra, kneading and pulling at her breasts with a rough caress that made Miss Gageby's cigarette tremble as her own hand flicked faster and faster on her wet knickers. Prue reached out to tweak Miss Delahaye's stiff little clitty, which made the woman tremble and sigh, and as Jess stuck her index and forefingers inside her anus, she yelped and shook in a flooding spasm.

Nurse Heckmondthwaite too was trembling, her nubbin quite distended at the tonguing, and seeming about to climax. Prue and Jess grinned in complicity, and their lips met in a sucking tongue-kiss as fingers probed hot wet slits and trembling damsels. Nurse Heckmondthwaite cried in a throaty, tormented squeal of pleasure as her naked quim bucked frantically, buttocks slapping her subject's crushed face, in the fury of her orgasm. Prue felt herself come and gave herself to her friend's embrace and her probing fingers. Dimly, she was aware of Henrietta who, having freed Miss Gageby's breasts from their bra, was slapping the massive teats like fish on a slab until Miss Gageby too trembled and softly squealed as her fingers blurred on her soaked crotch.

Henrietta reached down and pulled Miss Gageby's panties, then took the cigarette from her mouth and put it between the Matron's engorged quim lips! She ordered naughty Miss Gageby to blow smoke rings while she disgracefully diddled herself, or she would get the lyre in the dungeon ... Miss Gageby's fingers did not leave her throbbing clit, but with astonishing grace, her quim lips sucked and twisted until perfect little smoke rings were floating up towards Henrietta, who took them in her mouth, inhaled, and blew the smoke over Miss Gageby's face and flapping bare breasts.

When the cigarette was finished, Miss Gageby's belly heaved and expelled the butt like a popgun. Henrietta moved to her front, and, still pummelling her breasts, lifted her own skirt and lowered her panties to reveal her own bare quim. Miss Gageby moaned, now, and kicked off her shoes as if obeying some implanted command. She pushed the stockinged cream toes of her left foot deep into Henrietta's stretched quim, and began to thrust in and out, while with her right toe, she plucked at Henrietta's distended clit. Her stockinged feet were drenched in Henrietta's fluid; soon, Miss Gageby gasped and shuddered, and moaned with a kind of despairing song as she climaxed, and at this, Henrietta too gasped in heavy spasm.

There was a moment of contented stillness. The nurses replaced their clothing and smoothed their hair, and turned again to Miss Gageby as though nothing had happened, and their attention had been on their subject all the time.

'Well!' said Miss Gageby in a smoky drawl. 'I think the sea air makes good nurses of us. Except for one thing. Nurse Heckmondthwaite, you had bare quim with the subject, and took pleasure from her treatment – against my orders.'

Nurse Heckmondthwaite flushed.

'Well! I scarcely think – I mean –'

She looked round for moral support, and found none.

Miss Gageby ordered the subject released from her splints and clamps, and as this was done, she lit another cigarette.

'There is also the matter of Mrs Araval. She informed me that you were negligent, did not give her proper treatment, which must include a proper flogging.'

Miss Delahaye was helped to her feet and stood, still swaddled, rubbing her limbs and her sore bumhole.

'I – I didn't think –' Nurse Heckmondthwaite began.

'Exactly. You didn't think.'

Miss Gageby picked up the cane, still shining with the sweat of Miss Delahaye's flogged bottom, and swished it in the air.

'A beating has been missed. A beating must replace it. You choose, Nurse. Make good the beating tally, or have your negligence entered in Nurses' Records?'

Nurse Heckmondthwaite paled, then gulped.

'I accept beating, Matron. But here? In front of all?'

'Here, Nurse. On bare, and bagged.'

'Ooo . . .' moaned Nurse Heckmondthwaite, but did not resist as Henrietta seized her and attached her wrists to the clamps, then hoisted the pulley so that the false brunette was suspended a foot from the floor.

She dangled, squirming and moaning. Roughly, Henrietta pulled off her panties and lifted her skirt, then pulled the waistband up over her breasts, under her armpits. Prue giggled: the stubble on Nurse Heckmond-thwaite's shaven fount, and the straggly anus hairs, were red. Henrietta ripped the bra and bared her breasts, then pulled the skirt right over her head and tied it with a belt so that her head was sheathed and hidden by her own skirt.

'Matron,' whimpered Miss Delahaye, 'is it time for my treatment yet?'

'You impudent slut!' retorted Miss Gageby. 'Look what a filthy state your floor is in! Chicken bones and slops everywhere. You shall clean it and pick up every bit.'

Miss Delahaye was still blindfold and swaddled, but she had to kneel, supporting herself on her arms and ankles, and search the floor for every scrap, which she was obliged to pick up with her quim, and deposit on the dish with her own pubic hairs. Miss Gageby caned her four times on the breasts, which made her shriek and shudder, with another four on the bare buttocks, before she was allowed to begin her task, sobbing with the pain and humiliation. Miss Gageby then turned to the naked Nurse Heckmondthwaite and lit another cigarette before tapping her bottom with the cane. The nurse dangled helpless and naked from her straining wrists, and whimpered softly.

'I advise you to keep very still, Nurse,' said Miss Gageby, puffing contentedly, 'otherwise who knows where my strokes will land. It's Nurse's Discretion, you realise . . . an unlimited chastisement.'

The first cut landed on the buttocks, leaving deep pink; and the second, third and fourth, all in the same spot and with devilish precision. Nurse Heckmondthwaite squealed and began to whirl helplessly in her bonds, overcome by her smarting, but Miss Gageby did not move. As the nurse's twisting body presented her with a moving target – now fesses, now thigh and now belly – her cane landed implacably until the nurse's entire body was streaked pink. Miss Gageby spared neither teat nor belly, nor the swelling mound, when Nurse Heckmondthwaite's anguished dancing presented her lady's place.

'O no!' she cried, sobbing. 'Please . . . please, Miss.'

'Please *Matron*,' said Miss Gageby sternly as the tip of her cane landed squarely in her victim's furrow. 'No mention in Nurses' Records, remember?'

'Yes, yes,' sobbed the nurse brokenly. 'I submit . . . you know I must . . . Matron.'

'Must is not enough, Nurse,' said Miss Gageby, with a fierce cane-crack across her bare belly. 'There is another little word . . .'

'You know I *want* to submit!' screamed Nurse Heckmondthwaite. 'Damn it! You know we *all* want to . . .!'

Miss Delahaye was permitted to finish her task by picking up the smallest scraps with her tongue, while Miss Gageby casually beat her upturned buttocks with a lazy but severe cane. Nurse Heckmondthwaite said in a small voice that she was desperate to go to the privy. Miss Gageby ignored her. When the floor was cleaned, the subject was released from her rubber swaddling, and stood shivering, sobbing and naked, rubbing her bruised bottom and her body where the livid marks of her binding were apparent. She was ordered to dress in her school uniform again, after going to the privy, her evacuation supervised by Miss Gageby, who did not permit her to wipe or cleanse her bottom before putting on her panties. When she was dressed and tidied, Miss Delahaye asked when her treatment should begin.

Miss Gageby responded furiously by lifting her dress and dealing a further six cuts to her wobbling panties, and gasping that such a naughty slut did not merit a lady's treatment.

'We must go,' she said, 'since your time is up, mademoiselle. On second thoughts . . .'

With the cane handle, she pushed Nurse Heckmond-thwaite's livid lady's place, making her spin helplessly.

'It seems unfair that we have had exercise and you have not. You may kneel, and feed Nurse Heckmond-thwaite before releasing her, Miss Delahaye. First, your panties, please.'

Miss Delahaye took off her soiled knickers and handed them to the Assistant Matron, who with great ceremony wadded them in Nurse Heckmondthwaite's mouth, then tied her in a gag with her own garter belt. Then she took the dish containing Miss Delahaye's mink-hairs, and the greasy chicken scraps, and rammed the contents into her mouth. She was to separate her own hairs and chew them to a pulp, then feed Nurse Heckmondthwaite's quim with her tongue and lips. Nurse Heckmondthwaite was to hold the delicacy inside her gash for later inspection . . .

She opened the door, as Miss Delahaye knelt and began to kiss the tethered nurse's quim.

'*Au revoir*, mademoiselle,' cried Miss Gageby. 'And Nurse Heckmondthwaite is *not* allowed to go to the privy.'

'It seems unfair, Matron, that Miss Delahaye was denied treatment, with all that correction, and us nurses having . . . you know,' said Prue in the corridor.

'Heavens, that *was* her treatment!' cried Miss Gageby.

'But – O, I wonder why women can be so cruel to each other.'

'Cruel! She was lucky I didn't treat her in our dungeon . . .'

8

Honey Birch

The nurses' evening out together was put off, drifting in the vagueness of small choices: there were numerous 'togethers', which formed and re-formed like a kaleidoscope. Prue attended Mrs Shapiro once or twice, with others, but did not see Mrs Araval or Miss Delahaye again. But every day brought new subjects and new treatments, and Prue found that 'the new blonde London nurse' was actually demanded by some of her subjects, who had heard of her reputation for firmness. Henrietta and Nurse Heckmondthwaite were haughty.

'Do your subs tip well?' said Jess, who liked to abbreviate everything.

'Why, tip a nurse! I should think not,' replied Prue.

'Well, they should, you know. I don't see why they shouldn't tip a hygienist.'

Prue was called that morning to treat a young male, who was the image of young Jeremy Pleasant, except that he had no moustache and his hair was cropped short. Prue greeted him, then consulted, or pretended to consult, her notes.

'It seems you require special treatment, Master Raitte,' she said gravely. 'What made you request my services, sir?'

'O . . . Gemma – I mean, Flight Lieutenant Pleasant, you know – he spoke most highly of you, Nurse,' stammered the young man with an engaging blush.

'I see. You have your subject's kit?'

'Yes, Nurse,' he said, lifting a flight bag.

'Why are you not already changed?' she asked sternly. 'Do so now – but I am displeased at your timewasting.'

He began to undress from his crisp civilian suit, and asked if he had been naughty enough to incur punishment.

'Punishment!' snapped Prue. 'There is no punishment here, sir, only treatment. And since you have aroused my displeasure, I fear your treatment may be uncomfortable.'

'Ooo . . .' he said softly, and she watched as he changed into the shorts, white shirt, striped tie and blazer of a schoolboy! She noticed with approval that his striped boxers bulged noticeably; she drew a deep breath, so that he saw the swelling of her breasts, and the bulge in his trousers grew more alarming still, to his evident, yet not unhappy, embarrassment.

'You think this an occasion for rudeness, boy,' she rapped, ostentatiously picking up and flexing the stoutest cane from the neat rack with which this chamber, like all others, was provided.

She tapped his erection with the tip of her cane, which did nothing to diminish his swelling.

'Haven't you ever been alone with a nurse before?' she said. 'My, I can't imagine what flying does to you boys. We shall have to bring you down to earth before your treatment, sir. I suppose you know what that means?'

This time she swished the cane in the air, and he winced as it whistled.

'No . . . please, miss, I beg you,' he intoned numbly.

She swished the cane so that it raised a cloud of dust from the sofa.

'Please *Nurse*,' she said sharply. 'I see from your notes that you have had treatment before: lavage from Nurse Gageby, the expansion tube from Nurse Farle, and gluteal stimulation from Nurse Rise. That means she spanked you?'

'Y – yes, Miss – I mean, Nurse,' he mumbled.

'On bare?'

'I had to take my panties down, yes.'

'But not the cane?'

He shook his head.

'I have taken cane, but . . . not on the bare, Nurse.'

'Well, *I* am going to cane you, for your own good, boy, and definitely on the bare. I want to see every detail of your pain as I redden your skin, and make you smart and squeal and glow for a woman's pure delight. Do you agree? If so, lower your clothing to your ankles, and bend over the back of the sofa.'

He obeyed, shivering.

'I have never been caned on the bare, before, Nurse. I suppose it will hurt dreadfully.'

'Yes, it will. The more so, since I think you are lying.'

He shivered quite violently. His erection was very proud, a lovely huge cock that strained up against his belly, with the balls tight and tempting beneath.

'A dozen should see you right, and that horrid stiff thing back to normal,' she said in a businesslike tone. 'Now, spread your thighs a little more – that's it – and get ready for a nice slow dozen, plus one for luck. No squealing or flinching, mind, or you get the cut over. I won't have unruly subjects, Raitte.'

'Please be gentle, Nurse,' he whispered.

'Gentle!' she exclaimed. 'You don't really mean that, do you, boy? Else why did you ask for *me*?'

'O . . . I don't really know what I mean, Nurse,' he murmured wretchedly, and Prue told him that after a caning, his smarting bum would tell him.

She gave him a little poke in the balls, and said they would soften as his bum reddened; then without warning she delivered the first stroke. He clenched his bum but did not cry, except for a low moan that

131

wracked his body, and she forgave him this once. Thereafter he took his beating in silence. It was slow and leisurely, Prue making each stroke as juicy as she could, and making sure his whole croup was well coloured by the time she delivered the fourteenth – for one stroke had to be repeated after he jumped at a cut to the furrow. Between strokes, at intervals of two minutes, she asked him about life in the Air Force, and in particular what sort of lewdness the 'boys' got up to. He was hesitant, but when she increased the strength of her canestrokes, he sobbed a little and confessed that as cadets, they had, 'sort of initiation rites': endurance tests, beatings . . .'

'Beatings?'

'Just with a paddle, and certainly not bare,' he insisted. 'How I hate it! Our American friends are very fond of that, they call it "hazing", but we Brits – well, one of our intitiation tests is that we have to dress up as girls. It is so shaming! But there isn't really much to do at base, you see, and – well, it is a way of passing the time between exercises. Goodenhall is a bit of a relic of the Cold War, and it would be embarrassing for them to close it down. They are worried that if we were all to take early retirement, who knows where we would sell our services?'

'If you hate being beaten, why do you come to Hydro for treatment?' asked Prue. 'You must be aware of our rigorous approach to discipline – especially the male's.'

'Being beaten is normally horrible, even a paddling – some of those navigators lay it on hard! – but it feels sort of glowy afterwards, and nice from a *lady*'s hand.'

'And do you get hard when your comrades beat you? Or you beat them?'

'Certainly not!'

'Not even when you are dressed as a girly?'

'O! Ouch! That's tight!' he sobbed as the cane stroked. 'Certainly not as a girl! That would be too shaming, Nurse!'

132

Prue delivered the last stroke and tapped his balls again. His erection was now straining, with patchworks of crimson on his naked bum. She pretended to consult her notes again; in reality, they consisted of a neat line from Matron Bream, saying 'Lieutenant Raitte is a frisky pup, so treat him strictly, at Nurse's Discretion.'

'Well, you may stand up,' she said, 'but the problem hasn't been solved, has it? You are still disgracefully hard. How I hate mucky little school pups like you. Girls are much sweeter and more decorous. What *shall* we do? First, I'll have you *entirely* nude, boy.'

He gulped; Prue did too, still awed at her female power, as she watched him strip naked, and ordered him to fold his clothes neatly. As he was doing so, she took off her cardigan, then unfastened the buttons of her blouse; she let it hang loose, then undid the catch of her bra. She unfastened her skirt, unwrapped it, and threw it at him. Dumbfounded, he caught it. Then she slipped out of her blouse and bra, and gave him those too, relishing the firm shiver of her naked breasts and the boy's wide-eyed desire. The feeling made her quim seep, and she knew that her knickers would have a visible damp patch, but such was her own cool excitement that she did not care.

Suppressing a tremor, she unfastened her suspenders and rolled down her stockings, until she stood only in her bonnet and panties, and he clutched the fragrant bundle of her nurse's uniform. Today, her bra and panties were virginal white, but the bra still daringly scalloped and the panties thin and high. Harshly, she ordered him to put it on, bra and everything. In girly's clothing, his cock would be shamed into softness.

The male swallowed and rubbed his flaming bottom, but did as he was told. Slowly he donned the nurse's uniform, which fitted him neatly, and Prue kicked off her shoes and made him squeeze into them too. Finally she stripped herself of her panties, which were sopping and steamily fragrant, and told him to slip them on. His face was bright red as he put on the woman's knickers, and Prue folded her arms over her breasts, relishing her own nudity after her sweating exertion. She adjusted her nurse's bonnet at a jaunty angle, and smiled at him.

'Now I'll be more comfortable for your *next* treatment,' she said, 'for I'm afraid your cock is still wilful, isn't she? And there is the small matter of your lying about never having been caned bare before. I suppose you thought that would make me feel sorry for you, and go easy. Well, it won't. It shall make me give it to you extra hard, for your deceit and your stupidity in trying to fool me. You got hard from your bare caning, and a dozen from my cane would normally skin any virgin to a quivering, blubbering wreck, so it is perfectly clear your bum's well used to it!'

Raitte looked down in embarrassment: Prue's nurse's skirt bulged with the rise of his stiff member.

'But maybe you've never seen a naked woman before?' she taunted him. 'Perhaps not a naked nurse. Well, *my girl*, you'll wish you hadn't by the time I've finished with your girly's bum. First tickling caning was just a warm-up – I fooled *you*, you see – and now that I'm comfortable, I can tan you long and slow. You didn't seriously think you'd get off with a mere dozen! You have heard of the tawse, I suppose, girly?'

Prue noticed that at her contemptuous 'girly' he actually blushed and simpered, as if secretly thrilled. She selected a black tawse with three thick leather tongues, each studded with silver, and said a mental thank you to Miss Macardle.

'I have been a very naughty girl, Nurse,' Raitte whispered, 'and my bum deserves the tawse, if you please.'

'It'll be a full one hundred,' she said briskly. 'This time, not the sofa – I want that cock in full view. So, knickers down and skirt up, girl, and then bend over and touch your toes.'

'I don't know if I can take it, Nurse.'

'All girls take such treatment.'

Prue began to flog him, the harsh slap of the tawse-thongs echoing in the chamber. The red of his bum turned darker and darker at each stroke, until his croup was a shivering delicate purple. At each fierce stroke, the boy trembled, and seemed about to squeal; she felt her breasts bounce hard, her stiff nipples tingling like diamonds, and a warm trickle of seep flow down her inner thighs, as far as the calves' swell. She paused to stroke his flaming bare fesses, beautifully hot from her whipping. And still his cock stood!

Prue flogged him to one hundred, then told him to rest for a moment, before his treatment continued with another set of the cane. There was dismay but utter submission in his wet eyes; he pleaded that he was so raw he did not think he could stand it without some restraint, and she said gravely that, for the privilege of being bound, he was to take six extra. Glumly he nodded his agreement, and, fetching straps, she pinioned him with a briskness that hid her excitement.

She selected a compact flogging-horse with anklets and wrist-cuffs, and a leather waist-strap, and, careful not to sully her own uniform, she soon had him neatly bound. She said he should probably be gagged, as the cane on top of a tawsing was even more painful than he could imagine, and he did not protest as she removed her own still wet panties from his crotch and stuffed them into his mouth, where she fastened them with his own elastic snake-clasp belt wound twice around his chin. As she began the second cane-set, he seemed to lose control, and at each hard stroke to the bare, he jerked and quivered like a marionette.

She told him she would take her time with this second set, and he moaned prettily, with a brief squeal as the fresh stroking began. Her hand went between her thighs; she was sopping with love-oil, and at each lash to the squirming bare of the male, she flicked her clitty quite sharply, so that her moans joined his. At last the caning was complete, and his livid flesh glowed with twenty-six caresses – 'a nurse's dozen for fibbing, and a nurse's dozen for having a disgraceful huge cock'. The cock still stood; quickly, and with trembling fingers, Prue fetched from the medicine cabinet in the bathroom a double-pronged dildo made of soft rubber, its prongs bigger than most cocks. Beneath it was a hollow squeezy ball-sac, which she filled from the tap with hot water, then coated each prong with her own copious love-oils. This done, she told Raitte that a girl must receive a girl's proper anal treatment.

He groaned through his panty-gag, in protest or perhaps delight, and again as she parted his livid bum-cheeks and began to tickle his anus with her dripping finger, pushing her index and forefinger inside him, and making him squeak and wriggle. His arsehole felt soft and elastic; gasping, she inserted the oiled dildo and squeezed it inside him, meeting resistance at first, although she ordered him to relax, and then, when it was halfway inside, his anus seemed to yield, and the whole rubber prong slid joyously and completely into the bumhole.

Feverishly, she balanced herself on top of him, and put the other prong inside her own quim, where it sank easily and filled her. Breathing hard, Nurse Prudence began to ride her subject, squirming herself now in the delightful thrusting of the rubber cock inside her, and relishing the male's groans as the other dildo plunged fully inside him. A nodule on her dildo tweaked against her damsel, and her groans were as loud as her subject's. Her hand clasped the shiny smooth helmet of the cock, and began to rub.

'My,' she crooned, 'what a big stiff clitty you have, girl. I wonder if she'll spurt for me?'

She felt the cock tremble and tense, and knew he must

not be far from his creaming. In readiness, she gave way to the flutter in her belly, allowed herself to come to the plateau of climax, and when she could no longer hold back, gave way to her spasm with deep anguished cries of her joy. At the same time she squeezed hard on the rubber ball-sac, spurting the hot liquid into her own quim and the male's arsehole, and changed her gentle caress of his bulb to a strong rubbing pulse across the peehole. She took off her nurse's bonnet, and held it before his manhood; she felt a droplet of fluid; the cock began to buck; then he was squealing in his own ecstacy, joining her, as a great jet of hot cream washed her caressing fingers on his smooth throbbing glans, filling her upturned bonnet. In the high warmth of her own spasm, her vision blurred; she looked down and saw her own clothing on the male's writhing body, and felt as though she were poking herself, and at this gorgeous wicked thought, her moans of pleasure rose to a squeal.

After this treatment, Prue became very businesslike, and permitted the male to light a cigarette for her. She watched him shower, and dress, and when he was decent, she donned her own bra and panties but nothing more, and saw his limp cock begin to rise again. She consulted her notes, pretended to write something, with the cigarette dangling sluttishly between her lips, and asked nonchalantly whether his treatment had been sufficiently cleansing.

'O, yes, miss! I mean, Nurse! I never dreamed . . . O, Nurse, please may I kiss you?'

Prue looked up po-faced, making no attempt to remove the cigarette from her lips. She said it was permitted, not on the mouth or cheek, but in the place where he should make proper obeisance. The male knelt and pressed his lips to her wet panties, full on her swollen quim lips, and then, at her direction, kissed her feet.

'Nurse . . . did you enjoy giving me my treatment?' he gasped. 'O, I hope you did.'

She stared at him with a coolness she did not feel.

'Certainly not,' she rapped. 'I am a nurse, a professional, and I perform my duties impersonally. However, if you wish to express your appreciation, sir, you may do so in the traditional way.'

Without taking her eyes from his, she lowered her panties and revealed her naked quim, then, blowing smoke at him, parted the glistening quim lips and held them open showing him her wet, pink lady's place. Stammering and blushing, he took his wallet, and extracted a £20 note, which he rolled tight, then pushed it delicately into her waiting quim. When it was all the way inside her, she closed her lips like a limpet and pulled up her panties without giving any acknowledgement of his gift save a single frosty nod of dismissal. Lieutenant Raitte left the chamber sighing with joy. When he had gone, she rubbed the creamy bonnet all over her naked breasts and quim, and rubbed her clitty hard and quickly to another spasm. She sobbed in relief, then removed the £20 from her soaking quim, and licked it before stowing it safely in her knickers.

At luncheon, Jess remarked on her nice new perfume.

'It has the scent of a man's cream!' she cried.

'It is chestnut blossom,' said Prue.

'But chestnut blossom is out of season.'

'Cream isn't,' Prue replied.

Thereafter, she learnt that tips were to be had in plenty from supplicant males, and that the more they were humiliated, beaten, and treated as 'naughty little ticks', the more they clamoured to reward their nurse. If she was feeling particularly generous, she would allow or compel them to address her as 'Mistress'. With females, the rewards of tips were also plentiful, but females had to be approached in a slightly different way. They responded less to harshness than to sympathy. A female needed to feel that her hygienic correction was pampering designed for her specially, that her needs were shared by no other female.

'I'm awfully sorry, but this might be a little uncomfortable,' Prue would say, as she bound her naked subject most sternly for a flogging. 'But you are a special case, and need the most individual treatment, Madam.'

'O, I know, I know,' the subject would groan, in the delicious complicity of submissive and dominant.

While males loved to be scorned as one of a mass of wretched mucky boys, all the same, who only understood the harshest of thrashings, a female wished to think that all her squirmings and very real anguish at treatment was designed for her alone, and that no other female could possibly take such a fierce lavage, or so many strokes of tawse or cane on her quivering bare bum.

'I have never seen a bottom as red as yours, madam,' Prue would murmur, 'nor one which glows and quivers so tight and beautiful, and responds so well to her treatment. It is almost a shame Nurses' Code obliges me to be so strict.'

'That is because only you really understand my needs, Nurse Riding.' (Or the needs of her best friend who recommended Nurse Riding specifically.)

Females baulked at the direct matter of cash tipping, but were forthcoming with discreet little gifts.

'For you, dear Nurse Riding,' they would whisper, putting something gold in a velvet box into Prue's palm; and on that, it was Prue who offered *them* a kiss of obeisance.

One female, who slipped easily into a pleasant and generous chemistry with Prue, was Miss Tallinn, who appeared for her first treatment dressed as a police constable. She shyly admitted that she actually was a police constable, WPC Tallinn of Berwick. She was a tall and big-boned woman, with the healthy beauty of the north, the high cheekbones and strong body a joy of harmony. Her breasts were firm and thrusting, although their compact muscled beauty would not be fit for the lyre; yet they perfectly balanced the rest of her athlete's frame, the long filly's legs and rippling thighs. WPC Tallinn demurred at taking a shaven mink, saying that she had to be careful in the station, and if spotted in the shower she might be thought 'odd'. Nevertheless she kept her ash-blonde mink cropped as short as was commensurate with non-oddness; after much pleading, Prue allowed her a brief glimpse – 'amongst girls' – of her own gleaming fount, and WPC Tallinn was impressed, being allowed to touch it wonderingly with her dry, cool palm before Prue coquettishly pulled her knickers back up.

WPC Tallinn was but a few years Prue's senior, and told her she was addressed simply as 'Tallinn'.

'I like the no nonsense approach,' she said. 'Proper northern common sense. No fancy remedies or therapies or London tomfoolery, just cold showers and a good session of bash and spit. And old-fashioned herbal medicines, none of these cursed pharmaceuticals, which are no good for right-minded god-fearing folk.'

Prue raised an eyebrow at 'god-fearing'.

'I didn't say what gods,' Tallinn said rather primly. 'This is Northumberland, remember.'

Tallinn's treatment took place in 'the pit', a sumptuously equipped privy with sauna, a variety of tubs and basins, and an elaborate lavage machine of the type which Miss Bream used to service her nurses. Prue's notes, gnomic as always, indicated that Tallinn was to be given 'ice and fire' treatment, at Nurse's Discretion.

'Right,' said Tallinn briskly, 'let's get this kit off. Mine, I mean. You are new – I asked for you, as I've heard good things, and I like to check the new girls on my manor. But I know my treatment begins and ends with the hygienic birch-rods, Nurse, so I hope you have a strong arm.'

As she prattled, she gaily stripped off her dark-blue pantyhose, knickers and skirt, then the white blouse, rather quaintly leaving her checked cap until last. Prue watched her neatly fold her crisp, bright uniform into a neat pile. When Tallinn was naked, she slapped her thigh and gestured to the rack of disciplinary implements, which included a selection of birches, varying from 'hard' to 'fluffy'. Tallinn chose the hardest, a sheaf of pickled rods a good three feet long, and threw it to Prue.

'Let's get started,' she said. 'I'll take your hardest birching, Nurse, and you'd better tie me to the frame, for it is Nurse's Discretion, isn't it? In my experience, you wicked nurses want to lay it on very hard, once you've seen how much my bum can take. One day, I'll be permitted the Northumberland birch . . . one day.'

Her proud body trembled.

'I will lash you purple, miss,' said Prue softly.

Tallinn smiled. Her teeth gleamed white, like a puma's.

'A girl with spunk. I like you, Nurse. Now bind me, and gag me too, then give me a proper seeing to.'

She stood docilely by a tall whipping-frame, with cuffs for wrists and ankles, which was tilted slightly forward. Prue dutifully bound her limbs, then strapped the waistband very tightly, pinioning her to the crisscross frame. Tallinn gasped as the leather thong crinkled her waist flesh, and said she must be gagged too. She craned her head round, smiled beatifically, and said that Prue's own panties would make a good gag. Prue blushed! She obediently stepped out of her panties, balled them and wadded them in Tallinn's mouth. The policewoman went 'mmm' in mock protest or real appreciation. Her firm thighs and the slabs of her muscled buttocks rippled in anticipation; they were spread wide, and Prue saw dangling little blonde hairs beneath her quim and at her bumhole, where the

141

cropping razor had not reached. She picked up the heavy cluster of birch-rods.

The birch fell with a fierce crackling noise on the naked croup of the strapped policewoman, who shifted and moaned softly. Her buttocks clenched; when Prue withdrew the rods, she saw that already there was pleasing pink on her bare, mottled by little darker nodes where the birch tips had struck. She whipped her subject again on the buttocks, and again, to a full dozen; at each stroke the policewoman gasped and exhaled sharply as though in satisfaction, then began to gurgle softly in her throat, like a cat purring. When the fesses were blushing deep red, Prue began to beat her on the stretched upper back and shoulder-blades. To her surprise, this flogging made the woman stiffen and jerk quite hard, more than when the soft skin of the nates had been stroked. After a dozen to the back, Prue completed her treatment with a dozen to the backs of the thighs, which flushed instantly as the twigs scored them, and made Tallinn whinny and shake in very real anguish.

This treatment was repeated three times, with pauses of four minutes between treatments, until the police-woman's bare body glowed hot crimson. Released, she took out her gag and wiped the sweat from her brow, then gravely handed it back to Prue. Tears shone in her eyes and on her cheeks.

'Thank you, Nurse,' she whispered, smiling bravely. 'You laid fine fire. Now it is time for ice.'

From the freezer, Prue took a huge plastic bag full of ice cubes. Tallinn lay in a snug bath, just big enough for her lanky frame, and Prue poured the ice cubes over her until the bath was filled and only her trembling stiff nipples peeped from the icy mountain. Tallinn's flushed face turned rapidly white, tinged with blue, and the ice cubes rattled as she shivered. Prue took another container from the fridge, this one a tall jar containing a pulpy orange fluid, and set it atop the lavage machine. She cleared a path through the ice cubes, and found Tallinn's well-chilled quim and anus, then greased the tubes with petroleum jelly and inserted them fully into both Tallinn's nether holes.

She began the lavage; the machine hummed as the pulpy fluid was pumped into Tallinn's holes, and the woman groaned as she was filled to bursting in both anus and quim. She was obliged to hold her chilly cargo until Prue gave the word to evacuate; Prue sneaked her hand beneath the ice, and placed it on Tallinn's belly, feeling it swell and swell until the woman groaned she could take no more: even then, Prue waited for another cruel twenty seconds before giving the command to evacuate; Tallinn did so with a shivering gasp of relief, and the melting ice cubes turned brownish orange.

'O, that is gorgeous,' cried Tallinn, trembling with the cold. 'It is passion fruit, you know, wonderfully soothing: there is an alkali in it called harmine, which the Aztecs used, and the ancient reindeer keepers of Lapland.'

Prue asked where the ancient Finns got passion fruits, and Tallinn replied, probably from the Aztecs of Mexico.

'The ancient peoples of the north went more places than most people realise. Anyway, being a policewoman is very stressful,' she said proudly, 'and only the most sensitive merit treatment at the taxpayer's expense, which I ensure is well justified.'

Prue diplomatically agreed. Her hand slipped from belly to cropped fount, and the cold swollen quim lips. Tallinn told her to stroke her there, as it was very nice, and soon Prue's fingers found her acorn, all cold and shrivelled. Her hand moved through the stained ice water, stroking the little damsel as though to coax her back to life; at each tickle she felt Tallinn jerk, and not from the cold. Gradually her clitty warmed and stiffened like a bud in springtime, and colour suffused her face. The machine still pumped, and her belly was well swollen before Prue ordered her to evacuate, and this time her hand felt the powerful gush of warmed fluid from the anus and quim.

'You have brought fire from ice,' said Tallinn shyly, nodding at her stiff acorn. 'Please don't stop, Nurse.'

'Just for you, my special constable,' said Prue, her own damsel tingling with desire.

She flicked faster and faster as the pump continued its lavage, filling Tallinn's belly even as she writhed in the pleasure of Prue's fingering. Her belly swelled and swelled, and the woman writhed under the ice, which her body heat was now loosening to messy slush. Tallinn began to gasp and moan quite loudly, and suddenly Prue knew she was going to make her come. She redoubled her tickling, and rubbed the swollen quim lips quite roughly, taking them between thumb and forefinger and pinching, to Tallinn's evident delight.

'Nurse – may I evacuate?' she gasped. 'O, please.'

'No, you may not,' said Prue. 'Not until . . .'

She rubbed the stiff clitty harder and harder.

'You rotten bitch,' groaned Tallinn. 'If I had you alone in the cells, I'd . . .'

'You'd what, policewoman?' said Prue viciously, raining hard little finger-spanks to the clitoris.

'I'd . . . O, no . . . I'd . . . come! Yes! O! I'm coming! O, Nurse! Don't stop! O . . . O!'

Tallinn's swollen body writhed in her spasm, and Prue cried that she should evacuate; the woman's moans of pleasure turned to a gasping yelp, then almost to a scream, as the fluid spurted from both her holes, engulfing Prue's thrusting fingers with their bright stain, and Prue felt her own quim gushing wet. She bent down and kissed Tallinn firmly and wetly on the lips. Their tongues met; the policewoman did not resist.

'That is a lovely part of my treatment,' gasped Tallinn.

'It is just for you,' said Prue, brushing her hair from her brow and smoothing her uniform. 'I have never kissed a subject before, but –' she grinned impishly '– since you are a policewoman, it doesn't really count.'

Tallinn frowned.

'Policewomen aren't really human, are they?' said Prue airily, and Tallinn laughed.

'Doesn't my bum squirm like a human's?' she said. 'Just let me get you in a cell, and *I'll* show you human.'

'Never,' said Prue and kissed her again.

The jar of lavage was empty, and the ice cubes almost melted; Tallinn rose, blue with cold and stained with her own juices and the lavage, and said it was time for cleansing sauna. She went at once to the little cabin and stretched out on the top bench. Prue watched her through the spyhole. Tallinn threw water on the coals, and began to birch her own reddened breasts and bottom with fluffy birch twigs, and after a while she gestured that Prue must join her. Prue hesitated only an instant before daintily stripping off her nurse's uniform. Soon she was sitting beside the tall policewoman, idly flicking the birch twigs across her flat sweating belly and even allowing the twigs to stray gently to the quim lips and nipples, a touch which Tallinn appreciated, for she went 'mmm' several times. Tallinn brusquely sat up, and equally brusquely put her hand on Prue's shaven quim.

'So smooth,' she whispered, and their lips met again in a long kiss. Now, both hands were wet quims, the fingers probing deep inside the wetness and thumbs kneading eager damsels, which throbbed and tingled in the fragrant sweaty heat of the bathing chamber. Tallinn whispered that all were equal before the law, and an eye for an eye . . .

'You made me come, cruel Nurse, so I must have revenge,' she murmured. 'Spread your thighs while I plate you.'

Prue obeyed; her belly heaved in pleasure as she felt

145

three, no, four of Tallinn's gentle fingers thrusting deep into her wet slit, and the woman's tongue caressing her throbbing clitoris, while with her other hand, Tallinn had both her breasts crushed in a fierce yet tender grasp, squeezing and kneading her nipples until they were squashed and swollen like bright purple plums. Her own hand plunged between Tallinn's parted thighs, and the women fingered each other in a slippery bliss of tribadic joy, until both came, Prue gurgling deep in her throat as her belly and quim heaved in spasm, and her lips clawing at Tallinn's in a sweet, fierce kiss.

The final part of Tallinn's treatment was to be a surprise, Prue said on impulse. In the fridge she had seen a large jar of honey. When the two women left the sauna, lathered in sweat, Prue showered briefly, but forbade Tallinn to do so. She reached for her knickers and bra, then stopped, looking at the pile of Tallinn's uniform. Then, feeling very daring, she dressed herself in Tallinn's own costume, while her subject looked on with wide eyes. There was a rather coarse navy-blue bra and knickers, and blue pantyhose, not stockings. She put them on, together with the blouse, heavy skirt, and tunic, and then perched the policewoman's checkered cap at a gay angle. She smiled.

'I have always wanted to be a policewoman,' she said. 'Now, you miscreant, you are to receive the honey birch.'

She watched as Tallinn, on her orders, smeared the honey all over her body, laying it generously on her fount and bum; the honey mingled with her sweat, and her copious love-juice, to form a pungent fragrant paste which soon gleamed all over her skin. Prue took the flowers from a vase of roses and stripped them of petals, then made Tallinn lie down on a horizontal flogging-trestle. She proceeded to stick the petals all over her bum, teats and quim, and when she had fastened Tallinn's wrists with her own police handcuffs, said that she was to be birched anew, but this time until every rose petal had been dislodged.

'That will take ages!' protested Tallinn.

'We have ages,' Prue replied, and began to apply the heavy birch for a second time to Tallinn's bare buttocks.

'O,' cried Tallinn, 'it's good, Nurse!'

At each stroke, the bare bum writhed, the dark crimson skin a swirling mosaic of beauty. Prue grasped the heavy truncheon from her belt, and detached it, then began to beat Tallinn's upraised bum with her own truncheon. It made a heavy whacking noise, and the crimson of the birching was soon suffused with a deeper purple.

'You are so damn submissive, you bitch!' she cried suddenly, and paused in her beating to bend and part Tallinn's cheeks still further.

She reached down and tickled the quim lips with the tip of the truncheon, then suddenly pushed it to the hilt inside the slit, and began to thrust. Tallinn squealed, and her loins began to buck frantically in time with the thrusts. Prue now recommenced the birching, accompanying each stroke with a firm thrust into the writhing quim of her helpless subject, whose wrists strained raw against her cuffs. Prue's sweat drenched her police uniform, and she panted. The rose petals stuck to the birch twigs, and she shook them off, but many still clustered around the woman's two holes.

She put down the birch, and bent to Tallinn's glistening furrow, and began to lick the petals one by one from her honeyed bumhole, still thrusting truncheon into quim. She licked until all the petals had gone, and the anus was clean, then stuck her tongue inside the anus to a depth of half an inch, and thrust in and out, the tickling causing Tallinn to giggle between her shrieks of discomfort. Prue's own clit was stiff again, and she felt herself wetting the policewoman's knickers with copious draughts of her fluid.

Panting, she pulled the truncheon from the quim, and it plopped out, gleaming with oil; without pause, she inserted it between the petals of Tallinn's arse-bud and pushed hard. The truncheon sank in with surprising ease, as though Tallin's anus was accustomed to it, and the woman began to writhe anew as Prue poked her arsehole with the big truncheon. The fount was unattended; Prue slipped down on her back, beneath the low flogging-horse, and positioned her own fount directly beneath Tallinn's. Her knickers came down; her thighs rose, until her naked quim and stiff protruding clitty met Tallinn's, and still continuing her buggery of the groaning subject, she rubbed against her, bucking up from her crablike position, so that the two clits rubbed together. She felt the sticky rose petals detach themselves from Tallinn's mound at her frantic rubbing, and stick to her own, and all the time she continued her thrusting into Tallinn's anus until her thrusts became demonic, and her belly heaved in a delicious orgasm, and at her Nurse's cries, Tallinn too gave way to her own pleasure. Prue felt a gush of hot love-juice cascade over her dancing belly, and the two women's voices mingled like dove-calls.

When each participant in the healing drama was properly dressed once more, Prue said that time was up. They exchanged kisses, and then, giggling like schoolgirls, exchanged knickers. Tallinn kissed Prue's wet knickers then pressed a gift into Prue's hand.

'A token of appreciation, Nurse,' she murmured. 'I have never enjoyed such personal treatment.'

'I hope the taxpayers of Northumberland can afford for you to have more,' Prue replied, 'for I have never taken such personal delight in giving it. I bet you have never been buggered by your own truncheon before.'

'Well, I have,' said WPC Tallinn, 'but not as sweetly.'

In Prue's hand was a shiny pair of police handcuffs.

The twins scampered in to clear things up, and Prue

lit a cigarette, yawning happily, and rubbing her quim. She took out the key of the handcuffs, and secreted it in her quim, then sat with a wide grin, swinging the handcuffs round and round.

'Send in the next, please,' she said.

9

Hell Fur Leather

Indecisive discussions still took place about the evening
of clubbing – should it be in Berwick, or Tweedmouth,
or Cloughton itself, where there was apparently a
private and rather discreet club called 'Hell Fur
Leather'. Prue suggested to Jess, whom she was lazily
caressing in their nightly sauna, that she was flush from
tips, and she might treat just the two of them to a
sensuous evening, as she was itching to join the 11.59
club . . .

'Never been tipped less than twenty pounds!' she
claimed proudly.

'In there?' said Jess, her own fingers deep and gentle
in Prue's gushing slit, and her thumb expert on stiff
clitty.

'The very place,' gasped Prue.

'You probably qualify for the 11.59ers already,'
murmured Jess, her voice muffled by Prue's breasts.

She said, however, that it might be politic to invite
Miss Gageby as well – Prue remembered the promised
mauve undies – and she supposed Henrietta would get
wind of things, and the twins would scamper round like
nuisances, and Heckmondthwaite would sulk if the
bitch were snubbed, and . . .

At length, it was a merry and intriguing cortege of
taxis which made its way to Berwick past the mysterious
twinkling of Goodenhall Air Base. Prue had haggled

with Miss Gageby over her uniform, panties and things, then got hold of the coveted cream stockings with the brown seam, and all the rest of her things too, Miss Gageby simply stripping and throwing them to Prue in her haste to get the mauve undies. Naked, Prue rolled on the stockings with Miss Gageby's very own panties, which gave her a lovely wet sort of feeling, and then simply couldn't decide what to wear with them.

She tried all sorts of daring things she had from Miss Macardle, before her rescue by Jess, who interrupted to ask why she didn't just go as a nurse. Go as Miss Gageby herself, with her bonnet and blouse and everything. It would be wildly kinky . . . Jess herself had a black leather micro-skirt and black stockings with winkle-picker bootees, and a very tight black silk shirt, open to her navel, and with no bra at all, so that her big soft teats with their huge nip-rings threatened to flop out of their covering absolutely any minute. Prue, envious but tickled, nodded agreement.

With gusto, she dressed up as the Assistant Matron herself, and she and Miss Gageby exchanged winks of complicity. She was tightly corsed beneath her service blouse, in a crimson hygienic garment of stiff shiny rubber, held together by zips and safety pins instead of laces, that pinched her waist to a pin's width, and thrust her breasts up so that Miss Gageby's bra scarcely contained them. The dark crimson waspie, clearly visible through the tight blouse, contrasted well with the cream ensemble.

'I've never been a very clubby person,' Prue confessed as, equipped with a brightly coloured drink, she watched Jess's face bathed by the stroboscopic rainbow.

'This is just a slave market,' cried Jess with a frown. 'Just jiggle your stuff and see if anything rises.'

Miss Gageby indeed jiggled, and her silver chain-mail dress clearly showed the mauve undies beneath, which gleamed garishly in the flashing colours. Miss Gageby seemed very contented and her hips moved with relish in a mime of copulation, while her lyred breasts were almost all revealed in full glory, pushed up by tight corsing and the nipples clearly outlined under the thin cloth. Henrietta stood aloof, strangely gorgeous in a black robe of seamless latex, that covered her from neck to ankle, though its tightness showed every inch of her rich curved body, with no panty line to mar her smoothness, though the indentations of her piercings, rings and chains were quite sumptuously evident. She wore boots with spiked steel toes, and spurs, and Prue surmised she had only a corset under her dress, since her waist was pencil-thin. Prue insisted she was having a good time.

Her nurse's outfit attracted whistles and leers – how daring, how cool and fetishy to have a nurse's uniform ... But perhaps her sheer daring made her seem too cool and unapproachable, as indeed did the glowering Henrietta's black rubber dress, as though challenging any onlooker to an immediate duel. They drifted from club to club; gradually, there were assignations. Prue saw the twins disappear into a big BMW with a single gold-decked young man, Nurse Heckmondthwaite into a Mercedes with a mousy-looking young man in blue velvet, which excited a sneer from Henrietta; eventually, Henrietta insisted they go to the 'Hell Fur Leather'. Prue found herself in the back of a taxi with Henrietta and Jess, and Miss Gageby in the front, heading along the coast road to Cloughton. Prue breathed the freshness of the dunes and sea; it was a warm night. Henrietta and Miss Gageby seemed reserved now, and even Jess was apprehensively silent.

The Hell Fur Leather Club was a villa slightly out of town on a low clifftop, perhaps two miles lower down from Hydro. There was no plaque in the gateway, no neon or any sign, except a small nameplate saying 'Miss F Furbelow, M.A. Oxon.' but Henrietta seemed sure it was the right place. They got out, dismissed the taxi, and rang the entrance bell. There was a big iron gate and an attendant appeared, a willow-thin but full-breasted woman taller than Henrietta, in fur coat and leather boots, just like Barker – except that she carried a massive four-thonged whip. Henrietta said curtly that they sought the Hell Fur Leather Club.

'Are you aristocrats?' thundered the woman.

'Of course we are, you oaf,' snapped Henrietta. 'We have even brought our own nurse, in case of mishap.'

'There may be discomforts in the Hell Fur Leather, Milady,' said the woman, 'but no mishaps, only *haps*.'

'I should whip you for insolence,' said Henrietta.

'Yes, Milady, you should, please,' said the woman. 'Naked and bound.'

She placed the thongs of her whip between her teeth, licked them, and opened the gate. They crunched up the short gravel path to the house, a pleasing eighteenth-century mansion; there were no lights to guide them, only the moon and stars, with the crash of the waves nearby. There were plenty of vehicles in the forecourt, and they picked their way through limos and sports cars to the main door. The lights inside were bright, but hooded by thick drapes, and there was no raucous music. Miss Gageby rang the bell, and the door creaked open. Behind it, the hallway was softly lit, not like a club at all, but like a genteel suburban mansion, with a mirror, coatstand, and flower vases.

The lady who opened the door was dressed in a sober grey striped suit, with a white blouse and a flounced necktie. She was of Miss Gageby's age, but her dress made her look more mature, and her blonde hair was cut straight and short, cupping her face. She wore little gold-rimmed spectacles, rather like a girls' headmistress. She smiled pleasantly and said she was delighted to see her new guests.

'I am Miss Frideswide Furbelow,' she said, 'and of

course you are not required to use your real names, if it would spoil your fun. A *nom de plaisance*, as we say, is quite sufficient. I take it you are the nurses from Hydro – the High Mistress advised me to expect you sooner or later. Now, who is Nurse Farle?'

Henrietta identified herself, and admitted with a little smirk that she had heard of the Hell Fur Leather from High Mistress herself. Miss Furbelow nodded and began to finger Henrietta's rubber dress, letting her hands play on the body beneath, and cooing in approval.

'You'll do, Nurse,' she said. 'We have a very strict dress code, I'm afraid, but I am sure my checking you will just be a formality.'

She inspected each nurse, and they gave their real names, seeing no reason not to. Miss Gageby passed – her mauve undies were specially approved. She whispered to Henrietta that she didn't know she had had audience with the High Mistress, and Henrietta said with a mixture of smugness and guilt that she had not actually been received, she had overheard her talking to Miss Bream – actually, she fancied Miss Bream was *taking treatment* – and that was how she knew of this club. Prue passed inspection, their hostess saying that a real nurse's uniform was the most ironic conceit, but she frowned when she came to Jess.

'A micro-miniskirt – hmm, yes, and a blouse rather daringly opened ... daring is all very well, Nurse, but ...'

'A nurse must do better than all very well,' murmured Jess, and knotted her blouse flaps round her neck, so that her whole breasts and belly were bared.

She swivelled her body so that the heavy rings in her nipples and navel jangled against the chain that bound them. Then she turned so that only Miss Furbelow could see and lifted her skirt to show her panties. She swivelled again – there was further music from the rings at her quim, and Miss Furbelow said that Jess was now proper, and admitted with pleasure. Jess smiled in satisfaction.

'But to complete the picture,' murmured the lady, and bent down, extended her black-painted fingernails which were two inches long and sharp as talons, then ripped a jagged gash in each of Jess's stockings!

'There!' she said, 'the perfect slut! You may follow me to the first circle.'

As she led the way to the rear of the house, she explained that the club was not organised like other clubs, but was more of a social centre. There were a number of chambers, or 'circles', each with a different ambiance, and guests were free to wander between circles at will. But they would find that guests tended to stick together, and move in groups, which was a rather jolly *esprit de corps*. The nurses were shown into a large drawing room, with the most gorgeous rococo ceiling, powder blue with white and gilt edging, and all sorts of nymphs and Eros figures floating among the clouds, all naked and all either rampant or receptive . . .

The room contained a dozen males and females sipping drinks from crystal goblets. All were dressed well and quite formally, in expensive lounge suits or sumptuous but demure cocktail dresses. It was like a gathering at a country manor; even Henrietta seemed taken aback. Their arrival was greeted with warm interest, but no astonishment, not even a raised eyebrow, and after Miss Frideswide's invitation to mingle, Prue found herself making small talk with a quite delightful group of young men and women, sleek of face and hair, and groomed immaculately. In fact 'delightful' was a word that figured largely, along with 'super' and 'amusing'.

'A nurse . . . wonderful! You like Northumberland? Super!'

Prue whispered to Jess that she didn't understand

156

how were they to pay for their entertainment, for a start? Jess said maybe they were to be the entertainment. There were two maids serving drinks, each in an adorably frilly French outfit, with black chiffon skirts like ballerinas' tutus standing high over the loveliest frilly black lace knickers; black stockings and garter belt, and teetering high heels, and a little white pompom on their rumps. Tight blouses clearly showed the lacy black bras beneath, which seemed in tune with Miss Furbelow's taste for the sluttish.

'Isn't Frideswide ever fascinating!' Prue heard wafted. 'We must mingle in the other circles.'

'But I'm having such a good time, and the kraken hunt hasn't begun yet.'

'Did you know that Frideswide is the patron saint of Oxford? And that she was scourged to death by the Romans?'

'Really?'

'On her bare bum!'

'How lovely!'

Suddenly one of the maids stumbled slightly, and a dribble of drink spilled on to the Persian rug.

'O! I'm sorry, Mistress!' she blurted to Miss Furbelow, who said nothing, but smiled thinly and raised an eyebrow.

The girl was no more than eighteen, willowy and svelte, tall and with strong lips and eyes and pert upthrust breasts that sat ill at odds with her submissive demeanour. She blushed, and moved quietly to the side of the room, where there was a long low sofa in cream leather. No one paid her any attention, not even when she bent over the sofa, lifted her skirt over her back, and pulled down her knickers to her knees. She still held her drinks tray high, and stared stonily ahead of her into the middle distance. Her bum gleamed alabaster white in the twinkling glow of the chandeliers. Beside her, a male and female were talking in languid animation.

'. . . They call it kraken soup: had it when I was hunting up near Utsjoki: vodka, cranberry juice, dollop of reindeer cream, and their version of kraken, of course.'

'Fascinating! But, darling, I must have that lovely saffron-yellow dress from that shop in Chelsea . . .'

'Of course you must, darling.'

'Edward . . . that maid . . .'

'What . . .?'

'She is bending over in position, so she is *deserving*, and we are closest. You know Miss Furbelow's rules.'

'O! You be Mistress, Arabella.'

'But I was Mistress last time.'

'Well, I'll get you the frock, then.'

'Deal!' cried Arabella.

The coiffed and elegant female quite casually raised her long violet silk skirt, slit in the thigh like a cheongsam, and revealed her white-stockinged legs and bare fount – no knickers, and gleamingly shaved like Prue's own. She seemed quite unconcerned, and no one paid attention, as she rummaged at her waist until she extracted a pretty little dress cane, with a pearl handle and sharp, sparkling metal studs on the shaft.

She raised her martini glass to her lips and continued to make conversation, while with her other hand she raised the pearl-handled cane and brought it across the white globes of the servant's bum, very sharply so that a pink flush at once appeared. Arabella did not tremble, nor spill her drink nor even quicken her breath. She stroked again, and again, quite rapidly, and with a deft and practised flick of her wrist, as though swatting a mosquito.

The flogged serving girl gave no reaction to her beating even as the wicked studs on her bare made her wince, and neither did anyone else in the room. At each stroke, her Mistress interrupted her prattle to insult her victim, not looking at her nor raising her voice, bu observing mildly that she was the filthiest slut, the most disgusting, stinking bitch and slag and tart in Northumberland, and that no punishment was enough for her miserable whore's buttocks. She scored the naked fesses a good twelve or thirteen times before she said to Edward that he should have a go, her arm was getting tired.

'Well, how many is she due?' he said peevishly. 'Honestly, these sluts!'

'I think it's twenty-one,' said Arabella. 'She spilt a drink, didn't she?'

Suddenly Prue stepped forward and smiled.

'I'd be glad to help,' she said. 'At Hydro, we are trained in proper discipline of errant maids.'

'How awfully kind of you!' cried Arabella, clapping her hands in delight, and handing Prue the cane. 'I absolutely can't remember how many the slut has had, so you had better start at the beginning.'

'Twenty-one on bare?' said Prue, aware of envious glances from Henrietta and Nurse Gageby, and Arabella and Edward agreed that the whore Gemini could take as many as she cared.

From Arabella's choice vocabulary, it seemed that Gemini needed cleansing. Prue lifted the heavy little rod and began to beat the naked globes as hard as she could, yet imitating Arabella's stance of nonchalance and joining in the small talk as she flogged the maid's quivering bare bum.

She sneaked a look as often as she could, and saw to her pleasure that the arse-globes trembled like lovely thick jellies at each stroke, and that Gemini's face was flushing slightly, her lips pressed tightly. Still she did not let her tray tremble, and her moist eyes were wide and unblinking, even at the harshest cuts, including several to thigh-back and furrow. Only the other nurses were paying her any attention, although Jess was entrancing some male admirers by twirling her nipple and belly rings.

At last Prue came to the twenty-first stroke, and handed the cane back to Arabella, who thanked her profusely for being such a darling. Gemini silently replaced her knickers, which Prue saw were stained wet, and smoothed her skirt down, all with one hand, and still balancing her tray of drinks. Then she continued on her way, and Prue found herself talking to a beautiful mulatto woman in a black velvet ankle-gown and high black boots, who introduced herself, in a soft American drawl, as Virginia. Her elfin face was wreathed by a shining black mane, and her body was lithe and muscular under her sheer dress. Her green eyes twinkled mischievously, and she licked her thin lips with the tip of her tongue.

There was something delicious yet sinister and intriguing about her sinuous features; she wore no make-up save for dark saucers of kohl at her big cat's eyes. Prue explained herself, and Virginia said that she loved nurses, and especially nurses with firm hands. Prue suggested a Hydro treatment, and Virginia slipped her a visiting card, which carried simply her name and phone number. Prue giggled, and, asked to explain, said it reminded her of the London phone boxes.

'I am a rather private person,' murmured Virginia, smiling too. 'Perhaps you could call me sometime, come to my place for tea – it isn't far – and tell me more about Hydro. Perhaps even a private demonstration of your treatment, as you were so firm with sweet Gemini. Isn't her costume adorable? Any treatment would be rewarded, of course, Nurse Prudence – nothing good is ever for free. I am such a romantic! Don't you love Miss Furbelow's hunt? I'm not going tonight – my best dress! – but it is such a thrill anyway.'

Prue was about to ask what hunt she referred to, when the maid Gemini exclaimed that she had quite forgotten the time, and begged Arabella's pardon. Arabella said it was quite all right, she was having such fun, handed Edward her drink, and proceeded to strip

160

off her violet gown and matching lacy bra and knickers, while Gemini did the same with her maid's costume. Arabella made a face as she put on Gemini's knickers, and accused her of peeing herself under the nice nurse's caning, and Gemini said calmly that Arabella knew very well it wasn't pee. Then, solemnly, the females exchanged and donned each other's clothing, and now the haughty Arabella was the maid. She offered a drink to Prudence, her face calm, and with no hint of recognition or explanation. Prue jogged her elbow and a drink spilled.

Still impassive, Arabella placed herself in position over the sofa, knickers and skirt up and bum bared; exactly as had Gemini, who was now talking animatedly to Edward. He looked down at Arabella's naked fesses.

'O, bother!' he said. 'I suppose it is my turn now. I can't buy *you* a frock as well, Gemini.'

Gemini parted her violet skirt, and handed him the cane.

'O, Edward! Sometimes I think you should have married Arabella instead of me,' she pouted.

Edward began his languid beating of the woman's bare bottom and, as he flogged, Miss Furbelow clapped her hands and said the hunt would begin in a few moments. Some of the females left the room with her, and returned minutes later, having changed into their bizarre hunting kit. The females were sheathed in shiny black plastic, thin and crinkly, that swathed them from neck to toe, with seamless hoods covering their faces. The only openings on these costumes, apart from eyes and mouth, were the breasts, buttocks and founts left naked. All the females carried two items of correction, a thick leather whip, and a trident with three thick prongs, not sharp, but full, like hygienic dildos. They had glossy plastic boots, with spurs and sharp metal toecaps.

'Isn't it exciting?' cried Virginia, and explained the rules of the 'Kraken Hunt'.

161

The hunters had to bring the sea monster home from her ocean lair, driving and marking her well with whips, for a whip-marked monster could not return to the stinging ocean salt . . . But the prey was armed as well, and if they returned marked on their own bare, that was a sign of imperfection, and they would be punished accordingly. Virginia whispered that meant they would be corrected until their naked skin was no longer distinguishable from their black costumes. Prue asked the fate of the prey . . . the 'Kraken' of old Norse legend, who, it seemed, was always female.

'If she is captured, she will go to the third circle, and suffer extreme correction,' said Virginia.

'And if she wins? Evades capture, I mean.'

'She wins,' said Virginia, 'when she attains the third circle proudly alone, and submits to extreme correction.'

Miss Furbelow entered, leading a woman by a leash. Her hands were knotted behind her back, and her ankles were roped, so that she shuffled in awkward shame. A few strands of dirty, matted blonde hair peeped below a leather pixyhood which showed only her nose and eyes. Yet she was gorgeous in a saffron-yellow two-piece, with white silk stockings and white shoes. She knelt. Contemptuously, Miss Furbelow lifted her talons, and began to slice and hack at the young woman's clothing, reducing the sheeny expensive garment to shreds before the eyes of the company. When the garments were tatters, she ripped them contemptuously from the girl's body, revealing a white basque and suspenders to the stockings. All of these were shredded too, until the trembling girl was left naked and goose-pimpled. The pale gold of her skin, the full, thrusting breasts and firm thighs below a croup like peaches, made her seem not proud, but vulnerable and helpless.

All this time, Arabella had endured a vigorous caning from Edward's hand, but when the last shred of clothing was ripped from the kneeling prey, Miss Furbelow slashed the ropes binding her, and helped her gently to her feet. Suddenly, the flogged Arabella blinked, and looked at the yellow shreds on the carpet.

'O, no!' she wailed. 'You bitch! That was to be my dress!'

She dropped her tray of drinks, and rushed clumsily, knickers round her knees, to the ruined dress, where she knelt sobbing, picking up and caressing the useless rags, as though touching them would bring the garment back to life. There was a deathly hush in the room, and the naked prey disdainfully pushed Arabella aside. She stood, proud now in her nudity, and bowed to Miss Furbelow, then to the company. Edward handed her the jewelled cane with which he had beaten Arabella. Then, swiftly, she walked from the room and they heard the front door open and shut. For half a minute, Miss Furbelow looked at her watch, then nodded, and the huntresses bowed and sped after their quarry. Then their hostess turned icily to the sobbing Arabella.

'Your attachment to *things* is disgraceful, miss,' she spat. 'You know the rules of the Hell Fur Leather Club.'

There was a ripple of excitement as Arabella was pinioned by three immaculate ladies, and her wrists bound behind her back. Prue felt Jess's hand on her haunch, and heard her hot breath of excitement; then Henrietta moved beside her and touched her croup, resting her finger in her furrow. She smelt Henrietta's dark smoky perfume, and shivered. Nurse Gageby clasped Henrietta's waist, and all the nurses glanced at each other in sly excitement at the guessed fate of the miscreant.

'O, gosh,' said the other maid, putting her fingers to her mouth and stifling a sob. 'Poor Bella!'

The voice was strangely familiar, and Prue peered into the throng, at the pert, fresh face, the swept-back blonde hair under the maid's bonnet, the lithe, muscular young figure superb in her frilly maid's attire, and the fine mesh stockings as smooth on the hairless legs as a second skin. She jumped in surprise. It was Jeremy Pleasant, shorn of his luxuriant moustache, and with the girlish cuteness of his features artfuly enhanced by maquillage! He saw her penetrating glance, caught his breath, and went pale. Prue smiled at him and put her finger to her lips, and he beamed shyly in gratitude. She moved beside him, and whispered that she wondered where the Air Force officers went on Saturday nights, and he blushed hotly.

'You don't think ill of us – of me?' he stammered. 'Being a maid . . . a slave?'

'Of course not,' said Prue easily. 'I like being a girl – why shouldn't you?'

'My servants,' said Miss Furbelow sternly, 'I suggest we join our friends in the second circle, and deal with the slave Arabella as she deserves.'

Miss Furbelow led the way, with the hapless Arabella on a leash, struggling on hands and knees to keep up. Her knickers were still rather forlornly round her knees, and they were indeed sopping wet, as were her gleaming thighs where her juices had flowed under flogging.

'O, no . . .' she moaned, and Miss Furbelow snapped for silence.

Miss Furbelow's very real anger indicated a distressing fate for her captive. Her pert arse-globes waggled very prettily, pressed against the tight grey cloth, as though swelling with indignation, or themselves shivering under whip. She said loudly that she would exercise her privilege and take charge of this miscreant, and there were respectful murmurs. They seemed to agree with Miss Furbelow that love of *things* was somehow wrong. Prue heard muffled cries, as though from far away. They were not screams so much as long desolate moans, broken by occasional shrieks. She looked at Jess, puzzled, and Jess said it must be seagulls, but her eyes said she did not believe that. The guests followed Miss Furbelow to a padded door, which she opened into a vast chamber, like refectory at Hydro.

The walls too were padded, and it seemed more a grotto than a chamber, with nooks and crannies, twisting little alcoves and the aspect of a labyrinth, so that its denizens were concealed from casual view. It was not bright like the salon, but bathed in dark soft light, here sinister red, there turquoise shading to blue, or purple or emerald, as though the room were lit by a thousand precious stones, their luminance blending in a warm dark rainbow. There was delicious, wicked scent, a mixture of incense and perfume and sweat, and the smell of raw pain and fear. Miss Furbelow smiled grimly in the dark red glow.

'Feel free to mingle, and sample the social pleasures on offer,' she said, 'or you may begin by watching me attend to this wretched girl and her *things*!'

She pulled Arabella savagely by the hair, and the maid squealed. Then she pulled the struggling woman, on her knees, into an alcove lit by the garish red, where two masked females stood by a wooden table whose straps, chains and cuffs indicated an instrument of supplice. The belly-piece was short, and four prongs stretched out for the victim's arms and legs. Arabella was groaning and sobbing, and Miss Furbelow slapped her face and pulled her hair most cruelly, then kicked her bare rump and told her to shut up. Snuffling, Arabella calmed, and her wide eyes looked at her tormentors. The two females were masked, like executioners, and bare-breasted, wearing only curious and tight black leather trousers, with bare feet. They made noises of satisfaction at Arabella's entrance, like carnival touts waiting for custom.

In a short time, Arabella was hoisted on to the wooden table, her ankles and wrists fastened and her breasts and bum suspended openly in mid-air, so that she had to balance herself awkwardly on the narrow belly-strip. The legs were splayed so that her whole lady's place and bum-crack were cruelly and helplessly exposed. She was then stripped roughly of her maid's uniform, which came to shreds in Miss Furbelow's deft talons. The 'executioners' also had nails painted in black, with sharp long claws. Their naked breasts were tattooed with orchid petals swirling in purple and red around their nipples, so that their breasts looked like two large orchids, or the lips of a woman's fount. Their navels were pierced, and nipples too, with silver rings dangling, and around their necks they wore spiked chains.

The leather breeches of the two muscled females were open at the crotch; each female had pierced quim lips through which passed a heavy iron ring, and in the ring was coiled a heavy whip and a chain, so that their lady's mounds bulged like a soldier's armaments. The whips and chains dangled ominously between their thighs, brushing the leather trousers, and the quim lips of each female were stretched with seeming permanence into great flaps of tissue like asses' ears. As if on cue, one female suddenly flicked her wrist like a gunfighter and magically the whip was in her hand and cracking the air. She laughed; her companion did the same with her chain, and it thudded dully on the table legs, wrapping itself round and clinging like a snake. Arabella moaned, and Miss Furbelow demanded the chain. She was handed it, and began to stroke it across Arabella's bare, clinking and slithering into her furrow and bum-crack, and over her glistening exposed quim lips.

'Such a pretty girl,' she cooed, 'you really are a dream, Arabella. Such teats, such a gorgeous bum and a quim to die for! A pity that you must be so sternly corrected. But you do deserve it, don't you, sweet?'

Arabella lifted her head and sobbed 'yes'.

Miss Furbelow adjusted her spectacles, and bent

down to peer at Arabella's mottled nates, fresh from her caning. She stroked the fluffed skin, and said that men were awfully cruel, weren't they? But unfortunately, men were *things* which a lady had to put up with, and hopefully tame. She retrieved Arabella's shredded panties, and commented playfully on their wetness, then said that in consideration for Arabella's ladylike decorum, she would aid her to stay silent under correction. Again, Arabella agreed; the panties were ripped in half, and one half placed in her mouth, gagging her, the other wadded right inside her gaping quim! Miss Furbelow said that harmony must be observed, and took the maid's bra, balled it, and, prising open Arabella's anus with her talons, pushed the bra inside her bumhole until only the straps dangled rather comically between her thighs.

'There now,' said Miss Furbelow in a businesslike voice, 'I think you are ready to learn the error of your ways, Bella. You've already had cane, so I think something more subtle is required. And you know that a chastisement in first circle is twenty-one, but here in second circle, we are beyond rules, beyond the world, and there is no limit.'

She delivered three or four sharp spanks with her palm to Arabella's bare buttocks, and the maid shifted slightly in her bonds, then she took one of the chains, and nodded to the 'executioners'. She lifted the chain and brought it down with a loud ringing slap on the naked bum, which at once clenched in the pain of the heavy metal on bare. At the same time, one of the girls flexed her wrists, reached underneath the tethered maid, and began to rake her sharp fingernails across her breasts and belly, and across the open quim lips. The second executioner lifted her own whip, and as her partner proceeded away from the breasts, began to whip Arabella on her teats, with vigorous undercuts that flicked hard on her stiffened nipples, and curled lovingly

167

round her back in cruel caress. Lustfully embracing, Edward and Gemini murmured approval as they watched with sparkling eyes.

The first girl raked all of Arabella's naked body with her talons, leaving awful marks, and at the same time the crack of chain and whip married in an unearthly harmony of correction. The buttocks rapidly darkened and became livid, and Arabella's body was now squirming frantically in her bonds. She was helpless to move; her eyes brimmed with tears, and at each stroke she jerked like a marionette, and she bit deeper into her knicker-gag, her lips white with anguish. Miss Furbelow placidly flogged her writhing croup with the chain, pausing only to lift her skirt and wipe her misted glasses on her white petticoat, and observing that Arabella *did* squirm quite beautifully, didn't she? Prue noticed that Miss Furbelow had a lovely garter above her stocking top, made of a lily-frond and seaweed bulbs.

When about thirty strokes had been delivered to both croup and teats, the two chastisers changed places, and now it was the chain which lashed the quivering flans of Arabella's breasts, while the whip flogged her naked buttocks. The second girl dealt most harshly with the soles of Arabella's feet, and made the flogged girl almost giggle at the harsh tickle of her claws. Then she began to pinch the maid between thumb and forefinger, taking generous folds of pain-blushed flesh and squeezing them white. Miss Furbelow transferred the chain's lashes to Arabella's shoulders, allowing the girl to begin pinching her breasts, and the nipples themselves, which she fastened in a vice-like grip until they were squeezed to envelopes of tormented flesh, the nipple buds popping as though trying to escape.

This torment of soft, innocent breasts was not enough! Grinning fiercely, the girl applied her fingers to the lips of Arabella's quim, kneading and pinching and pulling until the tortured flaps stood as long and thick as the girl's own. Arabella's moaning had become an unbroken bleat of misery, and when the girl began to flick her clitty in mocking caress, she writhed even more than at the rain of whipstrokes, swinging herself to and fro as though to escape from pleasure more than from pain. Droplets of liquid fell from the wadded knickers in her quim; in the midst of her torment, the maid was making love-oil! And the correction did not stop until Arabella's moan became a scream, and the dark wealed body of the naked maid heaved in a savage spasm of ecstacy.

At this, Miss Furbelow called a halt; Arabella must have taken eighty or ninety strokes with both whip and chain, the chain leaving a harsher impression on her skin. Unbound, and helped to her feet, she murmured, 'Thank you, Mistress, I am corrected.'

'And pleasured, Maid.'

'Well so, Mistress.'

Arabella murmured that if Miss Furbelow permitted, she would like to stay in red zone, with her chastisers. Miss Furbelow nodded in approval, and the group seemed to split up, with couples and singles wandering into the rainbow haze of the labyrinthine second circle. Prue looked back and saw Arabella kneeling before her tormentors, licking their feet while they resumed their lashing on her bare striped shoulders. At their instruction, she had three fingers deep inside her own anus, and four inside her gaping slit, while she vigorously frotted her bare clitty with thumb.

Prue found herself separated from the stern Mistress and was glad to explore by herself. Couples and bodies came and went in the smoky incense haze; some clothed, others nude, and some in articles of restraint or correction such as chains, leg-irons, masks and studded corsets. All around her, the vast maze throbbed with the rhythms of discipline, the elemental music of leather on bare flesh, with the counterpoint of low anguished

169

moans and hopeless sobbing which did not come from any seagull, but from tormented human throats. Jess caught up with her, and kissed her.

'Whatever you want, Prue, you'll find it here.'

'I know, and it frightens me,' said Prue. 'What if I wanted something really bad ... to really hurt someone?'

Jess laughed.

'You think Arabella wasn't hurt? And you think she didn't want to be hurt? There is no badness in pain, when it is desired ... when a subject realises correction is what she has always deep down wanted. Look at lovely Nurse Crennet.'

In a niche shrouded in velvety turquoise light hung Nurse Crennet's nude body. No longer in businesslike nurse's starch, she was hanging upside down, the entire weight of her body taken by chains attached to her thimbled toes, her nipples, and her long, beautifully straight quim-hairs. She was suspended by her very own mink. Her body was streaked with glistening fluid from her open, pegged quim lips, and the juices ran down over her breasts and face, to pool on the floor where the ends of her lustrous mane were sopping as they lay in the puddle. Two figures attended her. Her legs were stretched wide by her anklets, revealing open quim, which was being beaten softly with a fluffy birch, the strokes landing with precision right on the wet pink between the fleshy swollen lips. The stretching of her mink hair pulled the whole skin of her mound right up like a satchel and made her fount seem like an extra eerie limb.

Alternating with the birch strokes, the second figure delivered strokes with a cat-o'-nine-tails to the bare buttocks, the impact jolting her so that Nurse Crennet writhed in her bonds, gently shuddering like water on the boil. However, this was no ordinary treatment on bare, for Nurse Crennet's already abnormal bum-swelling was now distended into two fleshy bulbs, beautiful in their enormity. She wore a tight metal strip around her waist, to which was attached a vice, or constricting ring, very like the lyre. This was screwed so as to exert pressure at the base of the already ripe buttocks, and squeezed the flesh until Nurse Crennet's magnificent tight bum-globes bulged to bursting point. It was this engorged skin, stretched thin as paper, which now purpled at each cut of the cruel tails. Her correctors were both females, completely nude, and rubbed their clits and wet quims merrily as they worked. Both were clean-scalped: the twins, Helen and Angela!

They giggled as they recognised Prudence, and said they thought they should find her here.

'Best club in town, isn't it, Nurse Crennet?'

'The only possible club,' sobbed Nurse Crennet.

Prue went further; she came on Henrietta, in the process of slipping from her rubber robe to reveal her pierced and chained body, the waist pinned in a latex corset as narrow as a schoolgirl's ankle. Robed, her body had the appearance of a smooth chocolate bar freckled by nuts; nude, she was a crag, an alp, her body bathed in gleaming blue light. She seemed not to notice Prue's presence; before her trembled the maid, Jeremy Pleasant.

'You are a filthy little pig, a pup, a slut,' sneered Henrietta. 'You dare to dress as female, an outrage, hiding your filthy maleness in a maid's frillies. We are in second circle, and no one shall heed your cries for help as I thrash the impudence from you.'

'Yes, Nurse,' murmured Jeremy.

'We have all night ahead, and by dawn your bum will be raw, you dirty slut. What have you to say?'

'I . . . I deserve everything from you, Nurse.'

'What? Louder!'

'I deserve to be beaten, Nurse. Please thrash me, I beg you, thrash my bare until I faint with pain and shame!'

'Still not enough,' growled Henrietta, 'I shall have to

teach you your manners. Grovel before me, worm, and worship a lady's feet.'

Jeremy knelt and began to lick and kiss Henrietta's pointed toecaps, which she contemptuously ground into his mouth, pressing his tongue and lips as he made obeisance. He moaned in discomfort, and Henrietta took a long cane dyed a bright, oddly sinister blue, then flicked up the hem of his frilly skirt to reveal the knickers stretched over his nates. Prue thought them quite taut and pretty, and so, evidently, did Henrietta, for her eyes softened and her mouth creased in a grin of cruel pleasure. She flicked the cane tip twice against the panties, and the male jumped.

'You'll jump when you feel full cane,' said Henrietta. 'In fact, I think I'll bind you for treatment, dirty girl. Lick harder! My boots are not clean!'

She kicked him quite hard in the mouth.

'And when my boots are shiny, you may attend to my lady's places. I haven't washed today, nor yesterday, and I am quite stinky. Your tongue will cleanse me, girl, before you are fit to take treatment.'

10

Bare Fists

Henrietta now splayed her thighs and parted her bum-cheeks, and the kneeling maid put his tongue into her furrow and began to lick feverishly; she grasped his head and pushed him against her anus and made him tongue her there, well inside, which he did with muffled grunts and slurping noises which could have been disgust or relish. All the time, Henrietta idly frotted her glistening stiff clitty with the handle of her cane, until it was time for the maid's attentions to be transferred to her open quim lips. Jeremy plunged his tongue into her slit, and began to lick her, while her cane-handle still played on her clitty, and then the tip of his tongue found the stiff damsel, and Henrietta sighed deeply as he tongued the clit. She made Jeremy do this for some minutes, and her quim and thighs moistened copiously, the trickle of fluid from her lady's hole shining wet on her thighs. Henrietta ordered Jeremy to lick and swallow all her secretions, and he did so, his eyes tightly shut in dreaming supplication.

Then it was time for treatment, and Henrietta gestured to a small vaulting-horse with a padded rubber cushion and four splayed legs with cuffs at each foot. On this, Jeremy was stretched, his panties down and skirt up to reveal his quivering bare. Henrietta took her time about fastening his wrists and ankles as tightly as the cuffs would allow, then said it was still not tight enough, and produced a long thin chain, with which she bound his waist over and over, until he groaned that he could scarcely breathe.

'So you know what it is like to be girdled as a maid,' spat Henrietta, and, without warning, lifted the cane and cracked it savagely across the boy's naked nates. He jumped and cried piteously, and she whipped him again, and again.

'How many must I take, Nurse?' he gasped. 'Those were so tight, and I smart so, I don't think I can bear a full set. There is no mercy in your treatment, Nurse, I think you are the cruellest nurse of all.'

Henrietta seemed pleased at this protest.

'A naughty maid needs a cruel nurse, to beat her on bare until she screams, specially when the naughty maid is a male! Doesn't she? Don't *you*? Isn't a girl's bare bum, smarting and wriggling in deserved agony, the only beauty?'

'O, yes, Mistress! I adore it, I need and deserve it! I am a naughty girl. Please beat me bare!' cried Jeremy.

Henrietta snarled that the bitch must be silenced. She ripped the white pompom from the skirt, and pressed it into Jeremy's mouth. Then she continued with the flogging, and now she grasped a second instrument of supplice, sneering that she now had a reputation for cruelty to maintain. The second instrument was a thick, heavy tawse, and Henrietta said Jeremy was to receive a harmonious treatment, five strokes of tawse for one of cane. The vicious flaps smacked across the squirming buttocks, five times, before another hard crack of the cane descended, adding a thin stripe to the garden of crimson blossoming under the tawse-thongs.

'Of course,' said Henrietta casually, though panting a little from her exertion, 'if you were a real girl, you'd be corrected with the eel, like the Norse maidens of old Northumberland. An electric eel, applied to the quim, eh? You have no quim, worm, but you do have another orifice . . .'

She parted his bum-cheeks and put a finger on his anus bud, pushed it inside him, then joined it with a second and a third finger, until her three fingers were pushed all the way inside his anus, thrusting like a penis, to his obvious discomfort. As she frigged the boy's bumhole, she continued corporal punishment, bending her torso back so as to get a wide aim, and the poor maid squirmed doubly both at the rain of strokes, and the horrid torment of the fingers poking his raw bumhole. But the male organ beneath the wriggling buttocks was timber, and the ball-sac stretched like a drumskin beneath Jeremy's massive erection. The harder Henrietta flogged, the stiffer and more trembling his penis seemed to grow. His moans added to the chorale of distress which echoed around the musky labyrinth, in a cawing lament which did seem to be the melancholy cry of seagulls.

Henrietta paused, and struck the ball-sac quite hard with the tip of her cane, which made Jeremy writhe quite frantically. Then she raised her boot, and reached between his thighs to press her foot tightly against the balls and risen shaft of his penis. She began to grind him there, and he squealed in discomfort, tears springing to his eyes. A final crunching grind to balls and cock, then the foot was removed, and the toecap placed in the male's anus, where Henrietta thrust it where her fingers had lately stretched. The toecaps were thin and sharp, and penetrated the anus to a depth of a few inches; she began to kick in and out, in a savage mimicry of the movements of love. Henrietta was now beating him alternately with tawse and cane, one stroke for one. His buttocks were now darkened all over, the stripes scarcely discernible in the mass of mottled and blackening skin that had once been two pearl-white, smooth globes.

Jeremy began to mouth through his gag, trying to form words of supplication.

'No more . . . it's enough . . . stop, please Mistress . . . stop, stop, O, stop now . . .'

Yet there seemed no measure to Henrietta's fury. And the cries of the tormented were indeed lost in the scented labyrinth of pain. She delivered two lashes with tawse and cane, at the same time, gasping in her own satisfaction, and the love juice now cascading in rivulets from her swollen quim lips. The boy squealed in despair; Henrietta's flogging became a fury, and she whipped him henceforth with both implements at once, so that no sooner was one vicious crack ringing than it was followed by a second, an awful third, a fourth . . . The boy's wails through his gag were quite pitiable, and suddenly his head slumped forward. As beseeched, he had fainted at the pain! At this, Henrietta emitted a cry of satisfaction, followed by a long sigh as she frotted her quim and clitty very hard, then moved to the maid's head, cupped it between her thighs, and began to frot herself with Jeremy's crown against her damsel.

Rhythmically thrusting her loins, and the magnificent points of her breasts stiff as the prow of a ship dancing in the waves, she bucked and pleasured herself against the flopping blonde hair of the insensate male. Her love juices trickled and matted his tresses as she moaned closer to her spasm and, as she bucked, her trembling cane hand continued to flog the male's inert croup. Prue darted forward and cried, '*Enough*, Henrietta!' and wrested the cane from her, then pushed the bigger woman to the ground and cradled Jeremy's head, kissing his brow and lips. He opened his eyes and smiled, and whispered, 'Thank you, Nurse' in a cracked voice. But his thanks were to Henrietta!

Suddenly Prue staggered, and toppled as she felt Henrietta's teeth bite savagely into her ankle, and her arms clasp her calves in a bear hug. She fell heavily on top of Henrietta and, on impulse, slapped her face hard, crisscrossing her cheeks with angry blows, and found herself squatting on the struggling nurse, whose breasts were bobbing in her fury, almost in Prue's face. She transferred her hand to the teats and began slapping and punching them as Henrietta struggled to get up, but she had Henrietta by her hair and pulled fiercely to keep her pinioned to the ground. Henrietta's nipple rings jangled harshly at Prue's furious blows, and she stuck her fingers through them and pulled, making Henrietta squeal in pain. Her knee was on Henrietta's jewelled quim and viciously she stabbed her lady's place, making her moan. She bent down and took Henrietta's rock-stiff nipple in her teeth and bit hard, causing the tall woman to writhe and squirm, but with her head still pinioned by the hair.

'You vicious beast!' cried Prue. 'You horrible cow, to hurt so!'

On and on she pummelled and bit and stabbed, her anger growing at Henrietta's very helplessness, until Prue realised that Henrietta's hands were no longer desperately clawing at Prue's body, to release herself, but that she had dropped her hands between her legs, the skin stroking Prue's stockinged flesh as she resumed her self-pleasuring on clit and wet quim lips! Henrietta had gone slack, her head lolling and her eyes no longer blazing with anger, but droopy and lost in the strange pleasure of her humiliation. The more Prue bit her nipples and breast-spanked her, the harder she frotted her own clit, until Prue felt her heave, the nipple rings jangling in a sweet music of submission as Henrietta groaned and yelped and bucked in a climax. And Prue became aware that her own belly was fluttering, her own quim soaking wet and dripping with oily love-juice, drenching her knickers and stocking tops and thighs.

Henrietta's dominant fury had turned to an ecstacy of submission, and Prue's own sympathetic rage on Jeremy's behalf to a desire to subdue the proud Henrietta. She could not understand; she was too far in lust to wish understanding. She removed her knee from Henrietta's crotch, and fumbled at her wet knickers, pulling them down so that her own shaved fount was naked. She pressed her thighs in Henrietta's like scissors, and their naked quims met. Still squeezing and nipping Henrietta's bruised teats, Prue began to rub her quim against her subject's; she found the clit, and their damsels touched in soft frottage, and Henrietta began to squirm and yelp with new pleasure.

Prue reached down for Henrietta's cane, and raised it. Henrietta saw what was in her eyes, and smiled, her nostrils flaring and her eyelids heavy with desire. She nodded her head, and Prue stretched out her arm and swung the cane. It whistled through the air and lashed full across Henrietta's bare breasts, and the nurse jumped as a vivid stripe coloured her pale teat-flesh. Prue whipped her again, and again, on the bare stiff nipples this time, which puckered softly as though crying out at the cane's kiss, yet stood stiff again in trembling readiness for the next.

All the time, Prue's soaking quim pulsed against Henrietta's, her cries of clit-joy matching her subjects until she too felt the welling of ecstacy in her belly. She heard a male voice sighing in excitement, and looked round to see Jeremy's eyes wide and bright at the spectacle, his lips creased in a smile and his penis hard as oak.

'You impudent slut!' cried Prue, and twisted round to deal him a swingeing crack with the cane, which stroked on his back and bumhole. 'You dissembled! You *can* take more.'

She repeated it, this time laying the cut across the bare purpled nates, one buttock after the other, and as she continued her frottage, she swivelled like a weathercock, caning now the throbbing crimson breasts of Henrietta, now the buttocks of the helpless male. Jeremy's body was jerking against his bonds at each cane-stroke, and through her sweat-blurred eyes Prue saw that a drop of creamy moisture had appeared at his peehole. His moans grew louder and quicker, and suddenly he gasped, and a fierce jet of cream spurted from his penis, which bucked and spattered Prue's ruched-up skirt and stockings with the hot fluid of his ecstacy. Prue could no longer hold back; she cried out loudly in her own orgasm, and as her quim washed Henrietta with her gushing love-juice, she knew that Henrietta's body too had submitted to spasming pleasure.

Prue gradually stopped her own writhing, wiped the sweat from her eyes, and sat gasping with her partners in joy.

'O, Henrietta . . .' she moaned, and leant to kiss her.

'Release me, you bitch!' cried Henrietta. 'You have made me submit to pleasure, slut, and I shall have you for it!'

'What is this unseemliness?' cried a new voice. 'It's the law going to have you both!'

Before she could react, Prue felt her wrists forced behind her and handcuffed! She was hurled off Henrietta's body, and she too was pinioned, turned over, and cuffed. The two females peered up aghast at a female with whip and baton. The two sets of handcuffs were linked by a chain, like an animal's leash, and she forced them to their knees, then made them crawl further into the labyrinth by pulling their arms painfully up above their backs. Prue shuffled wretchedly, her sopping knickers still down, and leaving an embarrassing trail of juice-spots on the floor, with Jeremy's sperm-drops gleaming on her stockings.

They came to a chamber in shadow, with an iron grille door, and were hurled inside, to hear the door clang shut on them. Prue pressed her face to the bars, still dazed from her orgasm, but her glow of pleasure giving way to chilly dread. There was no help here.

'I'll go and unbind your accomplice in crime,' said the woman pleasantly, 'and leave you a few moments to contemplate your miscreant's fate.'

'What crime?' stammered Prue.

'You took pleasure with a male, without licence.'

The woman pressed her face to the bars and allowed her soft lips to touch Prue's.

'I said I'd get you in a cell one day, Nurse Riding,' said the cruel, radiant face of WPC Tallinn.

Prue smoothed down her nurse's uniform and pulled her knickers up properly, and made sure her garters were fastened. It was suddenly cold in this police cell, and the floor was bare stone. In the corner, Henrietta crouched strangely forlorn: her nudity, now, not the nudity of power, but of capture and shame, her magnificent bum tattoos seeming merely the wan fancies of a prisoner. Their cell seemed to be a large ceilinged enclosure within the labyrinth, and in the half-darkness Prue saw a handsome array of disciplinary instruments. The aroma of naked power was chill in her nostrils.

She was aroused by a faint groan in the depths of the chamber, and crept to the source of the noise. A stretched, upright figure hung from the ceiling in a splayed 'X' position. Prue approached and cried out when she recognised Mrs Shapiro. The pretty dark woman was suspended by chains from her wrists, with similar chains cuffed to her ankles and rooted in the stone floor.

'O . . . if Dennis could see me now,' she crooned, in strange contentment, her chains jangling softly. 'Why, Nurse Riding! What is your penance here? And who is crying by the bars?'

The dominatrix Henrietta was quietly sobbing.

As Prue's eyes adjusted to the light, Mrs Shapiro's 'penance' became hideously obvious, as did the cause of her sparkling eyes. She was at last taking the lyre! Her breasts were squeezed in the vicious appliance, so that they bulged like pumpkins, and the nipples were clamped at the end of two more ceiling chains, so that they were stretched out thin and wide like gloves, with the points squeezed into tight grapes under the cruel pincers. A further clamp, like a furry clam, was applied to Mrs Shapiro's naked quim, pressing the lips shut; Prue looked at Mrs Shapiro's back, and saw a lattice-work of whip marks that extended from shoulder to calf, the buttocks being so darkly coloured as to be scarcely recognisable as the firm olive smoothness she remembered from Hydro. As a final supplice, a heavy plug stopped Mrs Shapiro's anus.

'O,' said Mrs Shapiro, 'I am not allowed to make commode, you see, so my holes are clamped for self-control, to hold it in. Tallinn has been attending to my flesh all night, with whip and cane! It is for the circulation, you know, as well as correction and endurance. The blood circulates more vigorously, and flows to my titties, and . . . well, see how big I am! Have you earned the lyre, Nurse Riding? I do hope so. We can hang, and take whip, naughty girls together.'

The cell door clanged open and shut, and WPC Tallinn threw another human bundle into her domain. This was the trussed body of Jeremy, still in his maid's uniform, who was left groaning on the flagstones while Tallinn, after locking the cell door with a flourish, occupied herself with fastening a curious harness around the naked Henrietta. She touched a switch, and the dim light brightened a little.

'This is the brace,' she said cheerily, 'and it will keep this miscreant proper while we attend to business.'

She undid Henrietta's handcuffs, and forced her to sit on the floor with her legs outstretched, head down at her upraised knees, and her hands stretched under her ankles. The wrists were cuffed again; then a metal collar was fastened around Henrietta's neck, with a tongue that hung down between her breasts, forcing them out on either side, and two cuffs, one on each side, which snapped shut on Henrietta's upper arms just above the elbows. The simplicity of this device meant that Henrietta was only slightly uncomfortable, but totally immobilised. Her face was pressed to her knees, held by the metal brace; her arms were pinioned and wrists cuffed, and it was not even necessary to restrain her ankles, for the movements of her legs below the knee were severely limited. Henrietta took this with glum submission, looking up once to ask that her punishment, whatever it was, be applied soon, rather than make her wait. Miss Tallinn said with the same cheerfulness that the anxiety of waiting was part of the pleasure – *her* pleasure.

She approached Prue and the tethered Mrs Shapiro. Tallinn was magnificent in her full dress policewoman's uniform: the crisp blue skirt, and dark uniform tunic with shiny silver buttons, covering a white blouse immaculate over her full breasts, the calves and thighs now in proper shiny stockings and rippling with a tiger's force. Her shoes were not clumpy police boots, but very high, teetering stilettos of the same midnight blue, with long, thin toecaps and spiked heels to match. She held a whip in her dark-gloved hand, and a truncheon, but not the smooth one Prue knew: this had lumps and striations, like a gnarled Scottish knobkerry. She gestured to a scroll on the wall above the rack of canes and whips. It read 'Norgjmerland'.

'Welcome to the old domain of Norgjmerland,' she said, 'whose guardian I am. This is my true manor, Nurse Prudence. That is the old, and the proper name, before the weak times, the days when an errant maiden was whipped naked one hundred times round the sacred fir tree, then whipped into the sea, and ordered to swim to Finland, braving the krakens' teeth. You see, Nurse Riding, I am a very special constable indeed, and Hell Fur Leather is my reality.'

Tallinn laughed. Suddenly she turned and bent down. lifted her skirt and pushed aside the thong of her knickers, revealing her naked furrow; then parted her bum-cheeks and pushed the cell key right into her anus, which swiftly enclosed it.

'Now the key is lost,' she said with a cold leer. 'But my uniform holds you here in my power, just as your nurse's uniform empowers you. Power and submission, there is nothing else in this world, and all our longings are to submit, or subdue. Wearing uniform is itself enslavement, giving the magic to enslave others. Do you agree to take the punishment that my uniform of Norgjmerland decrees?'

Far away, Prue thought she heard the cawing of seagulls, wheeling high in the air above the darkness of the sea where even now the hunted woman, the 'kraken', was plunged, naked, pursued by furies with whips.

'I submit, Tallinn,' she murmured. 'I am here of my own will . . . I'll take what is decreed.'

Tallinn nodded, and said she could now make herself more comfortable for the treatment to follow. She laid down her whip and truncheon, and stripped off her jacket, holding it out as though to let it fall.

'Slave,' she said, and Jeremy sprang forward and caught the garment just as it dropped.

Prue saw the fullness of Tallinn's breasts clearly outlined and thrusting against the white fabric of her blouse, the big berries of her nipples clear through the cloth, as she wore no bra, but a dark patch at her waist indicated a girdle or corset. Then, to Prue's surprise, she casually unbuttoned her blouse, and held it out.

'Slave,' she said again, and Jeremy caught it.

Swiftly, Tallinn unfastened her skirt and stepped out of it, letting it slide down her dark blue stockings to her ankles, and Jeremy crouched to catch it before it touched the floor. It glided slowly, as though borne by wings, revealing the shining of her silk stockings, the magic swelling of thigh and calf and the curves of her superb legs, then the gentle bumps of her ankles as the stocking-silk dived into the delicious mystery of her shoes.

Now Tallinn was wearing nothing but a midnight blue corselet, a satin waspie which pinched her waist to a lovely slenderness and was cut daringly high over her hips. She retained her gloves, which were revealed as tight blue gauntlets, which extended halfway up her forearms and were made of clinging shiny rubber. The crotch-piece of her corselet was a mere string, which Prue had seen tantalisingly shifted from her furrow to stow the key in her bumhole; there were no panties beneath, and almost all the thick slice of her fount bulged beneath the corselet.

Her garter straps went straight from the waspie to her stocking tops, and these, like the panty and bra of the corselet, were trimmed in fetching fluffy white lace. But there was really no bra; her breasts were bare and thrust forward like hard melons, under a pretty lace scaffolding of scalloped bottom-cups. Miss Tallinn scrutinised her whip, and her truncheon, then looked at Prue, and instead picked up a heavy blue cane with its tip splayed into three wicked tongues a good five or six inches long.

'How do you find me now, Nurse?' drawled Tallinn, as Jeremy carefully folded and stowed her uniform things on a chair.

'You . . . are gorgeous, Officer,' said Prue shyly.

Tallinn's nostrils flared, and she slashed the cane against her own clothing on the chair.

'I am a police officer,' she snapped, 'and it is not your business to find me gorgeous, Nurse. You will bend over and take a set of the cane before I decide on your further punishment. And you, worm,' she added, looking over her shoulder at Henrietta, 'shall watch with your big wide eyes, and think what is coming to *you*.'

'O, Miss,' said Prue, embarrassed more for Henrietta's sake than her own, 'must I?'

Tallinn put her lips a hair's breadth from Prue's and Prue smelt delicious cruelty in her soft, fruity perfume.

'There is no must,' she said. 'There is only *will* . . .'

Prue silently bent over, raised skirt and lowered panties, then, on Tallinn's orders, touched toes, right in front of the hanging Mrs Shapiro. She felt the cool air caress her bare bottom, and steeled herself for a harsher caress. Mrs Shapiro jangled her chains.

'O, Tallinn!' she cried. 'Must I watch? I shall be so excited, and it hurts so much to hold it in!'

Tallinn smiled grimly and said that she might slop out at the appointed time and not before.

'We'll give you a set of twenty-one while I think about your further correction, Prudence,' she said in a kindly voice, and delivered a searing cut to Prue's bare, lashing her naked fesses so hard that she squealed loud, and almost lost balance.

Tears leapt to her eyes; she looked round and saw that Mrs Shapiro's face was flushed and anxious, and Henrietta's face wore a sulky grin.

'I don't know if I can bear it!' Prue heard herself pant, peering round in anguish to see the stockings of her tormentor, gleaming in cruel beauty.

'A mere twenty-one? You've had worse. Is it the freedom you can't bear, Prudence, the knowledge that you *will* take it?'

She delivered two more cuts in rapid succession, and this time Prue moaned, her eyes springing with tears, but did not wobble from position, although her fesses clenched tight.

'Nice and pink,' said Tallinn thoughtfully. 'You see, Prudence, love and kisses and coming vanish as quickly as a seagull's cry. But a beating is precious, for her marks never leave you.'

Prue took a full twenty-one on bare, without any protest save a mewl of agony at every third or fourth stroke. At each cut, her buttocks trembled madly and, by the end, each lash brought her legs up ramrod straight as though trying to lift her from the cold floor, away from the pain.

'There!' said Tallinn, her voice kindly and cheerful, but, as Prue was rising, Tallinn delivered a hefty kick to her buttocks, the toecap of her stiletto shoe catching Prue squarely in the bumhole. Now Prue toppled, into a bundle on the floor, and her tears flowed unabated.

'You bitch!' she cried. 'That was cruel!'

Grimacing, she rubbed her flaming bottom and struggled to pull up her knickers in a semblance of dignity. Tallinn lashed the cane scornfully across her breasts, and kicked her again, this time on her fount which was revealed by her uplifted skirt, just as she had got her panties on again. Prue wailed and covered her face in her hands.

'You feel just like a helpless slave, a convict?' said Tallinn, as though guessing her thoughts. 'You have no rights here, and no dignity. In jail, you fight for the meanest scraps, all shred of self-esteem beaten from you. Survival of the cruellest, girl.'

'What about Mrs Shapiro?' said Prue. 'Surely she doesn't deserve –'

'Mrs Shapiro is *paying* for it,' snapped Tallinn.

She kicked Prue again on the bum, three times, followed by two kicks to the breasts, and Prue took it, sobbing in a miserable heap and cupping her hands to protect her crotch.

'No fight in you? No spunk?' sneered Tallinn. 'Kneel and crouch, slut, and get your panties right off, I want to see how your arse is marking.'

Snuffling, Prue obeyed, and threw her panties away now, regretting their leaving as the leaving of small but important friends. A prisoner with no panties seemed a prisoner shorn of all humanity. Tallinn inspected her buttocks, roughly prising the furrow wide to see where her tipped cane had lashed the bumhole and quim lips.

'Not bad,' she said, 'she's purpling nicely.'

Tallinn thrust her hand roughly between Prue's thighs, and put three or perhaps four fingers well inside her quim.

'Well, well, well,' she said, squeezing the pubic bone. 'Wet, eh? So a little punishment makes you excited.'

Tallinn lifted her truncheon, and smeared it with Prue's own love-oils, and Prue felt the tip nestle against her wide bumhole, tickling her. She squealed again as the knobbly shaft was pushed hard into her bumhole, hurting her dreadfully, and Tallinn told her not to resist. She sobbed that she couldn't stand it, she could feel every cruel notch and bump scoring the tender fabric of her anus.

'Enjoy what you cannot stop,' Tallinn hissed.

With a wail of anguish, Prue gave up, and relaxed her entire anus as though to make commode, and suddenly the shaft of the truncheon plunged all the way to her root. She took it with open bumhole, moaning deep and long. Jeremy was silent in fearful obedience, but the bulge at his crotch made his frilly skirt stand up. Poking her roughly with the truncheon, Tallinn ordered Prue to crawl like a puppy. Prue obeyed, crawling on the floor and jumping at the brutal thrusts of the shaft in her bumhole, until she was kneeling before the male's stockings and skirt, powerful with the acrid odour of his arousal. Tallinn pulled aside her string, this time to delve between the swelling quim lips, which glistened with moisture. Prue saw that her nipples too were stiff in excitement. Tallinn felt inside her quim, and from the dripping folds of her slit retrieved a large purple leaf, gleaming with her oils.

She ordered Jeremy to lift his skirt and reveal his naked penis. He did so, nervously, and Tallinn wrapped the leaf firmly around his erect cock, tearing it in strips at one end which she knotted around his balls to secure it, so that the male's organ was now stiff within a purple tent.

'Dulse,' said Tallinn. 'I have warmed it for your supper, slave. First, hold your hands on your head. Now eat it, and don't take your lips from the maid's cock till you have swallowed every bit.'

Prue felt her head pushed down on Jeremy's penis, and began to suck on the leaf. She sucked and sucked, and Jeremy's cock stood rock-stiff, but the leaf would not melt for her, and Tallinn sneered that she must bite and chew. Trembling, she obeyed, biting gingerly on the nut of Jeremy's helmet, and feeling him wince with a little groan. But she followed her orders, and as she chewed on the male's stiff cock, it seemed to tremble and grow more rigid even in his obvious distress! She managed to break the leaf up, and force some of it into her mouth, feeling her spittle cascade over the cock, and she swallowed it.

Gradually, she had the dulse eaten, and felt the naked flesh of Jeremy's glans at the back of her throat as her lips and teeth approached the base of his shaft, and his balls. She paused to gag, and eventually felt her teeth stroke the tight balls. She moaned and bit into the leaf where it was stuck to the tender ball-skin. As she sucked, she felt the painful thrusting of the truncheon in her anus.

Her lips were on his balls, she bit, and felt something hard underneath; Jeremy jerked in anguish, but the leaf came away as she pulled it with her teeth, and, gradually, she felt the leaf fragments enter her mouth, her tongue was on the naked balls, and the cock thrust deep into her throat, almost choking her as the glans stroked across her palate. She heard Jeremy cry out and felt his hands clutch her head – at the back of her throat a drop of spunk crept from his peehole. Then, as his cock began to throb and buck, she instinctively began to suck, for his pleasure; her saliva bathed his cock, creamy hot spunk washed the back of her throat, and she swallowed every spurt.

She stayed in position, feeling the cock dwindle to softness, like a lovely little fluffy toy, and she kept licking it as she did so, able to take the balls and organ quite comfortably in her mouth without straining. She still salivated, and when Tallinn pulled her hair to disengage her, the little cock was shiny with her own juices.

'Now, Nurse, you know about *spucktherapie*,' said Tallinn, as though she were Matron. 'It is Mrs Shapiro's turn.'

Prue was driven by her anus back to the hanging woman, and gasped as the truncheon was suddenly pulled from her bumhole with a liquid, sucking sound.

'O, that tickles!' she cried.

She looked at Henrietta again, and licked her lips with a victorious smile, and even when Tallinn kicked her again right in the anus, she groaned, but did not stop smiling.

'Am I to help with Mrs Shapiro's treatment, Police Constable?' she said shyly, and with bright eyes.

'Yes, Nurse, you are,' said Tallinn. 'First, I must give you a demonstration. Your bumhole is well disciplined now, and *this* is what Mrs Shapiro expects.'

The solid truncheon was now replaced in Prue's anus by Talinn's supple fingers, first one, then the second, until all four were inside her groaning bumhole, and still her filling did not stop, for she heard Tallinn grunt, and felt a squeeze and a push, and suddenly the thumb was in as well, making a fist. Prue bit her lip. Tallinn balled her fingers tightly, clasping the thumb, and slid her fist right to the root of Prue's anus, the walls of her shaft straining as she thrust remorselessly deeper. And then, it was the same sensation of relief and joy as when she had opened up to the truncheon's invasion: she felt her sphincter and her whole anus relax, and she became nothing but a melting receptacle for the hard fist and the woman's will.

Tallinn thrust in and out very vigorously, making Prue's bum jerk even more than under the cane. Her quim gushed with hot liquid as the harsh policewoman fisted her. Tallinn whistled, and cried, 'Dog!' and Jeremy approached on all fours, to be ordered to pleasure his Mistress in her lady's place. He seemed confused: Tallinn snapped that Prudence was just now his Mistress, that any lady, even a slave, was automatically the Mistress of a male cur. Prue cried out in joy as she felt Jeremy's obedient tongue lap at her tingling clitty, and she knew that her juices were gushing over his lips and mouth, for Tallinn ordered him in his turn to lick and swallow. It was not long before the awful, gorgeous pounding of the hot fist in her bum, the smarting of her buttocks, and the ecstacy of the tongue flicking her damsel, brought Prue to shudder and squirm and squeal in orgasm.

The fist uncurled, became fingers and thumb, and Prue shivered as the instrument of her pleasure withdrew from her anus. She rose unsteadily to her feet, and ignored the fright in Mrs Shapiro's eyes.

'O! I've never had that before!' squeaked Mrs Shapiro.

'And I've never done it before,' said Prue grimly.

'First I must make slops. O, please, Tallinn,' whined Mrs Shapiro, 'but not with everyone watching!'

Tallinn said that girls had few secrets, and prisoners none at all, and ordered Jeremy to bring the slop-bucket; it was placed under Mrs Shapiro's spread legs, and her arse-plug removed. Mrs Shapiro's whine turned to a sigh of pleasure as she noisily evacuated, but not for long, as Tallinn picked up her whip and moved behind her, urging her to hurry for her own comfort.

She dealt fifteen lashes to the buttocks before Mrs Shapiro groaned and sobbed that she was finished. Jeremy was ordered to attend with his tongue to the Mistress's cleanliness, and then clear her bucket. He knelt, and licked Mrs Shapiro's lady's places until she squirmed and giggled at the tickling of his tongue.

Bright red mottled Mrs Shapiro's pert olive bum. Prue needed no orders from Tallinn to grease her fingers with her own love-juices, then slide her fingers one by one into Mrs Shapiro's squirming crack, deep into the anus until she was able to get her whole hand in and, rubbing against the lovely silky fabric of the bumhole, she balled her fingers to a fist. She pushed and pushed, feeling the cavern give way and its owner writhe and squeeze in resistance, moaning that she couldn't, she just couldn't! Prue was behind the croup and with her free hand began to slap the silky flesh very hard . . . and at last, after she had spanked Mrs Shapiro at least forty times, the woman groaned, and Prue saw a great gush of fluid pour on her thighs to puddle the floor; the anus gave way, and Prue's fist was at Mrs Shapiro's root. She imitated her own fisting, and with her anus and flogged nates still glowing gloriously sore, she fisted Mrs Shapiro's anus with all her strength, marvelling at the depth and silky resilience of the woman's hole.

Now, the woman began to buck and squeeze not in resistance, but in pleasure, and the juice flowed down her soft inner thighs. She gasped to Prue that she must help her out of her gorgeous agony, must frot her clitty till she came, for her fisting was the most glorious attention her bum had ever had. Prue grasped her quim and balled a second fist, bending sinuously so that her second fist plunged easily into the slimy hot wetness of the gash. Vigorously, she fisted – punched! – the squirming joyous woman in both quim and anus, feeling her fists thus against one another through the thin separating membrane. At the same time, Tallinn picked

191

up her whip and began to flog Mrs Shapiro quite hard across her lyred teats and her belly, Prue artfully pushing her towards the whip with her fist-thrusts as she punched and pummelled inside the two soft holes. Mrs Shapiro screamed as she climaxed, and Prue's forearm was drenched in love-oil.

Tallinn declared this treatment over, and briskly lowered Mrs Shapiro from a pulley, until she was stretched on her back on the floor, her striped buckled teats quivering stiffly in the air. Tallinn said that she herself deserved relief, and pushed aside the string of her corselet to reveal her bare quim. She parted her wet lips between finger and thumb, and showed pink, with the dark thimble of the clit stiff and swollen above. Then she squatted over Mrs Shapiro's breasts and lowered her quim on to the upturned nipple of the left breast, and the teat sank into her quim. Tallinn began to bounce up and down, squeezing and sucking on the teat with her prehensile quim lips, and rubbing her clitty.

'A titty-fist, that's best of all,' she cried, licking her lips, and her shoe pressed Mrs Shapiro's gasping mouth. The muscles of her thighs and calves rippled under silk as her heels ground Mrs Shapiro's lips and tongue.

Mrs Shapiro was playing her part, thrusting upwards with her ribs to drive her breast deeply into Tallinn, and Tallinn twisted round to make room for Prue, who soon lifted her own skirt, and, happily knickerless, squatted over the other stiff teat and felt the thick breast, capped with the nipple's walnut, sink into her own quim. She and Tallinn thrust forwards; their founts touched, then their quim lips, and finally their swollen stiff damsels, and they both gasped as they writhed on Mrs Shapiro's breasts while frotting each other's clits in a sinuous dance of joy.

Tallinn ordered Jeremy to kneel before the buckled Henrietta and remove her boots, then she was to pleasure his organ to stiffness between her bare soles, making him spurt into her boots and then replace them on her feet. Jeremy obeyed, cupping the long delicate feet and making them a lovely false quim, and at the same time placing one of her shoes over his nose and mouth, where he sniffed with deep breaths. Her feet wriggled as they frigged his stiff cock, bringing him to a shuddering spurt in her other shoe, some of his cream jetting so hard it splashed on her ankles.

Jeremy moved to kiss her ankles and toes, and licked her soles lovingly before replacing the shoes; then he licked her toecaps for all the time Prue and Tallinn were gamahuching. There were tears of humiliation in Henrietta's eyes, yet as he smoothed his maid's skirts and began to depart, she begged him to approach once more, and called to Tallinn to witness her act of obeisance. She took Jeremy's cock in her mouth – it was still half stiff – and enveloped his balls too, just as Prue had, until the organ rose to full magnificence once more. She kissed Jeremy's cock with surprising tenderness, and there was a wet puddle between her pinioned thighs. Seeing this act, Tallinn called him rampant and insatiable and terribly wicked, and ordered him to make further obeisance to a lady: Mrs Shapiro.

Tallinn removed her foot from Mrs Shapiro's mouth and ordered Jeremy to lift skirt and adopt position with his cock over her lips, as if for press-ups. Jeremy straightened his body, his cock timber once more, and with his skirts up over his bare, lowered his glans and shaft right to the hilt into Mrs Shapiro's eager throat. She began to suck and bubble with spit, as he pumped, thrusting hard to her throat as though into a quim. At the same time, to the rhythm of his pumping, Tallinn seized a short four-thonged whip and began to flog his flushed bare buttocks into further blossom of chastisement. All the while, Henrietta watched, her face red and the puddle between her thighs deepening, as she struggled in her frustration to reach her quim with her fingers to relieve herself.

Prue, Tallinn and the two subjects all cried out in their joy and, within seconds, Jeremy was moved to give his sperm into Mrs Shapiro's mouth, so forcefully that it spurted over her convulsed lips; Tallinn and Prue spasmed together as their clits fenced in voluptuous frottage, and Prue, with a nursemaid's thoughtfulness, reached behind to Mrs Shapiro's vulva, found the clit between gaping wet quim lips, and flicked her throbbing damsel only a few times before she too convulsed in new ecstacy.

Suddenly there was a commotion nearby, and, panting, Prue blinked her eyes. She heard the sound of whiplashes, cries and scuffles, and then cheering. She followed Tallinn as she leapt to her feet.

'The key,' said Tallinn, 'quickly. The prey, the kraken, has returned, or been brought back by the hunters.'

She bent over; Prue, now with expert fingers, pushed into her opened anus, and retrieved the cell key. Tallinn smiled at Prue's fingers probing her bum, but pushed to help the key evacuate. They made their way to the door.

'When must I expect my punishment, Mistress?' said Henrietta in a small voice.

'Why, Henrietta, you've already had your punishment,' said Tallinn, as she released her. 'You've been obliged to watch . . .'

She pushed the cell door open, and tut-tutted, saying she was very remiss – she had left it open all the time; technically speaking, they hadn't been in a cell at all.

11

Nursebound

The masked woman's nude body was a mass of lashes. She crouched wet and shivering on the floor, like a beast waiting to spring. At her waist, she wore a garland of bulbous seaweed, like Miss Furbelow's garter.

'Get up,' said Miss Furbelow, elegant in her grey suit.

The woman stood proudly, hand on hips. All were gathered to see and the labyrinth was hushed. They were in a cell, open to the garden which sloped down to the dark waves, the swooping birds above. In the doorway stood the kraken's pursuers, shivering themselves despite their sweated bodies; each sheathed woman had whip stripes on her exposed places. Contemptuously, Miss Furbelow surveyed them.

'Your prey eluded you,' she said. 'She made her way back to the dungeon, *and* marked you prettily on her way. She wears the kraken's garland ... She swam to the holy rock.'

'Yes, Mistress,' growled a sullen female. 'We almost had her, but she tricked us –'

'Silence, ladies!' snapped Miss Furbelow, cracking her four-thonged whip. 'No excuses.'

She tossed her whip to the masked female, who caught it and held it cupped against her glistening breasts.

'Administer the just punishment,' she ordered calmly. 'Their skins are to be in harmony. You, ladies, line up.'

The sheathed women obeyed, their backs to the company, with white bare buttocks ready for chastisement. The nude female who was the victorious kraken lifted the whip, and serenely began to flog the buttocks of the first huntress. She flogged steadily and hard, and the huntress stood still, trembling a little, and not making a single cry, as her bare nates turned crimson, purpling after about fifteen minutes, her puffy arse-flesh as dark as her costume. She proceeded to flog the next in line, for the same time, and when all the huntresses' croups had been adorned with blushes, they were ordered to turn and face the company. They did so, all shivering, with moist eyes and white lips. The prey was now the huntress. Placidly, she raised her whip high, and stroked its tip over the trembling breasts of the first corrected, who, now, let out a soft, low moan.

'Continue with correct procedure,' said Miss Furbelow.

The small cell echoed to the merciless rhythm of the heavy little flail, as each huntress received a whipping on breasts and naked quim, and their lady's places were as dark-mottled as their fesses. They shuddered and sobbed, but there was no fury nor revenge in this flogging; procedure was correctly followed. The disgraced women were ordered to depart, crawling on all fours, and Miss Furbelow kicked their blackened croups as they passed her, right in the furrow. They wailed, kicked again until they reached the door, and the sanctuary of the labyrinth, but Prue disdained to kick a woman down.

'Isn't it exciting?' said a breathless voice beside her, and she felt a hand briefly brush her bottom.

She turned and saw Virginia.

'My, your bum's hot!' cooed the mulatto. 'You must have had fun in the police cell ... Word gets around. Maybe you'll show *me* what for ... Tallinn says I'm not naughty enough.'

Prue said she was sure she was quite naughty, and would select a suitable treatment for her. She saw Jess, and Miss Gageby and Henrietta, Jeremy and Tallinn herself were not far away in the throng. She saw another woman whose face was also familiar, in a very short evening frock of high-necked black ciré and tight around a rather adorable bum, who was whispering to Jeremy: she was reminded of the subject, Officer Raitte . . . Miss Furbelow murmured orders, and three women left the cell; moments later, Prue heard a rumbling like a steam-roller, and the women returned trundling a bizarre life-size figure made of gleaming brass.

It was not like a statue, more a curious suit of armour. Its 'feet' were slipped into metal grooves on the floor, where two bolts were snapped shut over them. These 'feet' were enormous brass boots, hinged to admit their wearer, with the doors hanging open at the back, and the buckles loose. They extended up to mid-thigh, and from their tops two shafts extended to meet in a central shaft, standing to neck height, and carved with two-headed fishy creatures wreathed by lilies. On this, at the waist, was a curved, hinged belt with a snap-buckle; and on top of the shaft was moulded a helmet, like a diver's helmet, with an eye-slit, and again with a hinged back, open to admit the wearer, or victim. At each side of the shaft were two hinged cylinders to admit the victim's arms. It was like the 'Iron Maiden', the mediaeval instrument of torture and execution, only there were no mortal spikes.

The nude blonde woman, still masked, bowed to Miss Furbelow, and stepped inside the brass boots, so that her face was pressed into the helmet, and her waist inside the belt. The boots were shut on her legs, and fastened, so that she was quite unable to move from their heavy anchorage. Next, the waistband was clamped around the small of her back, and her head was shut in the helmet, which closed with an ominous clang.

Finally, the arm-tubes were closed around her arms, pinioning her completely.

None of her bonds was tight, as they did not need to be; completely trapped in the enclosing metal, she was immobile. She might struggle in her prison, but she could not bend her legs, nor her waist nor arms. Two thin struts at the top of the boots supported a little cup, like a chalice, which was positioned an inch under her quim lips. Exposed were her proud naked breasts, her upper thighs, her back and shoulders and bare croup . . . and, at the front, the beautiful smooth hillock of her shaven fount, the quim lips thrusting out in a delicious swelling, as though rigorous treatments had drawn them to their full beauty; the acorn of the clit peeping shy but stiff amid the fleshy whorls of the quim. Miss Furbelow touched her hands together in approval.

'The sea monster has come to its lair, and been trapped in the brass monster of truth,' she said.

She picked up the four-thonged whip, and added two more. She tied their handles together, so that she had a whip of twelve thongs altogether. This she held in one hand, and in the other took the blue splayed cane. Without warning, Miss Furbelow lashed the woman's bare buttocks with the cane, repeating the stroke twice, and raising a blush. Prue heard the woman's body jerk inside her metal cauldron, making a hollow sound, and her groan of pain was eerily magnified by the brass helmet.

'Now, the truth game,' said Miss Furbelow. 'The sea monster shall tell us what led her to become that most sacred and delicious of earth monsters . . . a *nurse*! Any fault in the tale shall be rewarded with strokes, until the female emerges cleansed.'

Prue started: the kraken 'monster' was a nurse! Prue must have variously seen every nurse naked at privy, yet did not recognise her. Miss Furbelow was peering over her spectacles at Prue.

'You, Nurse, are properly attired, so you shall attend the front part of the female,' she said, handing Prue the whip of twelve tails. Prue gulped, and bowed in obeisance; it seemed she was to whip the girl's breasts and quim. She tried not to look into the eye-slit of the helmet, but the big blue eyes fixed her, calm and not pleading, but rather amused. Prue would do duty! She placed herself with whip readied, and the girl-monster began to speak.

'All women are monsters,' she intoned, 'because we hold the sea within us, in our salty founts, and the sea is the Mistress of life and of death, as Nurse is of Earth.'

There was a sharp cane-crack on bare flesh, and the eyes wrinkled as the girl shuddered.

'Enough dark secrets!' snapped Miss Furbelow. 'Your story, girl, and an instructive one. How came you to Nurse?'

'By power over the male, to enslave flesh and hearts.'

The cane whistled, and cracked twice against her fesses, jerking her within her metal shell.

'Schoolgirl stuff!' cried Miss Furbelow, lashing again.

'O . . .' she groaned, 'it is a story too beautiful . . .'

Miss Furbelow nodded grimly. Prue hesitated; shook her head, murmured that somehow she could not whip *that* woman's beauty, and handed the whip to Henrietta, with a bow of obeisance. Henrietta lifted the whip, staring coldly into her victim's eyes, then lashed her full across the naked breasts. The woman's eyes closed in a wrinkle of agony.

'I *was* a schoolgirl, then, treated as such, though in my womb and breasts and mink-hair I was a full woman,' she said. 'My Governess made me dress in girlish things, even to go outside, and I attracted male attention, which shamed me, though I was punished by my Governess as if it were my fault. As though to mock me, she dressed me in little short skirts, frilly knickers that you could see beneath the skirt, stockings with

199

seams, a tight blouse that showed my breasts shamefully to any eyes, for I was permitted neither bra nor corselet. I lived in luxury, in a pampered quiet village, and the cruelty of my Governess seemed a reasonable price to pay for my comfort.

'She was a woman of about twenty-five, and seemed vastly old, though in reality there were scarcely seven years between us. She was handsome, a stern, serious face, with big lips and high cheekbones framed by straight chestnut hair, very shiny, and cut short in a curious gamine style. She assured me that things were so everywhere, that naughty girls, even when ripe, had to dress as naughty girls. And naughty boys as naughty boys? I asked, and she smiled, and said yes.

'But whenever we went out, and I got glances, she would punish me for it later. I was very virginal – that was why my late father provided for my secluded education, with a few select Mistresses to give lessons, here in our peaceful village. They might not beat me, but must refer me to my Governess for chastisement, when I was remiss in study. So, all in all, I had frequent occasion to be chastised, and felt I deserved it. I did deserve it! When corrected for allowing myself to be ogled by males, it did not occur to me to protest that since her buttocks swayed as mine did, perhaps the looks were intended for us both, as males have not the taste to discriminate.'

She cried out suddenly, as three sharp cuts lashed her bare buttocks; a nod from Miss Furbelow, and Henrietta followed them with two strokes, quickly back and forth, lacing the breasts, and when Miss Furbelow nodded again, she lashed the woman's bare quim, her muscles rippling like a vengeful whirlwind.

'It is not your place to comment on the male,' snapped Miss Furbelow. 'That is my privilege, as Mistress here.'

'For small offences, I would be spanked,' the brass

figure continued in a trembling voice. 'I would bend over her knee. I remember the scent of her silk stockings, and the faint, acrid odour of her knickers and the rustle of her skirts – she always wore dark colours, as befitted a stern governess, but with a white or pink or baby-blue petticoat underneath – with the fresh blue sky outside the window. I would get thirty or forty spanks on my bare bum. I had to raise my skirt before bending over, and she would hook my panties and pull them down very slowly, making little clucking noises as though my bare globes held some impolite secret.

'She made quite a ritual of this before the spanking actually started, and sometimes, to taunt me, would sip a cup of tea, or even speak on the telephone. That serene clink of her teacup! I remember, at first I was so nervous I wanted to wet myself, and once I did, all over my knickers and stockings, and got a double spanking for it. It happened a second time, and after the spanking, she proceeded to the cane, and that was just after my eighteenth birthday, I remember, for she gave me a lovely cake with sugar mermaids.

'The cane was her preferred punishment from then on, although for lesser things it would be a spanking, a hundred spanks now, for she said a big girl could take it. I got used to spanking, and . . . and came to enjoy it, for I always associated it with the lovely smell of her stockings and petticoats, and fresh shoe-polish – she always made me clean her shoes before I was spanked. I took the cane standing, that is, bent over and touching my toes, with skirts up and my panties *and* my stockings round my ankles. It seemed ever so much more shaming to have my stockings down than just my panties, as though my stockings protected my virginity, and even my bare quim did not make me feel so vulnerable as bare legs – especially when the cane whistled and took me deliberately on my thigh backs, which hurt dreadfully.

'She was cruel – when that happened, and I knew she did it deliberately, she would say she had missed a stroke and repeat the cut on the bum, which added three or four strokes to a beating. Sometimes the caning was twenty-one, and then I was permitted to bend over the sofa, and hold on to the sides, to stop me jerking. And by the end each cut would make my feet leave the floor, and my legs stiffen in agony! O! O!'

She was interrupted by a further three to the bum, and Henrietta whipped a savage three each to the breasts and the mound, taking her right on the quim lips. She gulped.

'It was her conceit to keep a cuckoo clock, set to cuckoo at the twenty-four-hour clock, so she would set it for 21.00 hours, and the little thing would cuckoo twenty-one times, and at each chirp I got a cut. She called it a seconds beating, for my poor bare bum would be stroked at each second. Gosh, that was truly dreadful. But other times, she would give me a slow beating, and in a way that was just as bad, for she would leave me standing there between strokes, not knowing how long it would be before my croup jerked again, and dying to pee, while she would do it so casually, as if I were only an afterthought – when a beating, to me, made my searing hot bum the centre of the world!

'She was so cruel. She was playing with me like a toy ... would devise little fancies, like making me tie a coloured ribbon round the cane handle, and kiss the cane tip both cold before my beating, and warm afterwards. She would inspect my flogged bum, and my lady's place, most closely after each session, and came to see, to my embarrassment, that I was actually excited by my beating! She accused me and I falsely denied it: a strange loveliness welled up in my belly at each cut of the cane on my bare, and my nips hardened and my little clitty grew all big and stiff, and my slit got thick and swollen with my lips all gorged ...

202

'I couldn't understand it . . . perhaps it was that her strokes were so clean, and I felt she understood and cared for me. And it made me feel all grown up, although I was dressed as a girly, with pleated skirt and pigtails and everything – perhaps she wanted to be the girly! Despite my humiliation, she would address me civilly, and so, humiliated as a maid, I felt a lady. She made it clear that this was simply correct procedure, the necessary business of taming a wilful young girl, and her role as Governess did not permit any personal element to come into my correction.

'My denial of excitement made her furious and earned me beatings for the next three days, one beating of twenty-one in the morning and one in the afternoon. For these canings, she said she had to break me from pleasure. So I let her strip me entirely naked, without even my bra – I remember she took great pleasure in removing it, saying my titties flopped out like big canteloupes, and in rolling down my stockings and panties, very slowly, and unbuckling my shoes, caressing my feet very softly as she took the stockings off, and always whispering how much it was going to hurt me nude, and how sorry she was, but it was the proper way to correct a young maid.

'A naked flogging in her salon would be indecorous, as I might forget myself and soil her furnishings. I blushed deeply at this, for I had shamefully made pond before. The exercise room in the basement was equipped with the usual gymnastic furniture. She said I was to bend over the vaulting horse, and I did so, finding it a snug fit, as though purpose-built. I was shocked when she produced cords and tied my ankles and wrists to the legs of the horse, so that I was quite helpless! She told me not to be afraid, that restraint would help me take it like a lady, and she trusted me not to cry and blub, which would make a light gag necessary. She showed me the gag – a leather strip with a metal flap in it to keep the tongue down, and I shivered and promised to keep quiet.

'For the first of the six punishment beatings, she took a much longer and harder cane, about four feet or more. Tied and helpless, I felt dizzy with fear, but with excitement too, and I could feel my quim moistening. When the first stroke landed, I almost cried out, but shut my eyes tight and tried to squeeze away the tears as my bum wriggled in vain, to escape that awful smarting. How it hurt! I had never imagined anything could hurt so much. And there were another twenty to go! At five, I was in agony, and cried out again and again for her to stop the dreadful beating. I was squealing and blubbing just like a soft maid! And then she said in a kind voice that she had better gag me after all, but did I really want her to stop? I knew I deserved this just correction but, if I disagreed, I would be released, and no more said of the matter.

'I heard her kind voice, and dreaded the thought that she might be displeased with me. And deep inside, I wanted to take the thrashing! *Wanted* to be naked and helpless, and squirm for her! I heard myself say that I would take full punishment, and all the punishments thereafter, and would she please gag me. She smiled, and did so; the strap was tight around my chin, and the tongue flap cold, and now I could make no sound other than a tortured moan. She said, dreamily, that the Earth was ice, and that on the bare flesh of young ladies, must be created fire.

'How I got through the first awful dozen I do not know – the gag helped – but the pain was so intense that I lost all control. I wet myself copiously, feeling the hot pee flow down my bare legs, and I remember being glad I was nude, for I would not soil my stockings. She ignored my disgraceful wetting, and I felt we were somehow accomplices in my beating rather than Mistress and maid. The beating continued, and now I realised that my smarting bum had got used to the thrashing, and the agony had reached a plateau, where I was somehow in control. I was riding the cane . . .

'I stopped crying through my tongue-plate and gag, and began to gasp as I felt my clit all tingly and stiff, and a lovely warm fluttering in my belly, and there was still juice flowing on my thigh, but it was hot oil from my steaming slit! And as the twenty-first stroke approached, I gasped louder and louder, and at the twentieth, I shuddered and moaned and had my first lovely lovely orgasm! She knew that I had climaxed, and stroked my hair, and warned me that my next five special beatings would be no less fierce, and I said that I did not want them to be any less fierce, for I wanted my naked bum to be corrected until I was a proper maid. She laughed and said I was a very proper maid, and there were some things it was time I understood.

'I did not climax at my second beating, although I knew I was close, and had to take my supper standing up, I was so sore in my bum. Afterwards, she gave me a book to study. It was understood that on full maturity, I should study to be a nurse, which my Governess said was the highest of a lady's endeavours, and she said this book would help me understand true nursing. It was by a Scottish lady named Miss Bright, a headmistress of a young ladies' academy in the Victorian era, and concerned methods of disciplining young ladies, with an interesting addendum on the correction of young men.

'I read all of it that night, lying on my belly because my bum was so sore. I knew I would be beaten the next day, and the next, but I didn't care! I read the whole book, enthralled at the descriptions of the various instruments of correction: I had never imagined that discipline was capable of such intricate subtlety: canes, tawses, birches, chairs, stools, and horses for flogging or restraint; cages, corsets, Spanish boots and intimate clamps, and the healing unguents used after chastisement. It was these ointments which my Governess rubbed on my bottom every night, and I loved their cooling solace as much as the caress of her hands on my naked bottom.

'And as I read Miss Bright's book, I found my clit tingling, just as when I was caned, and fingered myself lovingly. When I read the description of a young lady taking a public tawsing of sixty on bare, her knickers at her ankles, followed by a caning of twenty-one, I thrilled to imagine myself in her place – to be watched by all – and masturbated myself to orgasm for the very first time! I read the book and masturbated every night after my beatings. My face wore a serene smile, and after the special beatings she made a special "bravery cake" for me, and said that there were other books I should read. She knew I had been masturbating, and was happy for me.

'The books told fearful yet compelling stories, of the sailors taking the cat-o'-nine-tails on their bare backs, tied to the mainmast, amid the lonely ocean, and I thought that awfully sad and brave and thrilling. Then there were the flogging contests where the young men of ancient Sparta would be bound naked and flogged without limit in honour of the goddess. I read Miss Bright's formula for young men's correction. My Governess asked if I had masturbated at these descriptions and I blushed and said I had masturbated quite a lot. I was excited by Miss Bright's recommendation that a rowdy male be tamed by female robes for his chastisement.

'My Governess said this was sound, and it was time I learnt about the male ego and its treatment. I said mischievously that the male ego and the male bum seemed to be one and the same thing, and she said it was. She said that a particular young man should come to tea one day soon . . . I had met him in the village a few times, and I was fond of him, though shy. My Governess said he would be sure to accept her invitation. I was thrilled and could hardly wait. I was allowed to dress grown-up now, and bought myself a lovely little black dress, not quite a mini, but quite high, and fabulous black stockings and really scrumptious red shoes which I thought daring.'

Miss Furbelow interrupted with three cane strokes to bare bum, 'for vanity', and Henrietta whipped her twice on breasts and quim; she squealed in surprise and sobbed.

'He arrived on the appointed afternoon, very polite in a grey suit and tie, and a bunch of flowers for me and one for my Governess. She made a fabulous tea, and I spilt lots of crumbs in my nervousness. The tea tasted unusually nice, and my Governess made sure I had three cups, and I was worried I should have to excuse myself to pee. I think he was nervous too. He told me he intended to join the Air Force. How I longed to be up in the air beside him!'

She yelled suddenly as four fierce strokes cut her bare, and Henrietta applied three whiplashes to her front, which was now striping nicely, the bare hillock of the quim well flushed and mottled, and Miss Furbelow said females were creatures of the Earth and sea; the air was for males.

'O! How it smarts, Mistress! ... Well, my Governess bustled merrily in and out, and suddenly she jogged his elbow, and he spilt his tea all over me, wetting my new dress and my stockings and knickers too! I was mortified, but my Governess was cold and furious. She said he was a disgrace and had insulted her house, and more, and I tried to say it was all right, but she hushed me and said he must be punished as a naughty boy, and make amends. He offered to pay to have my dress cleaned but that added to the insult, and after a hushed conversation between the two, it was agreed to my astonishment that he was to atone by taking a beating . . . from my cane! I cannot say I was displeased, or that my quim did not moisten at this lovely thought.

'I had never beaten anyone before, let alone a male, and I tried to imitate my Governess. I became all stern and said he was to bend over the sofa. My Governess said that I must not forget to instruct him about his clothing. She closed the curtains and lit a scented candle, as though for some sacred ritual, and I realised she meant he was to be caned on the bare. My quim began to trickle with hot moisture as I told him in a shaky voice that he was to bend over, then lower his trousers and panties to his ankles.

'I admit I was curious to see his cock, this mysterious organ which, according to Miss Bright, had a tendency to stand up under a lady's rod if the beating were not stern enough . . . He obeyed, very shy and trembling, and showed me the most delicious bum, two golden fesses that I just wanted to flog until they melted, then lick them all up and kiss them better! I swallowed hard and took hold of the heaviest cane! With all my strength, I laid a stroke that slanted across his bottom and blushed him. He groaned and his bum clenched, but I was told to aim straighter.

'I got my aim right, and soon I was beating this naked male as though born to it. He was to take full twenty-one and I was determined to relish every stroke, for by the fourth or fifth my quim and panties were sopping wet and my clitty stiff as a button! Each stroke made him jerk away from the sofa, and his legs straightened with his pain, and I saw to my delight that his cock was stiff! It was wonderful! His balls so sweet and tight, and that big frightening shaft all pink and hard as a lance, except that it wasn't frightening, for my cane made me in control. At the twelfth stroke, my Governess interrupted, and said his state was unseemly. If my flogging were not hard enough, we would use Miss Bright's method.

'She brought a dress, panties, stockings, and even a bra, and made him strip, and put on a maid's frilly skirt and apron. Now I had the pleasure of lowering the pink panties and white stockings, as he teetered on his unfamiliar high heels. His flushed bottom faced me again, and I continued to beat him as hard as I could, loving his delicious squirming and the trickling in my fount, until his bare bum was dark crimson. But still his cock stood! My Governess stood watching intently, with her arms folded, but I could tell she was excited by her flushed face and her fingers stroking her breast and nipples. I felt glorious in fierce control, and when I landed the final stroke on that bruised male arse, I thought myself a Governess!

'He tried to conceal his cock, still rampant, but my Governess stayed his hand and touched his naked cock, on his bulb! She said I should learn the proper method of correcting an unseemly male, and ordered him to lie down on the floor on his back. He did so, his cock up in the air like a lovely curving pole, and suddenly, my Governess had her skirts up and was squatting over him with her knickers down, as though to evacuate! She took her own swollen quim lips in her fingers and parted them, then gently lowered herself on the male's cock. He moaned and rolled his eyes and I thought him soppy, but my quim was gushing now and I pushed my fingers into my panties on to my throbbing clit.

'Spasms of pleasure flooded me, and I began to frot as I watched my Governess straddle the male, his organ glistening with her cascade of love-oil; she slid him very slowly in and out of her slit, at the same time masturbating herself on clitty and squeezing his balls as though milking them. I masturbated freely, and she looked at me with a knowing smile. Our clits were accomplices in our lustful masturbation! He began to wriggle and groan, and I thrilled at the male's submission, and then he cried out, and my Governess raised herself slightly and freed the tip of his cock, grasping his shaft with her hand and rubbing it fiercely so that his cream spurted in a great jet over her quim and knickers, and at that moment my frotting made me climax in the sweetest orgasm. I was breathless, and the scented candle smoke seemed to fill and inspire me.

'My Governess rose, and said that a male had more spunk than one milking could drain: the time had come for me to give up my precious cherry, blessedly under her control. I needed little encouragement. I had dreamed of this! Still glowing with my orgasm, I continued to masturbate as I pulled down my wet knickers and squatted over his soft member. She showed me how to rub and tickle him so that he would stiffen again, and I marvelled how easy it was. She whispered that I was not to worry – her special herbal tea would prevent any "eventuality". I smiled at her connivance, and watched her put her head to his bulb and suck his soft cock into hardness, while I squatted and frigged shamelessly, my quim touching her bobbing hair.

'She withdrew, and I sank down on the stiff cock. It thrust all the way inside me in a rush, and I felt a moment's pain as my membrane popped, but nothing to the glorious pleasure of being filled by that hot stiff flesh! I masturbated copiously as I bounced on him, feeling the throbbing bulb of his cock nuzzling at the mouth of my womb as I watched the flow of my love-juices over his balls. I came again before I felt his first hot drops inside me. My Governess told me to squeeze with the walls of my quim, and I was rewarded with a wonderful gush of hot sticky cream that made me come once more in a glorious gasping spasm.

'When it was over, and we were all dressed, we finished our tea quite decorously, my lustful glances meeting with shy blushes on his part, and my feeling of wickedness added to my enjoyment! It was only when my Governess was closing the door on our departing guest that I saw him slip a paper into her blouse: it was a cheque! Then I understood the nature of the event which had so beautifully transformed my life: that a male must be subdued for his pleasure, and that of his Mistress, and that he must pay token of his submission. Thereafter, we entertained numerous gentlemen to tea, and treatment; my Governess and I were indeed accomplices, with a financial arrangement agreeable to us both. Nursing is the kindness of true discipline, and it is also the business of healing with strokes ... Thus were my studies as Nurse enhanced by lucrative hygienic treatment to the naked bottoms of submissive males. I admit that, at one time, I even put a card in a phone box, for curiosity, and was positively inundated with callers. I felt truly Nurse!'

'You have merited full cleansing,' murmured the Mistress.

She began to flog the naked bottom rhythmically and hard, until the woman was jumping loudly against the walls of her prison. Henrietta, openly lustful, began to flog her naked quim and teats, darkening them to a lovely puffy purple as she unashamedly masturbated. The woman groaned, but managed to continue speaking even as she jumped in torment at her naked beating. Miss Furbelow seemed lost in her disciplinary frenzy, as though she were outraged and jealous at the nonchalance of her victim and her story.

'I do not know if he ever joined the Air Force,' the kraken gasped, 'but I imagine him flying high, his lovely bum smarting from other thoughtful Mistresses ...'

Suddenly, her cries turned from pain to triumph.

'There! The sea-monster has spoken under lash, until the first sun has illumined the cell – he peeps through the third bar, and the old lore says I am now Mistress, and claim my forfeit.'

Miss Furbelow paled in a surprised, angry grimace.

'I admit your truth,' she said. 'You gain forfeit.'

She stopped the beating, and let her cane dangle, then ordered that the brass prison be opened. Panting like a mare, Henrietta let her whip rest. The cup was removed from beneath the woman's quim: it overflowed with her juice, and was solemnly passed to each female of the company, who anointed her lips with the salty fluid, and Miss Furbelow proclaimed that woman had drunk of the sea of woman. The masked woman emerged, rubbing her inflamed nates and breasts, and hopping in agony, her cheeks wet with tears.

'Miss Furbelow, you shall take no less than I, and from a new and sweeter rod: that of the stern Nurse Riding. Lower stockings and knickers, please, and touch toes. Nurse Riding, you shall please take up the flail and the cane which have blessed me, and bless the Mistress in her turn. Her set will be thirty-nine each with cane and whip, the strokes alternate and on full bare: fesses, thighs and back.'

Miss Furbelow shivered and looked round, but the company's eyes were unforgiving.

'The old rules,' murmured Virginia.

'Yes,' whispered Miss Furbelow, taking off her glasses and stowing them in her breast pocket. 'The old rules.'

She took position, raised her grey skirt right up over her shoulders, until all of her back, and her taut bare buttocks, shone like a beacon to Prue's eager eyes. She looked at the masked woman and received a piercing stare. She would not fail her. Slowly, Miss Furbelow lowered her panties, which Prue saw were well moist, and fumbled with her stockings to let them fall to her splayed ankles.

'Nurse Riding?' whispered Miss Furbelow. 'I beg you –'

'Do not beg for mercy,' snapped Prue.

'I beg you, flog me on the bare, until I faint,' said the Mistress of Hell Fur Leather.

* * *

It was a chilly dawn as the party of nurses spilled into the driveway of the Hell Fur Leather Club. Prue suddenly realised that in all Northumberland, or Norgjmerland, they were unlikely to find a taxi at this time of the morning. The twins said not to worry, the High Mistress had sent her carriage. They showed Jess and Prue to an open wagon, sumptuous but unhorsed. The twins disappeared, and returned moments later with Henrietta and Miss Gageby, both wearing bridle and bit, just like ponies. Henrietta was splendidly nude, and Miss Gageby proudly displayed Prue's mauve underthings! They had heavy horseshoes, and just like ponies were smiling and clumping their shoes and frisking as they were harnessed to the carriage. Miss Furbelow appeared, her face flushed and radiant, and her gait very stiff, as she supervised Tallinn and Jeremy, loading a bundle into the carriage, which they said was a package for High Mistress of Hydro. Virginia blew a kiss at Prue, and said she must not forget to call.

'Thank you, Nurse Furbelow,' chorused the twins, and took off their wigs to wave a salutation.

'Nurse . . . ?' said Prue, and they giggled.

'Of course. She is one of us, Nurse Prudence. You have just visited Hydro's special dungeon, and Nurse Furbelow is its Mistress . . .'

The package squirmed and shifted, and Prue saw the masked nude woman, the kraken, now tightly bound in adhesive tape, her bruised body beautiful as a silkworm in a shiny cocoon of gleaming clingfilm. Helen and Angela climbed into the front seat, cracked a whip which snaked beautifully across the ponies' naked rumps, and ordered them to step off at a high canter. They did so, pumping knees and thighs as they pulled the carriage quite fast down the driveway. Henrietta seemed happy that she had been found worthy of proper humiliation, and Miss Gageby looked at her sister pony adoringly.

'I think last night should qualify me for membership of the 11.59ers,' Prue said as they approached Hydro.

Barker was asleep at her post, and her digital clock read 11.59. Jess laughed.

''fraid not,' she said. 'Barker's clock seems to have stopped, so it doesn't count.'

'O, rats!' cried Prue.

At the main entrance, they were greeted by Miss Bream.

'11.59 by Barker's clock,' she said with a mischievous smile, 'so you have just made it, Nurses. I believe you have a package for me.'

'We have a package for the High Mistress, Matron,' said Prue, as the twins gently unloaded the gleaming wrapped bundle of whipped flesh.

'In a manner of speaking,' said Miss Bream. 'You see, Nurse Riding, this *is* the High Mistress.'

12

Down at Heel

'Virginia?' said a male voice on the telephone.

'Isn't this her private number?' snapped Prue.

'O, *Virginia*,' said the voice, and chuckled.

A moment later, she heard Virginia's gentle contralto.

'Nurse Prudence! I have been so impatient for you to call, I was even thinking rude thoughts about your neglect ... O my! I guess that means I have been naughty.'

'Yes, Miss Virginia,' said Prudence, 'I confess I am shocked. Your unclean thoughts merit correction.'

'Then perhaps you would be gracious enough to visit me, Nurse? I know you are busy, treating your subjects, and I am so jealous of them.'

'Jealousy too is an unclean emotion,' said Prue, 'and I am not too busy to chastise you for it. My schedule permits me to attend you this afternoon at two.'

Virginia sighed happily, and said she would send a car for her at 13.45. Prue agreed.

She was still a little miffed that the events at Hell Fur Leather didn't count for her coveted entry to the 11.59 club. The club was the very dungeon of Hydro itself – Miss Furbelow the nurse in charge, so that didn't count, and it doubly didn't count because Barker's clock had stopped.

A saloon car punctually arrived, driven by a young man in a dark suit. Prue wore a long blue raincoat, and her best Nurse's uniform underneath, bonnet perched jauntily on her blonde tresses. Underneath, she had a corselage, a tight black satin waspie from Miss Macardle's hygienic collection, with pointed cones of steel for bra-cups, and an open crotch. Her stockings were black too, and she had shaved specially well, her fount-lips gleaming pink and full at her bare mound. Her briefcase held implements of treatment, and a pair of soft roll-up thigh-boots in calfskin.

'Why ... Lieutenant Raitte!' she cried as the driver greeted her. 'I hardly recognised you ... out of uniform!'

The car gunned down the driveway and past the glowering Barker, who had the gate already open for them. Her clock still read 11.59, as though the High Mistress had little interest, or influence, in its repair.

'They prefer us to be in civvies, off the base,' said Raitte, turning the car up away from town along the cliff road. 'It is more discreet, you see.'

'The air base?' cried Prue. 'Is that where we are going?'

'Yes, Mistress – I mean, yes, Nurse,' said Raitte.

They turned inland, across a bleak moor, and came to 'Road Closed' signs warning them of bloodcurdling penalties for trespassers. When they passed a high wire fence, with searchlights and guard dogs, and stopped at a checkpoint manned by gleaming military policemen, Prue saw a great expanse of hangars, airstrips and buildings, all drab grey. There were a few planes and helicopters parked seemingly at random, and the hangars were either closed, or their contents shrouded in tarpaulins. They drove past endless barracks, huts and administrative buildings. The airmen ignored her as they plodded about their duties. They came to a large administration complex, and slowed for the parking lot, which was full of American limousines. She looked at one, a huge stretched Lincoln Continental with the Stars and Stripes, parked in a space marked 'Colonel Virgil V. Althond, USAF', and beside it a gleaming Rolls-Royce with the Union Flag. They parked, and Lt Raitte escorted her into the gaunt grey building, which smelt and echoed like administrative blocks everywhere, until they passed through to the other side, to a courtyard with a fountain and flowers, and at the far end an old timbered house, which Raitte explained was the orginal Goodenhall Manor.

'Now it is the Ladies' Quarters,' he said, 'and the – and Virginia will attend you there. I wish I were permitted to attend you myself, Mistress – Nurse – but my duties . . . There is an exercise scheduled in a couple of hours.'

She touched his lips as he showed her into the shady, flower-decked vestibule of the Ladies' Quarters.

'You may call me Mistress, boy,' she said.

She was shown into a sweet little chamber, with flowers everywhere, a bed with starched crisp linen, a privy, and a view over a lush arbour.

'If you care to freshen up . . .' said Raitte vaguely, 'you will be attended in a moment, Mistress.'

She permitted the young man to kneel and kiss her toecaps before he scurried off to his 'exercise'. Then she yawned, and stretched herself. The small, timbered house was not empty; she heard girls' voices, and some male ones, and the clatter of high heels in the corridors. There was the dim hubbub of a bar, with clinking glasses. She started to rummage idly in the drawers and cupboards of her new home, however temporary it was. The room was perfumed, but musty, as though no one had been here for a while. The drawers were empty, but then she found a small suitcase in the wardrobe, and opened it. There were some lovely silk stockings and panties, still musky from their wearer's perfume, and a bit soiled. There was a skirt and a blouse, and a waspie corset just like Prue's own, and the same size.

Underneath these things was a double dildo, a four-thonged whip, a short crook cane, and what seemed a rather brutal cock-harness, designed for a male with plenty of inches. And there was a gas mask! There was also a letter, which she unfolded.

'Darling Mistress Wendy,' it started. 'How stiff my cock is for your touch and your chastisement! The punishment for my impudent tattoos must be without end. How my ass longs to feel the strokes of your cruel cane! My lips long to kiss your boots trampling me like the no-good worm I am! I am the naughtiest girl in the world and my croup needs your purgation. Make me smart to busting with your white-hot rod, for no Mistress is as cruel, no goddess so powerful . . .'

The letter gushed on in the same vein, and Prue skipped to the signature: 'Your slave for ever – Virginia'.

Prue frowned, and stroked her chin for a while. Then she rose, and made her way to the bar at the end of the hall. She found herself, not in a chintzy ladies' place, but in an old-fashioned beer-and-sawdust pub. There was a group of uniformed air force officers at the bar, drinking pints of beer, while some played pool or darts. But most of the customers were ladies, and while a few propped up the bar and talked easily with the males, most sat gossiping at tables. They seemed to prefer pints of beer too.

She bought one herself, sat down discreetly close to the largest group of females, and pretended not to eavesdrop. Oddly, they were all gorgeously dressed, in sequins and shimmering satins, earrings and maquillage, as though on their way to a ball, and not in a dusty air base pub at two in the afternoon. They were talking about a free fall parachute display – apparently the exercise scheduled for that afternoon – and whether the cloud cover would affect things. Prue said loudly that she had never seen a parachute display, and was admitted to the conversation.

'So you're a nurse! How wonderful! For Virginia?'

There were knowing winks.

'*She*'ll give you a hard time ... Don't let her show you her tattoos.'

'Don't let yourself become one!'

There was coarse but not unfriendly laughter, and she asked if a friend of hers, Wendy, had been round lately.

'Wendy? Blonde lass, from the Hydro? Your sort of build? Yes, Virginia likes them that way. Haven't seen her for a while. Maybe she wore her out!'

'Or maybe *she* wore *her* out!'

There was more raucous laughter, in which Prue joined. She felt them scrutinising her dress, like women, and spookily undressing her with their eyes, too, as men did. And then – she spluttered in her beer. They *were* men! She was rescued from further enquiry by the arrival of Jeremy Pleasant, in a plain blue skirt and sweater, with sensible shoes and stockings, like a servicewoman. He was greeted with cries of 'Hi, Gemma!' and was very flustered.

'Nurse Riding!' he said. 'I'm glad I've found you ... Virginia sends her apologies, it's a meeting to do with the air display, and she'll be some time.'

Prue rose and nodded civilly to the 'she-males', then said that Jeremy might escort her back to her quarters. He did so, and when she shut the door, she opened her bag and took out a long, thin, whippy cane and cracked it on the starched linen bed, sending up an eddy of dust.

'I am cross at being kept waiting, and with you – with all of you! Men – officers – dressed as women! Enough mysteries! I want explanations.'

She waved the letter at him, and demanded who Wendy was.

'I ... I honestly don't know, Nurse,' he stammered. 'She came from Hydro, to give treatment to Virginia, that's all.'

'More to the point, who is Virginia?' snapped Prue, swishing the cane again.

Jeremy held out a sealed blue envelope, addressed to Prue. It made the crackle of banknotes.

'Virginia sent your nursing fee,' he said.

'I warn you, a nurse does not expect to be treated so disdainfully, and does not intend to leave without seeing at least one bare bum corrected! Virginia's, or yours!'

The young man gulped.

'Virginia,' he said, 'is the big boss. "She", as we call her. Colonel Virgil V. Althond, USAF.'

Prue felt her envelope again. The banknotes were large.

'Well, Lieutenant Pleasant,' she said, somewhat more gently, 'it seems I shall have to wait for Colonel *Virginia*. I'm not sure I shouldn't take the cane to you, sir, for your casual attitude . . . or just to pass the time.'

Jeremy blushed, and smiled shyly.

'Would you, Nurse?' he murmured. 'O, would you? I haven't had treatment for . . . it seems ages!'

'And they let you fly planes with such a weak memory!' she cried. 'You have forgotten about Hell Fur Leather.'

'O, that,' said Jeremy. 'Please, Mistress . . .'

'I didn't give you permission to call me Mistress!' she rapped. 'That insolence certainly deserves correction.'

Her fount was beginning to tingle just a little.

'Yes, Miss – I mean, Nurse,' he said eagerly. 'Please order me to lift my skirt for you.'

'I suppose it is Nurse's Duty to inspect your previous treatment,' she said. 'Very well, *Miss*. Strip to bare, please, and bend over.'

Joyfully, the young man lifted his plain skirt, showing a tight thong of frilly pink lace in contrast. She ordered him to strip this completely, and unfasten his stockings. He stepped out of the panties and kicked them aside, then fumbled with his straps and assumed position. She licked her lips. His bum still glowed from the events at Miss Furbelow's, and her quim began to seep warm

220

moisture as she ran her palms over the mottled arse-globes.

'Well, I think your impudence could deserve a treatment,' she said thoughtfully. 'We should have time for a quick set before Virginia comes – say fifteen? But you must promise to tell me afterwards what this place really is, and what you and your beautifully dressed friends really are.'

He nodded eagerly; without ceremony, she lifted the cane and delivered fifteen strokes in rapid order to his bare buttocks. He made no sound, save a first little gasp of shock, but shivered in ecstatic relief as she caned his bare, and his cock rose. Prue's free hand strayed between her legs and touched her stiffening clit. When he had taken the fifteen, she made him sit beside her on the bed, and put her hand in his lap. She asked for the promised explanations.

'There is nothing sinister, Nurse. Goodenhall is a proper air base, under joint command. It's just that the personnel are ... rather special. Servicemen have the same urges as other men, including the urge to robe ourselves as ladies – and that is more than most people think.'

Prue was reminded of Miss Bright's observation that males appreciated being disciplined when robed as females ...

'And the RAF has always been tolerant of so-called eccentricity. As for the Americans, why, they have to be politically correct these days, and you can't discriminate against anybody, for anything. So here we are, tucked away in Northumberland. Happy and, thanks to the nurses of Hydro ... well disciplined. We have our own games and punishments, of course – the Americans are particularly fond of a "bare-ass paddling" – but it's only horseplay. Nothing surpasses a lady's touch. There is a magical day in every man's life when he discovers the true beauty of women, and the beauty of submitting to them; and his own vain need, not just to feel the touch of the beings he worships, but to feel *like* them.'

Prue cupped Jeremy's balls, and squeezed a little, making him moan and nestle his face at her breast. His male scent, and the hot stiffness of his cock against her body, made her quite wet. Jeremy blurted that it was his sweetest dream, to be robed as female, and flirted with, felt and caressed most intimately, by a stern and demanding lady!

'It is rather nice, to have a slave male robed, and submitting to caress,' said Prue thoughtfully. 'I can understand the love men have of female clothing, their crude excitement as they penetrate the divine recesses of knicker and stocking and silky things . . . And now, as we wait, you will tell me the truth of how *your* magical moment . . .'

'O! Well, I had left school,' murmured Jeremy, 'and I had the summer to spend before RAF College. To earn money, I did odd jobs round the village – near Chatham – gardening and so on. I did some gardening for a lady called Mrs Crowe, who had a cottage outside the village. It was one of those roses and honeysuckle places, and her husband was something up in London, mobile phone and striped suit . . . you know.'

'I know,' said Prue, stroking his stiff cock and tickling the tight balls, making him sigh.

'I had to do jobs like pruning, and digging, and I could have done them all at once, really, but she kept thinking of new things for me to do. She always gave me a cup of tea in her kitchen, afterwards, and she would smile very quietly at me, like a sphinx. I was shy. She was lovely, Nurse. Very shiny brown hair, and a very . . . regal figure. One afternoon, she set me to doing the rose bushes, just beside her bathroom window. It was very hot, and I had my shirt off. I heard the noise of water, and knew she was taking a bath. Then – I just peeked, I told myself by accident – and she was nude, in the bath, sitting with her thighs parted and her mink all glistening and wet, and washing herself there. It was such a lovely thick mink, all beautiful brown curls, and her thighs were so firm and pale and creamy . . . I made it more than a peek, Nurse. She began to soap herself, there on her lady's place, and then soaped her breasts too. They were very big, with wide brown nipples, and she took a long time rubbing herself, flopping her breasts up and down and from side to side, and squeezing her nips, as though they were her cuddly toys. Then she lifted up her arms and began to shave her pits, and trimmed her mink-hairs too, blowing the hairs from the razor as though she were blowing soap bubbles towards me, though she was looking everywhere *except* at me.

'She turned round in the bath, and lifted her bum in the air, all wet and pink and shiny, and parted her furrow, and began to trim the hairs on her bumhole! I was frozen with wonder. I had never seen such a thing! After that, she sat down facing me again, and took a pair of scissors to cut her fingernails, then squatted and bent her leg up to trim her toenails, very slowly, and taking the nails off in one slice, rather than clipping them. She put the nails carefully at the side of the bath. I don't know, Nurse, but I felt myself getting stiff as I watched her cut her toenails, and . . . and I longed suddenly to lick the nail slices, or to lie down and take her feet into my mouth while she stood crushing me with the weight of her nude body, and smiling cruelly with those rosebud lips!

'Suddenly, she stood up from her bath, and bent down, showing me her quim and bumhole, to take the plug out. She stopped in that position as though it would take a long time to pull out a plug, and all the time I watched her bottom shivering and swaying, as if on purpose. Then she turned round and, very calmly, walked to the window to shut it. I had no time to turn;

she looked out of the window, not at my face, which was beetroot, but down, at my bulging crotch! And she smiled very slightly to herself and shut the window.

'I was in such confusion – I went back to work until she called me in to tea as usual, and I went to get my shirt, but she told me I didn't need to put on false modesty just for her. She was sitting at the table, with her legs crossed and one hand on her lap under the table. With the other, she poured tea and told me to sit down. She was wearing a nice white blouse and a swirly cotton skirt with a flower print, and white stockings. She said wasn't it very hot and stockings a bit silly.'

' "But I have taken off my knickers," she said calmly. "It's cooler, and a lady's biscuit must be well cooled."

'I had never heard a lady's place called a biscuit, and was astonished, the more so when she said, "Does the heat give you an erection, Jeremy? Or was it the sight of me in the bathroom?"

'I started to mumble some excuses, knowing that I had none, so I drank down my tea and said I should leave.

' "Not so fast," she said with a funny smile that was very beguiling. "You must have a biscuit with your tea. Jeremy, I am sorry to say, you have been a very naughty boy, peeping at me. What will Miles say?"

'Miles was her husband. I wasn't afraid, but I didn't like that "will". I begged her not to tell him, said I was sorry, and she told me to prove it, by kneeling before her and apologise for being such a horrid little worm. I obeyed, awfully excited, and then, in a cold, imperious voice, she ordered me to lick her feet: she was wearing shiny shoes with sharp points and high heels, in white leather, and I licked them, and on her orders took the toes in my mouth and sucked them, making little gurgling noises which she said would indicate my apology. Her feet smelled sweaty and ripe, despite her bath. When I was sucking her toes, my erection came back! She told me to rise, and I half turned away in embarrassment, but she saw, and smiled cruelly.

'Then she lifted her hand from her lap, and she was holding a cane! It was a black sinister thing, about three feet long, with a crook handle, and she said I must know what this was. I nodded; she said that if I atoned for my rudeness, all would be forgiven. Surely I had been caned at school, and could take it like a big strong boy? I said that there was no cane at my school these days.

' "More is the pity," she said. "A boy like you, his bottom virgin to the rod. Well, I'll correct that, won't I, Jeremy? Do you accept my punishment for your rudeness?"

'I was so confused and miserable! And yet ... I somehow *wanted* this gorgeous, stern female to beat me for my shame. So I said that if that would satisfy her, I would take the cane. I held out my hands, but she laughed, and said that a caning was on the bottom. She turned round in her chair and ordered me to bend over her knee. Trembling, I did so, and smelled her fragrance, all flowers and summer warmth, and I could not stop my cock standing so very stiff! I lay on her knee and felt her fingers fumble at my belt.

' "Pants down, boy," she murmured, "it'll be on the bare."

'I let her strip me – how sweet it was to obey that cruel voice! – then felt the cool air on my naked bum. I was so ashamed, yet thrilled at my shame. I heard her flex the cane, then take a sip of tea, teasing me. There was silence in the kitchen, broken only by the birdsong and the tinkle of her teacup, and I was trembling as I waited for the cut of the cane on my bare bum. Waited as I knew I had always waited – to be helpless in the power of a strong woman!

'The cane whistled without warning, and I felt my skin laced by white-hot fire. It was indescribably painful, and I let out a great yelp. She told me angrily that I must not be soppy, that I could clench my bum if I wanted, and even wriggle a tiny bit, but I must make no noise, or else what would the neighbours think? I nodded miserably, and then the second cut landed, and it hurt ten times as much as the first! I couldn't help but squirm, and my bottom wriggled and clenched, but I could not drive away the terrible pain! Tears were streaming down my cheeks, and again and again she scored my bare, until my whole bottom felt on fire.

'She laughed, and said she liked to see men squirm so helplessly as she hurt them. Some women liked to tease, and hurt in the heart, but she liked to hurt where it really smarted, on the bare bum. I took great gulps of air, and each time my lungs filled with her flowery fragrance, and the ripe smell of her feet below. Her skirt rode up over her stockings. I peeked, and through my blurred eyes I saw her garters and suspender belt, and the thick trimmed fur of her mink, with her fingers buried in it, at her quim, and moving very gently as she tickled herself on her lady's place. Her knickers were lying on the floor behind her, where she had dropped them. I thought of those silky panties sliding ever so slowly down her bare thighs, and I felt my cock was stiff to bursting. I asked how many strokes it was.

' "O, there is far more to come, Jeremy," she said, delivering another really tight cut that had my eyes streaming. "Normally, a beating would be a baker's dozen – that's what I give Miles, when he is naughty – but you have such a juicy virgin bum, it seems a shame to waste this fine afternoon on such short treatment. Let us say, at my discretion – that is, until I get bored. Or to be sporting, until your erection softens. You'll get used to it."

'She tickled my balls, and said how tight they were. I moaned that I did not think my erection would ever soften.

' "Perhaps my beating excites you, Jeremy, because

226

care for you enough to punish you properly. A married woman! Luckily, Miles doesn't get home until I pick him up in the Volvo, so we have plenty of time for me to punish you for your naughtiness. Naughty boys today aren't thrashed as they should be, by a lady who *cares* about *disciplining* the male."

'On the last word, she cut me twice, thwap-thwap! in rapid succession, and I groaned in sheer agony. Yet I felt a strange thing, as though the spunk were welling up in my balls. How could such pain make me so exalted? After a while, she said I could rest, but not get up, and I heard her sipping tea once more, but the cup trembled. She brought it down to my lips, and let me sip, saying I was her prisoner in chains. O, Nurse, it was so lovely to be her slave, the plaything of a cruel Mistress! At the same time, I could feel the lovely swish of her stockinged thighs move as she caressed herself on her fount. I was imprisoned in the mystery of a lady, embraced by the smoothness of her stockings and the ripe sweet odours of her panties and her shiny leather shoes. I wanted those shoes to trample me, her toecaps to dig into my flesh, my mouth, my very balls and cock! How ashamed yet free I felt, her worthless toy, wrapped amidst her scented garments! After a few minutes, the beating started again, much harder and fiercer now, and I felt her thighs squirm and shift quite rapidly. There was a delicious smoky perfume coming from her lady's place, salty and sweet at once, and ... O, I can't describe it.'

'I know that perfume, Jeremy,' said Prue. 'I am a woman as well as a nurse, remember?'

Prue's own quim was flowing copiously at his words, and she began to flick her stiff clitty quite firmly.

'And Mrs Crowe was right – I was getting used to it! The pain seemed to have reached a plateau, and I felt it become part of me and I did not want it to stop. It was *her* gift to me! She beat me and beat me, so cruelly, and yet she stroked my hair between lashes, and told me I was quite a good subject. To take *her* cane on the bare seemed such a privilege. I felt my spunk coming, I knew I was going to spurt, and she sensed that – women *know* – for she suddenly took off her shoe and picked up her panties and placed them carefully inside her shoe. She put her shoe on my cock, with the panties in it, like a glove. It was narrow, and the silk of the panties squeezed my bulb, and I felt her fingers pressing the lovely soft leather on my balls, and moving my cock up and down, very firmly, while she continued to beat me, making her strokes in time with the sharp squeezes to my cock. I clutched her feet, one shod and the other stockinged, and – O, Nurse! – I spurted my cream into her precious lovely shoe!

'I was all soft and soppy, and said I wanted to kiss her in thanks, and she let me go, after one sharp cut to my bum, and said I was nice and crimson now, and could thank her properly for my punishment. I knelt again; she pressed my face to her fount, and buried my mouth in her forest of smelly wet curls. I had never dreamt of such beauty, but she guided me; I felt her little acorn all stiff and wet between the big fleshy folds of her quim, and she made me lick her there with the tip of my tongue. As I flicked, she moaned, and her belly trembled and her quim flowed on me.

'She stroked my bare bottom, and said I was very hot and sore, and I got a slow rubbing of cold cream, and then my cock was half standing, as though I hadn't spurted at all. She tapped it, and asked if I had ever done it with a girl before, all the way, as she put it, and I was ashamed, for I hadn't. So I lay on the carpet on my back, still with my jeans around my ankles, and she rubbed my cock and tickled my balls until I stood really hard again. She was so wonderfully efficient and impersonal, like a nurse.

'I felt helpless in her control. I lay back, and she

climbed on top of me, squatting and pulling her skirt up, and showing her quim all glistening with juices. Her stocking tops were wet, and her garters too, and then she undid her blouse right down to her belly button, and let her breasts flop out like two lovely big meringues. Her nips were all stiff like fruits, and she took her panties from her shoe, put the shoe back on, then began to rub her breasts with the panties until they were as shiny as her lady's place. All the time, her lips sneered as though I were just a thing, to be used for her own curiosity. I told her she could do what she wanted with me, as I was her slave. "I know," she said, and her words, and look of disdain were the most thrilling experience of my life.

'She opened the lips of her quim very wide, and I could see all the lovely shiny wet pink, that I had kissed and tongued, and as she rubbed her breasts she began to play with her clit again, tickling her with little grunts of pleasure as she squatted with her slit just an inch from my cock. She was teasing me again, I could tell from her sardonic mouth and her dancing eyes – she knew I longed to feel that wet place engulf my cock, and swallow me whole. Suddenly she lowered herself on to my cock, so that I sank into her hot wet gash, right to my hilt, and felt her quim lips squashing my balls. Her whole weight was crushing me.

'Then she swung her long legs up and put both her spike heels hard in my mouth, and told me to suck them. As I did so, she ground her heels on my tongue, quite harshly, and began to move up and down, her bum and thighs pressing my balls, and squeezing my cock with a control that made her quim seem like a hot wet vice. She told me not to move, then bent over towards me so that her breasts hung down between her thighs, and said that she would milk me, and I was to milk her too. She made me squeeze her nipples and pull them like a cow's teats as she rocked on me, gasping harshly as she ground her feet in my helpless open mouth.

'When she sensed me tensing to spurt, she lowered her hand to the base of my cock, which she squeezed very firmly and rapidly, until I felt my spurt ebb away, and she could start her milking over again. At the same time she fingered her clit, which stood all pink and gleaming like a little soldier in his chariot. I could feel her love-juice flowing on my balls, as though she had wet herself all over me – in my dreams! – and it was gentle as a perfumed ocean.

' "O, Mrs Crowe," I moaned through her wriggling heels, until she told me I was privileged to call her Mistress, though I must only do so when we were alone. My heart leapt – that meant there was to be another time! I had forgotten all about the world, there was no one but me, squirming under my Mistress. I watched her play with her clit as she writhed on my balls and shaft, and heaving rapidly as she came in a lovely shivering spasm, and when she did, her juices flowed like a river. But always she kept me hard by pressing my shaft with severe fingers; I felt my balls would burst with my spunk which longed to bathe her!

'I made the motions of a kiss to her lips, but she slapped my balls hard and said sternly that a slave must never think of kissing his Mistress. At last she let me spurt inside her, and I thought I should die as the honeyed milk flowed from my balls in worship. I was still not allowed to depart. She brought her slave a dish of biscuits, which I had to eat on the floor, like a cat, with my bum in the air, and she stroked my arse with her palm as I ate.

'She seemed playfully disdainful of me, for being so soft and adoring of her cruelty. Still crouching, I had a glass of wine, then she spilled some on her breasts and made me kneel and lick it off, taking the nips in my mouth and chewing them hard, which made her pant and sigh. Then I was given a hand-spanking on my bare, just because she felt like it, about a hundred slaps and real stingers, for I was still smarting from her cane. How proud I was that a dominant lady was pleased to spank me! After that I had to lick her biscuit again until she came, and this time she was sitting on the chair with her thighs apart and her feet raised; she had my stiff cock between the soles of her shoes and was frotting me, but so delicately that she stopped me from spurting until she had come herself . . . and then she permitted me to spurt in adoration all over her shoes, and made me hold them up to her lips, her stockinged feet pressed in my balls, while she rubbed the shoes clean on her breasts, and I slid them back on her soft, moist stockinged feet.

'She made me turn round, squatting on her upturned toecap. I was ordered to lower myself, and imagine my shock when I felt the point of her shoe inserted into my bumhole, and she began to wiggle it inside me quite deep. Her other foot dealt little kicks to the bulb of my cock, which was standing quite clean and bare of the foreskin. She would tap me right on the peehole with her toecap, and it was so unbearably thrilling that I begged her to cane me again, to calm me! That sounds crazy, doesn't it?'

'No, Jeremy, it sounds sweet,' said Prue.

'So, as she sat on the chair, I knelt and tongued her clitty, her thighs squeezing me so powerfully that I felt quite suffocated and it was all dark in that soft perfumed cavern. I was in awe that woman could come so much . . . I felt both her feet frotting my cock very hard, and she cracked the cane down over my back and across my bum-cheeks. She even got the tip to strike me on the bumhole where her sweet toe had just been, and that hurt so much that I could not hold my spurt any longer . . . O, the smell of her, like flowers and fruit, and the delicious pain that enslaved me! I creamed all over her stockings, and as she felt my spurt, she was coming

231

too. Well, after more wine, she . . . she thanked me for my work in the garden, and casually dismissed me.'

Jeremy sighed, and Prue asked what was the matter.

'O, Nurse Riding, I never saw my Mistress again! The very next day, the Crowes moved away, to an old mill in Sandwich! She explained that this had been arranged a long while, and she simply wanted the garden to look nice for the new owners. I begged – she only let me kiss her feet once more, before I left – in ecstacy at this final cruelty! The funny thing – when I worried she would be late picking up her husband, she laughed and said Miles was already home . . .'

Prue smiled, and squeezed his balls, then kissed him.

'Since then, I have worshipped woman, and the sweet pain of a woman's scorn and chastisement, with bare hand or bare cane, and the garments that adorn a woman's sacred body! O, Nurse, you women cannot conceive how beautiful it is to *be* a woman, to dress as one of those goddesses! The soft caress of silk or lace or leather, the fitting of the foot into the divine discomfort of a high shoe; the cruel fetters of bra and corset and panties, or the swish of a skirt or gown over the stockinged legs . . . For you, such things are normal, to me they are heaven. Just as when an implacable Mistress whips me for impudently wishing to be her!'

'Well, *sir*,' said Prue, 'now I know why you need to submit to a lady. And with total obedience, it is possible that this lady may permit you to call her Mistress. But we have not much time, I think, so . . .'

She bent Jeremy over her knee and, in silence, spanked his bare rapidly and hard; he squirmed with pleasure, and she took his rampant cock between the soles of her shoes. She rubbed his glans sternly, pausing to twist her foot and playfully tickle his balls, or his anus bud with her toecap, and all the time her fingers flickered like bee's wings against her throbbing clitty. It was not long before he bucked in his spurt, and the hot cream washed her soles, and she spasmed at the same time, her belly fluttering to her little cries of joy that mingled with his.

'You are a good girl,' she murmured, stroking his reddened bare bum.

'Thank you, Mistress,' he blurted, and the two had just replaced and smoothed their clothing when there was a brief knock, and Virginia came in, splendid in a purple robe that covered her arms and neck, and swirled around her black-stockinged ankles and high stilettos. Jeremy jumped to his feet and saluted.

'At ease, Lieutenant,' said Virginia. 'You look a suspiciously happy girl, my dear. Well! I think Nurse Riding has already exercised her skills somewhat, and I must see if there is any expertise left for me. Dismiss, Lieutenant.'

Jeremy saluted again, smoothed his clothing, and opened the door, with Virginia returning his salute!

'One moment,' said Virginia in her silky contralto, kicking something pink across the floor. 'A girl should never forget her panties, Lieutenant: people might talk.'

13

11.59

'We haven't as long as I'd like, Nurse,' said Virginia. 'The sky-diving exercise – have to hurry before we are socked in, and we have some important guests coming.'

'Colonel,' Prue said, 'this is all a surprise.'

'Call me Virginia,' said the colonel, quite firmly. 'That's an order – I am the boss here!'

Submissive, Prue bowed her head and said she awaited her colonel's command. Virginia laughed loud.

'Why, my first command is for *you* to command *me*, Mistress! And most rigorously, for my poor bottom is in sore need. And don't ask questions . . . all hush-hush here.'

'Well then, Colonel Virginia, you may strip naked,' said Prue sternly, and rummaged in her bag to get her thigh-boots and a specially heavy cat-o'-nine-tails. Virginia's eyes widened as she saw the braided, studded thongs.

'O, golly!' she cried. 'That is strong meat.'

'Strip, Miss!' said Prue. As Virginia removed her dress and underthings, Prue herself stripped for comfort, to her waspie corset and the bright polished cones of her bra. She rolled the soft thigh-boots over her stockings, where the head of each boot flared slightly, pouching her thighs and fount.

'I hear your tattoos are famous, Virginia,' she said.

'Don't ask, and don't tell,' whispered Virginia, now nude apart from her full black wig.

Prue flexed the whip, landing it with a dull crack on the bed, and told Virginia they had little time for niceties, so she was to lie face down and touch each corner. She assumed a military lady had no need of extra restraint. Virginia peeped at Prue's costume, and murmured her delight. Her hands covered her crotch, and Prue told her not to have false modesty. Virginia simpered and strode to the bed; her male's body was supply muscled and slim, with taut fesses that Prue found herself longing to lace. And then she saw between the thighs, and her hand flew to her mouth.

'You said, don't be modest,' said Virginia, exposed.

On the dark skin of this inhumanly monstrous and beautiful shaft, were tattoos, a myriad of little red rosebuds like a pincushion. And the cock was not even erect. She blushed, and blurted that it must be difficult to get clothing to fit.

Virginia laughed, and spreadeagled herself on the bed, putting a pillow underneath her buttocks to raise them. Prue went to Wendy's suitcase, and fetched the gasmask. It was a modernistic device, an aviator's helmet with nozzles and grilles for nose and mouth, and thick grey goggles. It fitted snugly round Virginia's head, her wig swirled up neatly, and Prue strapped it tightly, telling Virginia that she did not wish too much American intimacy, and therefore should see her subject as a thing, not a person. Virginia sighed, 'O, mmm . . .', her voice tinny through the mask, and sank down blissfully for her beating. Prue cracked the whip, and the flesh darkened; she flogged to a deep purple by the thirtieth stroke. Prue heard her victim's breath amplified and roaring like a whirlwind in the mask, as her bottom writhed.

'O, Miss Wendy,' moaned Virginia, and Prue furiously lashed in machine-gun rhythm, making the buttocks jump and twitch almost by the force of the whip's impact.

'Let me never hear you say that name again,' she hissed. 'My name – is – Mistress – Prudence!' and, pausing in the flogging, she raised her left toe and drove the point straight and deep into her subject's arse-bud.

She thrust it in and out until Virginia writhed in pain and squealed that she was sorry and would not offend her sweet cruel Mistress ever again. Prue withdrew her toecap in a corkscrew motion that made Virginia howl.

She had intended only fifty lashes, but she went to seventy in her rage, and, panting hard, put down the whip. The virile shemale's magnificent nude body was twitching and sobbing in her pain, and Prue began to stroke Virginia's bare bum. Virginia groaned hoarsely in a metallic rasp, and her cheeks were wet with tears.

'That was so good, Mistress,' sobbed Virginia shyly. '*You* are the best Nurse. Here's the proof . . .'

She twisted to show from her haunches an erection as long as Prue's forearm, and more. Prue put out her hand to touch the penis as though it might bite. It jerked suddenly and she jumped in surprise. Virginia laughed; she had squeezed her sphincter muscle. The bulb stood clear of the prepuce like a delicious chocolate lollipop. Prue's quim was soaking; her juices trickled on her stockings and split panties, moistening the tops of her calfskins. Time was short; she fumbled and removed her mask, then bent swiftly and clasped the cock's helmet in her mouth. It was far too big to take the organ in more than half way, and still she had him at the back of her throat, sucking and licking to bring cream from the monster as though to tame it.

Virginia yelped softly as she put her tongue to the sensitive undershaft of the glans.

'Cream for me, Virginia,' Prue murmured, half to herself. 'Spurt into your Nurse's mouth, fill her with your spunk from those lovely balls, help me join the club . . .'

She could feel the massive cock trembling, the balls

full of spunk for her. Just then, Virginia's pager bleeped. The cock wilted a little; Virginia ripped off her gasmask, gulped for air, then listened to the voice, and sighed.

'I have to go,' she said, '*now*. I'm flying lead, and we have to take off, or the cloud cover will be too thick.'

Prue sighed as she felt the giant cock wilt under her very lips, and suddenly insisted that Virginia should take her Mistress along. Virginia asked quizzically if she had ever parachuted.

'No,' said Prue, 'but a good slave will not let her Mistress come to harm, will she?'

She emphasised her words with a little whip-flick to that shining dark glans, and Virginia breathed hard, then nodded OK, and Prue was to wait here, without dressing: all weight on an aircraft was crucial. Virginia scooped up her dress and slipped into it, without underthings or stockings, and removed her wig; underneath, her skull gleamed like a coffee bean. She left, and returned moments later, as Colonel Virgil V. Althond, splendid in brown leather flying suit, with his own gasmask slung around his neck.

'Bring the mask, Nurse,' he said, 'and get in here. Even the big boss has to be discreet. Come on if you're coming!'

He held out a large canvas military kitbag. Prue gaped. He ordered her to hurry, and she obeyed. She clambered into the bag's mouth, slithered down inside, and heard its top zipped. Then she was hoisted on to Virginia's – on to Colonel Virgil's – back, and swayed to and fro as he marched briskly out of the Ladies' Quarters, and on to the tarmac. There were muffled shouts and orders, and the sound of motors whining, and she thought she heard Virgil say gaily, 'Chicken in a bag,' but was unsure. She cried out briefly as she was dumped on a cold metal floor; straps pinioned her to the bulkhead.

The motors roared, she felt the movement of the

plane, and suddenly she was pinned back as they left the ground, the incredible thrust seeming to drag her insides from her. She heard the crackle of the radio, and Virgil's terse commands to the co-pilot, and they soared steeply, getting colder and colder, until at last they levelled, and she was released from her bag. She blinked and shivered; she was stowed at the rear of a tiny cockpit, along with parachute harnesses, flares, a liferaft, and a jumble of other equipment. On impulse, she picked up a curious device about the size of an automatic corkscrew, which retracted and expanded at the push of a button. The label said 'oxygen nozzle dilator', which meant little to her, but on a frivolous impulse she stowed it as a souvenir in her only available place, next to her left breast in the small space between her nipple and her metal bra cup, where it tinkled.

There were dials and blinking readouts everywhere, and the forward window was hardly more than a slit. Though cold, it felt like a sort of cosy womb, illumined by a brilliant blue sky, and below them was a sea of solid fluffy clouds.

'Clouds came over fast,' said Virgil with a frown, and then grinned. 'Maybe nobody will see your first parachute dive, Nurse Riding. Maybe nobody should – we can finish our business in the air. *I'll* vouch for you in the 11.59 Club.'

'So will I, Mistress,' said the co-pilot.

'Why, hello again, Lieutenant Raitte,' she said smiling, with as much dignity as she could muster, goose-pimpled in her tight corset and thigh-boots, and still carrying the whip.

'What a marvellous corset, Mistress,' cried Raitte over the engines. 'How do you manage to fit into it? So narrow – it must be dashed uncomfortable. I wish I had one.'

'It is,' said Prue with a proud smile.

'We're a bit off course, Boss,' said Raitte uncon-

239

cernedly. 'This cheap Russian equipment ... Never trust the Helsinki mafia.'

'We'll get kitted anyway, Nurse,' said Virgil. 'Now, since you've had no training, I'll jump alongside you. Free fall is fun, with a friend ...'

He followed this with a series of instructions, plus the salient point, to pull firmly on the ripcord after receiving Virgil's OK: they had to spend a long time in free fall, breathing tank oxgyen, before they fell from freezing 60,000 feet to warmer air at 10,000.

'You'll find it bracing, Nurse. Like a cold shower. Some folk parachute in the nude, for thrills! Main thing is to avoid jerky motions, otherwise you may panic and flail around, get trapped in the cords, or tear the silk.'

Prue looked hesitant and a little giddy.

'You do want to jump, don't you?' and he patted the bulging crotch of the zip-pocketed leather flying suit.

'I ... I am in your hands, Commander,' said Prue with a shy smile, and blushing at her quim still seeping with excitement. 'I will not have vertigo, with *you* in control.'

Prue let him strap on her parachute, which was surprisingly light, and then he strapped on his own. He told her to put on her gasmask, which she did, and he tightened it for her, leaving her tresses streaming from the back. To this was fitted the nozzle of an oxygen cylinder. Virgil said she looked gorgeous wearing a waspie corset with open crotch, and black Mistress's boots, and a gasmask and silk parachute. She smiled and made sure her whip was tucked at her waist. The hatch slid open, and a howling gust of freezing air swept the cabin. Virgil held Prue's waist, and she looked down at all the fluffy clouds, like cotton wool.

'Niflheim,' said Virgil. 'Land of mist monsters – once you taste it, it never leaves you ...'

It seemed so harmless, despite the wind. Even so, she hesitated, until suddenly he took her by her unstrapped hair and pulled her out with him, to be buffeted by the slipstream. Prue's legs were flung from her, and her thighs flailed. Her naked quim lips felt the full blast of the wind, and she shrieked as the air seemed to penetrate her fount with an icy needle. Jerked by the shock, she accidentally slammed her wrist, then her parachute, against Virgil, knocking him spinning. Her hair slipped momentarily from his grasp, and she was sucked away, tumbling alone. She saw Virgil, a speck above her, but could not tell if he was fifty feet away or five hundred. In terror, she wet herself, and saw the scattering of droplets, like little globes of golden light in the sky. She heard herself wail a long, unheard scream as she plummeted towards the earth.

She clutched herself in a bundle, freezing and sobbing. The tears crusted at her eyes and she had to wipe them away, and the steel points of her breastplate seemed like vicious ice pincers in the awful cold. Then gradually, she calmed. She was falling towards the fluffy cloud bank, still vastly distant. Far away, the cloud belt ended, and she could see a sliver of brown that was the earth. She looked up and saw Virgil diving towards her, arms stretched like a bird's wings. To slow herself, she began to waggle her arms but only succeeded in tumbling around and catching her ripcord. She heard a click and a hiss, and realised to her horror that she had opened her parachute too soon: slowed at this height, her tiny oxygen cylinder would be exhausted before she reached dense air. She tried to right herself, but got further entangled in her cords and the parachute silk.

She could feel herself wet again, as she fought to control the unfamiliar billowing silk. Her contortions had succeeded in jamming it, and the parachute was half open, the rest of it twining itself inextricably around her spinning body, like a spider of the mist. The parachute slowed her fall a fraction; she tried to wave at Virgil, her arms and legs now tightly bandaged by cords and silk.

She was securely bound, her thighs pushed up against her breasts and her arms awkwardly trapped behind her knees, leaving the freezing wind to hurtle through her bare spread quim.

The parachute silk was meshed with her upper body, pinioning her metalled breasts in a vicelike corset. Worse, the silk had become wadded in her mouth, gagging her. But ice crystals no longer formed at her eyes. Above her, the sliver of parachute flapped impotently, dragging her descent. And the dark figure of Virginia approached.

The clouds rushed to greet her, and suddenly Prue was blinded by wreaths of mist, and soaking wet so that her corset and the bonds of parachute silk clung to her in a tight sodden mass. It was so silent, with not even the caw of birds, as though she were marooned outside of time.

'Welcome to Niflheim, Mistress, the mist sea between heaven and Earth, where the krakens come from . . .'

She felt a hand clasp her ankle, and she looked into the laughing eyes of Virgil. Her sobs turned to become ones of relief as he cradled her, gently rocking. He said that one parachute would be enough, and warmed her with his maleness.

'You have been a thoughtless nurse,' he cried in the masked tinny voice, 'and it is fitting you should get a lesson in parachuting. A *rigorous* lesson . . .'

Prue smiled with joy at his words. Helpless, she watched him detach the whip from her waist and then, still clutching her bound ankle so that her immobile thighs and buttocks were spread open to his gaze, he applied a sharp whipstroke to her bare buttocks! Prue sighed in delight.

'Ouch! So hot,' she mouthed at him.

Again and again, she squirmed as the whip lashed her cold bare fesses; in bondage of silk, her contortions of pain were unlimited by gravity as the hard strokes expertly laced her. She was upside down, her quim open to heaven, and the whip raining on her bare bum, her thighs too, and Virgil even laid agonising strokes on the naked quim lips.

And suddenly the male's waist was by her head, the zip open, and that magnificent organ erect and throbbing by her lips. She needed no encouragement; as he reminded her of unfinished business, the whip her merciless visitor, she accepted the cock full to the back of her throat and began to suck and lick as she fell swooning down through the warming air in sweetest submission.

Her quim was flowing with moisture, hot oil that floated into the clouds as little oily droplets of love-juice, and she giggled at the thought that there would be lustful rain on Northumberland. She sensed his spurt arriving, and he withdrew his cock from her mouth, gleaming with her spittle, a great dark weapon in the wreath of mist . . . This was her monster! She had taken over thirty whipstrokes, and her bum and quim were raw with agony; she craned and saw a deep flush spread all over her naked quim-flesh, like a crimson tide. And then, as the cock hovered in front of her eyes, she saw the tattoos in their full glory: myriad fine rose blossoms hard with virility.

She strained to open her quim and thighs as wide as she could in grateful and apprehensive welcome of the massive dark engine, and gasped as she felt it penetrate her soaking wet passage, the throbbing helmet right to her womb's neck. He began to thrust, and at each stroke, Prue groaned with pleasure.

'O, Colonel,' she gasped. 'O, I've never taken a cock so big. O, you *are* big boss . . .'

Her lashed arse-globes tickled her clit to new spasms of delight, and she came within seconds; still he fucked remorselessly, and suddenly they were out of the clouds, with the friendly green earth beneath them. He opened

243

the parachute, and their fall slowed, and now their fucking was as slow and smooth as their descent, his dark stiff oak in a sly, oily kissing of her womb's mouth. The land was naked and empty beneath them.

'What do your tattoos mean?' she gasped. 'Tell me!'

'Why, one for every female I have fucked. Not all of them in the air ... You've heard of the Mile High Club? Well, you have just joined the Eleven Mile High Club ... eleven point five nine miles to be precise, my *favourite altitude.*'

The little mystery made her laugh; she bucked, and her quim muscle squeezed harder, to milk him of cream.

'I wish you had two cocks, so that you could fuck me in the bumhole,' she said.

'Back at base, I have plenty of cocks at my command – and thus at yours.'

The ground neared; he cradled her, and when they were seconds from their impact, she felt the huge cock wash her womb in a lovely jet of hot sperm; he cradled her in his arms, and with his cock still throbbing inside her, they fell gently to Earth. As she touched the ground, and rolled over, Prue exploded in a searing orgasm, as though she were again swooning and falling through clouds ...

'O! O! O! ... Thank you, Virginia,' she gasped.

'Thank *you*, kind Mistress,' said Virginia.

'You said you had many cocks at your command?' said Prue through the wind streaming her hair. 'I am curious.'

Turning in the jeep's front seat, Virginia nodded yes.

'Perhaps your curiosity shall be satisfied back at the base, Mistress. I said there would be guests.'

The Ladies' Quarters were abuzz. After toilette, Prue entered the bar, radiantly accoutred from Wendy's suitcase: a scalloped bra and high g-string, of the softest black latex! Over that, a white silk blouse, open to

244

navel, and a micro-skirt in black leather, slit up the whole thigh. Shoes were the highest, sharpest black stilettos, and her fishnet stockings had deliberate sluttish rips on both thighs, below the crotch, where the swelling of her pantied mound peeped under the skimpy skirt; and she carried her own strong whip. The bar was joyously thronged with males, females and males robed as females. Applause greeted Prue's entrance, as though they had been expecting her. Virginia, demure in a little black cocktail dress, knelt and kissed her feet, saying she was sure Prue knew everybody . . .

Hydro was present in force. There was Miss Bream, and Henrietta, and Miss Gageby, wearing a skin-tight 'discipline', a mini-dress of spiky goat's hair, and the twins, and Jess . . . She saw many of her subjects, too: Mrs Shapiro was there, with Dennis in tow, handsome and rather coy in his wife's robes. Tallinn in her police uniform with handcuffs, whip, and quite an enormous truncheon; Mrs Araval, sheathed in white latex, a long skirt so narrow her ankles could scarcely move, her waist corsed to a pin's thickness, and her eyes radiant with pleasure above the large steel ball strapped to gag her; there was even Miss Delahaye, wrapped in a beguilingly tight sheath dress that proved to consist of rubber and leather strips gummed to her body. All faces were flushed with merriment, and her arrival seemed to be the signal for licence.

'Welcome to the 11.59 club, Nurse Prudence! You are our honoured and special guest,' sang Miss Bream, almost bare-breasted in a breathlessly low strapless gown of diaphanous scarlet silk that billowed above her knees like a ballerina's tutu, revealing frilly lace stockings, straps, and a tantalising knickerless mound entirely rouged. Her bare breasts were clearly visible, huge firm melons of lyred beauty, with faint cane streaks visible through the silk, and the nipples stiff and wide as glazed brown ewers.

Virginia explained that the air base was a convenient venue for large gatherings. Everybody was in the 11.59 Club! Except Prue, the new nurse ... not quite a member.

'I thought our airborne event would qualify me,' she said, but it seemed her parachuting was not novel.

To be formally admitted, a 'grand deed' was required, when Prue had thought it just a question of staying out late, for naughtiness.

'But soon I'll add a tattoo – yours, Mistress,' whispered Virginia.

Prue smiled; the air was heavy with sweat and scent, bare flesh and the crack of discipline. She inspected the myriad pleasures of her sisters, already advanced in lewdness. The twins were naked below the waist, and strapped tight in a curious double straitjacket. Their bottoms wriggled under the attentions of two canes, wielded by uniformed RAF bucks, and their flushed faces indicated hilarity and joyous submission. Lieutenant Raitte, splendid in a pink chiffon tutu with white stockings and frilly blouse, was carried struggling to a whipping block, where he was tied by a bevy of nurses, and given seven of the best on bare from each giggling female, until Henrietta pushed through, bearing a proper four-thonged whip, which had his bum wriggling in unfeigned agony.

She looked round for Jeremy Pleasant, and learnt he should arrive any moment. Raitte begged not for mercy, but for the touch of his Mistress, Nurse Riding, and Henrietta graciously gave way. The tattoos and piercings of her nude body were quaintly enhanced by painted RAF roundels and USAF stars. Prue lifted her whip and began to flog the male's buttocks, and swiftly moistened in her own excitement. When Henrietta shyly bent over, whispering she would be pleased to accept an 'airman's dozen' from Prue's whip, Prue willingly obliged the dominatrix's desire to briefly submit, the whorls and chains and roundels of her jerking bare bum seeming to wink at Prue in joyful complicity.

There was a beer-licking contest, where naked nurses were licked dry by males, and then the same tongues had to lick them to orgasm, the slowest male being rewarded with cane – and the winner with whip. There was much accusation of feigned orgasm, and these disputes were settled by Miss Bream, with a 'penalty shoot-out': the males in question would lick her own bare clit to orgasm, to prove their prowess. She caned them on bare as they tongued, the original dispute rapidly forgotten, and Prue found their moans of rapturous discomfort exciting, with their bums wriggling and their blue shirts knotted at their waists, and their lips stained with the rouge from Miss Bream's fount.

The shemales fared no better, and there was much yelping delight as the nurses, who were supreme over mere males, decreed forfeits and punishments. Miss Furbelow, in a charcoal pinstripe suit with grey stockings, delivered fastidious canings to errant bottoms with a tiny lady's cane, which was a steel rod studded with cut crystal: even the gentlest stroke with this made bottoms charming and frisky, and Miss Furbelow rarely stroked gently. Nurse Crennet, nude, caned male croups while her own distended fesses and breasts were clamped tight in their lyres, and Miss Furbelow beat their distended flesh. Her long mink-hairs were pulled cruelly apart with tweezers, and a squatting male supplicant fucked her with a dildo, one end in his anus and the other thrusting in her wet gash, while Jess, naked but for a rubber corset that consisted almost entirely of bulky zip fasteners, about a dozen of them strapping her torso, sucked the man's cock; the dildo she wore strapped round her waist on a string was energetically fucking another officer, skirts up, in his squirming bumhole. Prue remembered Virginia's dictum on robed males: 'Why be one thing when you can be two?' Or three . . .

WPC Tallinn had a young male stretched on a rack, which she was turning with sinister creaks as she buggered him with her truncheon, and urging him to confess. He confessed long and loud, and each confession got him thirteen with the cane before his buggery began anew. There was a chain gang of malefactors lined up before Tallinn's rack, bound together by their cocks and balls . . .

'I wish Heckmondthwaite were here,' said Miss Gageby. 'I am juicy to give the bitch treatment . . . a double dildo in both holes.'

'*That* would be a result, but you know she can't take it in anus,' said Miss Bream. 'Her arsehole is narrow as a worm's throat. I've tried.'

All beseeched Prue for the privilege of her whip, as though in special benison; the males for the privilege of beng handcuffed, by Tallinn's gleaming gift, to her ankle by their balls, and having to follow in abject humiliation every kick or pirouette she chose to make as she beat them. A nude female was strapped to the dartboard as target; the darts were coloured quills tipped in glue, and the nurse was a lovely quiver of feathers at teats and quim; in contrast, a naked nurse bent in position, thighs splayed, and the targets were gash and anus, both filled prettily.

At the pool table, ladies used their naked breasts as cues, and only the lyred elite could play, until a young robed male suggested the males could lift skirts and play too, straddling the table and propelling the ball with their erect penises. The nurses enlivened this strange snooker by caning bare bums as they manoeuvred. Miss Gageby endured the torment of having her body rubbed and flogged in her goat's hair shirt, and Prue saw Jess happily moaning as she was hoisted on chains passed through her nipple rings, while Henrietta playfully zipped her corset up and down, each swish of the tight zip puffing and scoring the naked skin.

There was fucking in every orifice amongst all three sexes: females pleasured each other with dildo, fist or tongue, or fucked writhing males two at a time with giant double dildos, while the males were obliged to pleasure other females with their tongues on clitties. Prue received unceasing obeisance, her throbbing damsel tongued to spasm by male and female alike. She liked watching rampant males fucking nurses, especially when two were at both holes of one female, and a third in her mouth. One male in particular seemed inexhaustible, the cock priapically rigid. He was sinisterly dressed in black leather jacket and skirt, with furry flying-boots, and as he drew near, Prue saw his secret: the massive pink cock was a dildo! She recognised Barker, who coyly smiled for the first time ever, and said it was lonely at her gatepost . . .

She particularly liked flogging the bare of the shemales as they tongued her, and fumed that these cock-bearers should be so softly pretty. Even the blushing Mr Shapiro was attractively robed! Imperiously, she ordered every single male and shemale line up, bare for her lash. At that moment a Rolls-Royce drew up outside, and a uniformed figure emerged. There were murmurs that the British CO was here! And through the door stepped Jeremy Pleasant, a hint of new moustache on his lip. He went to Prue and at once knelt to kiss her feet. She knocked his hat off with her whip and told him he was insolent to grow it without her permission.

'I'm afraid I told you a white lie, Mistress,' he blurted. 'You see, I'm really the Wing Commander here, Virginia's colleague.'

Prue snapped that 'Gemma' was insolent indeed, and was to join the line – triple beating, for one so exalted – but first she was to dress properly . . .

Resplendent in sky-blue satin, Jeremy – Gemma –

prostrated himself beside Virginia, and lifted her skirts to be thrashed until her bare bum was a rainbow. Prue flogged until every croup was mottled to her satisfaction, and masturbated openly at her glorious humiliation of the submissive males – *erect* males! – as they gazed at her in worship. She made sure every bum was purple, then touched with her lips each straining helmet of the serried stiff cocks; suddenly, without a word, she shook off her skirt and panties, and lay on the pool table, her legs splayed.

Miss Crennet fastened Prue's breasts in her lyre, and Prue swooned in the sweet agony of her teat-stretching. Her head and buttocks hanging free, cock after cock paid homage to the wet maw of her gash, and her nurses brought tongue and dildo to fill her bumhole. Her mouth sucked on still-creamy cocks, stiffening them for new entry to her soaking temple. She spasmed often, and lost count of her cocks after the thirteenth. And when she and her company were sated, she turned over on the table and ordered from each, seven strokes of her own whip to the quivering soft flans of her bare croup until her swollen buttocks were hot and dark as the Earth's core . . .

And then, with a roar of drums as though from distant mist and ocean, a tall figure approached, wearing a nursing matron's uniform, sky blue and razor starched. Her face was hidden by a leather mask, and she bore on a wide bronze platter an instrument of correction so fearsome that the company hushed. The figure spoke, her voice muffled behind her mask, and it was the voice of the kraken that Prue had seen flogged in her metal carapace: the High Mistress of Hydro.

'It is time for you to take what your virtue has earned, Nurse Prudence Riding,' she intoned. 'You shall feel the kiss of the Northumberland birch, from each of your sisters in turn.'

The bronze dish was taken from her, and she lifted

the birch. The flogging tool was more like a whole bush than a cluster of birch twigs, and these were no twigs, but branches of four or five feet in length; there must have been fifty of the rods, fanned like a giant peacock's tail. Prue was released from her lyre, her bruised breasts thrusting huge and swollen before her. Naked, she got down from the table and knelt to kiss the birch, then the feet of the High Mistress; then turned and crouched with her bare buttocks splayed high in the air. She saw Henrietta, Miss Bream, Miss Gageby, Jess, all eager for the honour of birching her.

The birch gently stroked her bare buttocks for a moment, its tips brushing her flesh and rustling like soft petticoats. Then, suddenly, it landed with full crackling force on her naked fesses, smothering them in a savage kiss that hid them entirely from gaze; when the rods slithered to rise for the next stroke, Prue's buttocks were livid with new fire. She was flogged for an hour, until every strand of the Northumberland birch was broken or fallen from its cluster, and the floor was a mass of wood splinters. The beating only ceased when Prue shuddered and screamed and slumped in a moment's unconsciousness at the intensity of the orgasm to which her bare birching had raised her.

'I have taken the Northumberland birch, and I have taken the flesh of all, in the bare holes of my willing body!' she sobbed. 'I must qualify for membership of 11.59.'

'Not quite,' said the High Mistress, muffled by her face mask 'You have not had the kraken, nor shall you.'

Prue sat up and gaped; the High Mistress removed her face mask, and all bowed.

'Wendy!' cried Prue, and fell sobbing into her sister's arms. '*You* . . . you knew all along . . . *You* brought me here.'

'Sort of,' said Wendy, 'and now you are to become me, Prudence. You've proved yourself worthy to succeed me as High Mistress. It's time for me to leave – there've been a few misunderstandings, nothing I can't sort out elsewhere.'

'Well, then, if I am to be High Mistress, surely that makes me Mistress of the 11.59ers too,' said Prudence.

'Hmmm . . . You still have to contribute some new or grand deed,' said Wendy.

'Surely *this* counts . . . I've been fucked and buggered and whipped and I've sucked every cock here!'

Wendy sighed, and looked at Virginia.

'Not exactly new, I'm afraid,' she sighed. 'Remember, I was here before you, Prudence . . .'

The door opened and Nurse Heckmondthwaite burst in, imperious with cane and full Nurse's Regalia over cream stockings. Prue thought that her first task as 'big boss' must be to make wearing cream stockings her own privilege . . .

'You are late, Nurse Heckmondthwaite,' she said loudly, 'and the High Mistress takes a dim view of unpunctuality.'

Nurse Heckmondthwaite was seized, and her bum bared for Prue's cane. The tempting globes made Prue take the largest dildo, and try to insert it humiliatingly inside the anus. It would not budge: truly, Nurse Heckmondthwaite's hole was impossibly tight! Heads were shaken: the Heck's anus was truly impenetrable.

Nonchalantly, Prue reached for the little oxygen nozzle dilator she had liberated from the aircraft. It went just into the tip of the squealing nurse's anus bud; Prue flicked the switch; it sprang open and expanded with a loud click. The gleaming pink cavern of Nurse Heckmondthwaite's bumhole was wide open to all eyes . . . and all cocks! There was a thrill of approval. Stiff cocks trembled in anticipation of filling the false brunette's squirming bumhole, where little red hairs cringed in anticipation of her buggery.

'At last! A nurse bum-pegged! Now that *is* something

grand,' said Wendy. 'For my last act as High Mistress of Hydro, I welcome you to the 11.59 Club, Nurse Prudence.'

Envoi

Old Scores

Two new subjects were arriving from London; Wendy said she would join Prue in her first greeting as High Mistress.

'They want full treatment,' she said. 'Names Rufus and Jocasta ... recommended by Miss Macardle of London.'

Masked, Prue welcomed the new arrivals, and said they were privileged to begin their full treatment straight away.

'What fun,' said Rufus, holding Jocasta, who looked at him rather coyly. 'Macardle is wonderful. Plenty of baths and carrot juice and mud packs, I suppose.'

'And much more,' murmured Prue.

When the pair were strapped naked, gagged and squealing on a cold slab, Prue handed Wendy the cat-o'-nine-tails.

'After you, sister,' she said. 'Your going-away present.'

'No, after you,' said Wendy.

'O, let dear Henrietta do it!'

As nude Henrietta vigorously flogged the two squirming, bum-plugged croups, Wendy explained her demission.

'The accounts, you see ... That Wing Commander Jeremy is an awful stickler for silly detail, and he does cane an errant nurse rather fiercely. So I'm off to start a Health Hydro in Finland, at the Arctic Circle.'

'Why there?'

'Best birch trees . . .'

The screams of Rufus and Jocasta were abject. But Prue said that their treatment was at Nurse's Discretion . . . every nurse's discretion. Then Prue asked why Wendy never fixed Barker's clock, stuck at 11.59.

'O, that's not a clock,' laughed Wendy. 'That is a digital calculator. It measures inches, in decimal points. And I think it'll be stuck at 11.59 until the Americans send a new commander to replace Virginia . . .'

NEW BOOKS

Coming up from Nexus and Black Lace

There are three Nexus titles published in December

Fairground Attractions by Lisette Ashton
December 1998   Price £5.99   ISBN: 0 352 33295 6
Beneath the glamour and excitement of the fairground there is a sinister world, undisclosed to the visiting crowds. Operating outside the restrictions of the towns they entertain, the fairground's owners are used to indulging their lewd appetites whenever and however they please. Georgia and Holly are reluctant recruits to the fairground and they soon discover the pains and pleasures of this barbarous regime, as both women endure a painful lesson in the fairground's rules. It's a lesson they will never forget. By the author of *The Black Room* and *Amazon Slave*.

The Warrior Queen by Kendal Grahame
December 1998   Price £5.99   ISBN: 0 352 33294 8
In the first century AD, the Roman army has invaded Britannia and its soldiers are sating their lusts on helpless Celtic maidens. A revolt is underway, however, led by Boudicca, queen of the Iceni. She loves dominating men as much as the Romans love dominating women, and surrounds herself with submissives who fulfil her every need, no matter how perverted. Seeking advice from a mysterious druid clan, she finds herself for the first time uncomfortably aroused by the idea of submitting to a man. Will she ever be able to satisfy her darkest urges? By the author of *The Training of Fallen Angels*.

Bound to Obey by Amanda Ware
December 1998   Price £5.99   ISBN: 0 352 33058 9
Master Francis and Mistress Lynne have appointed Caroline as their new maid. But this post requires more than the usual amount of submissiveness from the servant, and a far less substantial uniform. At times, Caroline will be expected to wear no more than a silk scarf bound tightly around her wrists. Just as she is beginning to get used to her kinky employers, Caroline finds that there are others with still more deviant proclivities – ones which she is soon to witness at first hand. This is a new edition of one of Nexus's most popular tales of submission.

The Test by Nadine Somers
January 1998   Price £5.99   ISBN: 0352 33320 0
When Rachel starts working for Michael, a high-ranking Government minister, she doesn't realise exactly what kind of job training he has in store for her. She is to be initiated into a mysterious and perverse group of female devotees of discipline; total obedience is expected of new recruits, and bizarre and lewd demands are made of them. Will Rachel pass the test?

Exposing Louisa by Jean Aveline
January 1998   Price £5.99   ISBN: 0352 33321 9
Anton and Magdalena are brother and sister, separated at birth but reunited as teenagers. The forbidden nature of their love for each other only serves to intensify their passion for experimentation – for the darkest of sexual games. Working as dancers, they fall under the spell of the manipulative Sophie and the masterful Dieter, both of whom have secret and perverse plans for the couple. By the author of *Sisters of Severcy*.

BLACK
l a c e

There are three Black Lace titles published in December

A Private View by Crystalle Valentino
December 1998   Price £5.99   ISBN: 0 352 33308 1
Successful catwalk model Jemma has all the wealth and status she needs, but she can't resist taking a friend up on a dare to pose nude for a world-famous erotic photographer. As she becomes ever more ensconced in his bizarre world, she discovers how far his friends are willing to go to pursue their varied sexual tastes – and how far she'll go to keep up with them.

A Secret Place by Ella Broussard
December 1998   Price £5.99   ISBN: 0 352 33307 3
Bel is a locations scout for a film company. When a big-budget Hollywood movie is made in rural England in the summer, she is delighted to be working on-set. Bel loves working outdoors – and with a good-looking and adventurous crew of technicians and actors around her, there are plenty of opportunities for the naughty girl to show off her talents.

Sugar and Spice 2 ed. Kerri Sharp
December 1998   Price £7.99   ISBN: 0 352 33309 X
Sugar and Spice anthologies mean Black Lace short stories – stories showing the power of the female erotic imagination to arouse and excite. With contributions from women in America, Australia and Europe, this second compendium in the series provides another dazzling variety of settings and themes. Explicitly sexual and highly entertaining, *Sugar and Spice 2* is the ideal introduction to the Black Lace series.

A Feast for the Senses by Martine Marquand
January 1998   Price £5.99   ISBN: 0 352 33310 3
Claira Fairfax leaves her innocent life in Georgian England to embark on the Grand Tour of Europe. She travels through the decadent cities – from icebound Amsterdam to sultry Constantinople – undergoing lessons in perverse pleasure from the mysterious and eccentric Count Anton di Maliban.

The Transformation by Natasha Rostova
January 1998   Price £5.99   ISBN: 0 352 33311 1
Three friends, one location – San Francisco. This book contains three interlinked and very modern stories which have their links in fairy tales. There's nothing innocent about Lydia, Molly and Cassie, however, as one summer provides them with revelatory sexual experiences which transform their lives.

Nexus

NEXUS BACKLIST

All books are priced £4.99 unless another price is given. If a date is supplied, the book in question will not be available until that month in 1998.

CONTEMPORARY EROTICA

THE ACADEMY	Arabella Knight		
AGONY AUNT	G. C. Scott		
ALLISON'S AWAKENING	Lauren King		
AMAZON SLAVE	Lisette Ashton	£5.99	
THE BLACK GARTER	Lisette Ashton	£5.99	Sept
THE BLACK ROOM	Lisette Ashton		
BOUND TO OBEY	Amanda Ware	£5.99	Dec
BOUND TO SUBMIT	Amanda Ware		
CANDIDA IN PARIS	Virginia Lasalle		
CHAINS OF SHAME	Brigitte Markham	£5.99	July
A CHAMBER OF DELIGHTS	Katrina Young		
DARK DELIGHTS	Maria del Rey	£5.99	Aug
DARLINE DOMINANT	Tania d'Alanis	£5.99	Oct
A DEGREE OF DISCIPLINE	Zoe Templeton		
THE DISCIPLINE OF NURSE RIDING	Yolanda Celbridge	£5.99	Nov
THE DOMINO TATTOO	Cyrian Amberlake		
THE DOMINO QUEEN	Cyrian Amberlake		
EDEN UNVEILED	Maria del Rey		
EDUCATING ELLA	Stephen Ferris		
EMMA'S SECRET DOMINATION	Hilary James		
FAIRGROUND ATTRACTIONS	Lisette Ashton	£5.99	Dec
THE TRAINING OF FALLEN ANGELS	Kendal Grahame		
HEART OF DESIRE	Maria del Rey		

HOUSE OF TEMPTATIONS	Yvonne Strickland		
THE ISLAND OF MALDONA	Yolanda Celbridge		
THE CASTLE OF MALDONA	Yolanda Celbridge		
THE ICE QUEEN	Stephen Ferris		
JOURNEY FROM INNOCENCE	Jean-Philippe Aubourg		
JULIE AT THE REFORMATORY	Angela Elgar		
A MASTER OF DISCIPLINE	Zoe Templeton	£5.99	
MELINDA AND THE COUNTESS	Susanna Hughes		
MELINDA AND SOPHIA	Susanna Hughes		
MELINDA AND ESMERALDA	Susanna Hughes		
THE MISTRESS OF STERNWOOD GRANGE	Arabella Knight	£5.99	
THE NEW STORY OF O	Anonymous		
ONE WEEK IN THE PRIVATE HOUSE	Esme Ombreux		
AMANDA IN THE PRIVATE HOUSE	Esme Ombreux		
PENNY IN HARNESS	Penny Birch	£5.99	July
THE REWARD OF FAITH	Elizabeth Bruce		
RITES OF OBEDIENCE	Lindsay Gordon	£5.99	
RUE MARQUIS DE SADE	Morgana Baron	£5.99	Nov
'S' – A STORY OF SUBMISSION	Philippa Masters		
'S' – A JOURNEY INTO SERVITUDE	Philippa Masters	£5.99	Oct
THE SCHOOLING OF STELLA	Yolanda Celbridge		
SECRETS OF THE WHIPCORD	Michaela Wallace		
SHERRIE AND THE INITIATION OF PENNY	Evelyn Culber		
STEPHANIE'S CASTLE	Susanna Hughes		
STEPHANIE'S PLEASURE	Susanna Hughes		
SUSIE IN SERVITUDE	Arabella Knight	£5.99	Sept
A TASTE OF AMBER	Penny Birch	£5.99	Nov
VIRGINIA'S QUEST	Katrina Young		

ANCIENT & FANTASY SETTINGS

THE CLOAK OF APHRODITE	Kendal Grahame		
DEMONIA	Kendal Grahame		
THE DUNGEONS OF LIDIR	Aran Ashe		
THE FOREST OF BONDAGE	Aran Ashe		
NYMPHS OF DIONYSUS	Susan Tinoff		
THE WARRIOR QUEEN	Kendal Grahame	£5.99	Dec

EDWARDIAN, VICTORIAN & OLDER EROTICA

ANNIE	Evelyn Culber	£5.99	
ANNIE AND THE COUNTESS	Evelyn Culber	£5.99	
BEATRICE	Anonymous		
THE CORRECTION OF AN ESSEX MAID	Yolanda Celbridge	£5.99	
DEAR FANNY	Michelle Clare		
LYDIA IN THE HAREM	Philippa Masters		
LURE OF THE MANOR	Barbra Baron		
MAN WITH A MAID 3	Anonymous		
MEMOIRS OF A CORNISH GOVERNESS	Yolanda Celbridge		
THE GOVERNESS AT ST AGATHA'S	Yolanda Celbridge		
MISS RATTAN'S LESSON	Yolanda Celbridge	£5.99	Aug
PRIVATE MEMOIRS OF A KENTISH HEADMISTRESS	Yolanda Celbridge		
SISTERS OF SEVERCY	Jean Aveline		

SAMPLERS & COLLECTIONS

EROTICON 3	Various		
EROTICON 4	Various	£5.99	July
THE FIESTA LETTERS	ed. Chris Lloyd		
NEW EROTICA 2	ed. Esme Ombreux		
NEW EROTICA 3	ed. Esme Ombreux		
NEW EROTICA 4	ed. Esme Ombreux	£5.99	Sept

NON-FICTION

HOW TO DRIVE YOUR WOMAN WILD IN BED	Graham Masterton	
HOW TO DRIVE YOUR MAN WILD IN BED	Graham Masterton	
LETTERS TO LINZI	Linzi Drew	

Please send me the books I have ticked above.

Name ....

Address ....

....

....

.... Post code........................

Send to: **Cash Sales, Nexus Books, Thames Wharf Studios, Rainville Road, London W6 9HT**

Please enclose a cheque or postal order, made payable to **Nexus Books**, to the value of the books you have ordered plus postage and packing costs as follows:

UK and BFPO – £1.00 for the first book, 50p for the second book and 30p for each subsequent book to a maximum of £3.00;

Overseas (including Republic of Ireland) – £2.00 for the first book, £1.00 for the second book and 50p for each subsequent book.

If you would prefer to pay by VISA or ACCESS/MASTER-CARD, please write your card number and expiry date here:

....

Please allow up to 28 days for delivery.

Signature ....